THE INNOCENT ASSASSIN

THE TRAVELING COMPANION SERIES

BOOK ONE

KIM BLACK

 Formatted with Vellum

For Riley,
my co-conspirator and forever love.

ACKNOWLEDGMENTS

Huge thanks to my best friend, Tammie, for always supporting my weirdness and sharing my love of all things books.

I want to thank my editor, James Quiggle, for all the hard work and expertise you bring to every manuscript. You're an inspiration.

To my priceless critique group, Donna, Kristine, Karen, and Cindy, love and hugs abound.

I wish to spotlight the women who have given (and continue to give) their time and talents to help change the tide of war, in whatever capacity they serve.

Special thanks to the Monuments Men and Women Foundation for the Preservation of Art. Your ongoing efforts to identify, recover, and return works stolen by Hitler and the Nazis are a valuable legacy to artists around the world. For more information on the organization, please visit https://www.monumentsmenandwomenfnd.org.

1

WEDNESDAY, MAY 2, 1945, MORNING

In Amsterdam, we learned how to hide—from Nazis, from the neighbors, from ourselves. The surviving Jews, the striking rail workers, and the last ragged edge of Dutch troops hid in closets, under floors, and in attics. Some of us disappeared into the silent shadows.

That morning, the sun rose with a yellow glow, and the tulip fields shook off the morning chill, though the rest of us in Amsterdam quivered to our marrow. Canadian forces had liberated parts of Holland, but we still waited for the Allies to march through our streets and free us from Nazi occupation.

I'd heard whispers last night at the club where I worked—a high-ranking officer of the Third Reich was dead. Some said by his own hand. I dared not hope; I'd heard rumors before.

A bicycle bell zinged at the gate in what was left of a sturdy stone wall in front of my little townhome, and I pulled on my tattered grey coat to see what the boy had for me.

"You must have wealthy friends, miss. You have a telegram."

The boy beamed with teeth too white and ground down from eating things that were not food.

My numb fingertips searched my pockets for something to give him. I found a two-and-a-half-cent coin, which might have been pure gold by the look on his face. "No, miss. I couldn't." He held it on his palm as though he was afraid to close his fingers over it.

I knelt to look him in the eye. He was a child. No more than nine years old, though by his size, he might have been as young as seven. His gaunt little figure resembled a doll, and I wished to wrap him in a blanket and take him inside to warm himself by my stove.

He should have been playing marbles or pirates or anything more suitable for a boy. I longed for a city where he could ride his bicycle in a park instead of around charred rubble and over mortar-pocked streets. A place where his family didn't have to worry if he'd come home each night. That's why I was in Amsterdam.

His cool blue eyes smiled with an innocence I barely recognized anymore. He had a job to do, and so did I.

"It's for your mother, then." I took the envelope from him and wrapped my hand around his icy fingers. "Take it home to her."

"Thank you, miss." And with another zing on his bell, the boy wheeled away.

When I turned back to the green façade of my building, Mrs. Dahlia Lundt was already watching from her window next door. I waved and offered a smile through rattling teeth.

The elderly widow raised her sash and leaned over her sill. "Good afternoon, Penny." Her posh British accent reminded me of home. "I made biscuits for tea, so I'm running a bit late. I'll be over in half an hour." She glanced toward my telegram. "Not bad news, I hope."

I shook my head. "I don't expect so. See you soon."

The old woman was an angel and a better neighbor than I deserved. We looked after each other, catching up every afternoon with tea and conversation. It was a respite for both of us. I'd ask if she needed errands run or letters posted. And she helped me forget, even if only for an hour, that we were in the middle of a battered shell of a city in the throes of a hellish war.

Inside, I pulled the butter knife from the jar on the table—I hadn't used it for anything in over a month—and slid the dull blade down the fold of my missive.

MOTHER NEEDS YOU HOME.

My fingers trembled from something other than the cold. I knew what the message meant. I was going back to London. It also meant I would see Jack Vogel tonight.

Without thinking, I peered into the little mirror on the wall over my washbasin. I pinched my cheeks and prayed Jack wouldn't notice how the war had paled me. Perhaps when I saw him tonight, the bare light bulb in the cloakroom at the club would be dim enough to hide it. He'd have to speak to me. Wouldn't he?

Was I to finish my work here before I left, or drop everything? Would he provide a way home, or was it up to me? I'd know for sure in a few hours.

I hung my coat on its hook and put on the kettle. I measured the tea leaves into the infuser as giddiness overtook me. I wouldn't have to ration my tea anymore; I decided to be lavish with today's serving. Mrs. Lundt and I would enjoy ourselves.

I tidied my room for company, fluffing the pancake-flat bed pillow and smoothing the coverlet. I picked up the book on my night table and pulled the torn strip of paper from between the pages. I read the name for the thousandth time. Yann Kohler. When I'd first received the note, the page had been longer, with five names above Herr Kohler's. It had taken me almost a year to find the others. Kohler was the last man left. What was I supposed to do about that?

"Knock-knock," Mrs. Lundt sang without knocking. "Sorry to be a few minutes late. I come bearing sweeties."

I dropped the strip of paper into my bra before I opened the door for the woman. She smiled sweetly, hugging her tea towel-wrapped parcel of biscuits to her small bosom.

"You're not late at all. Come inside and sit near the stove. I'm afraid this spring will never warm up." I directed her to the chair on the opposite side of the table.

"Nonsense," she chimed, unfolding the napkin of sweets over a plate. "Before we know it, we'll be glowing from the heat of summer."

An almost-forgotten aroma floated to my nose, rousing my attention. "Sugar?" I blinked as the tiny woman beamed at me. "How did you manage sugar?"

Her eyes sparkled, and she sat down with a quiet sigh. "You should know better than to ask questions like that. The proper response is a gracious *thank you*."

I dipped my chin. "Thank you." With a quick sweep of my towel, I poured two cups of tea and placed them on either side of the plate of biscuits. "Are we celebrating something?"

"Certainly," the old woman said, holding her cup under her nose. "Didn't you hear? That horrid little man is dead. The war will be over soon."

"Who?"

"Hitler. It was in the newspaper this morning." Mrs. Lundt crinkled her nose, which had been the last inch of her face that wasn't wrinkled.

A swell of relief flooded over me. I almost laughed that she called the underground reports *the newspaper* and that she called Hitler *little*, as she was no more than four-foot-ten.

"Then it is a celebration." We clinked our mismatched teacups. But my thoughts were already in London. I would miss my tea parties with Mrs. Lundt. She was my one real friend in Amsterdam, apart from Jack.

"Oh, my! And at a time like this. I hope it's not ill health." The woman's voice dripped with sadness.

"What is it?" I asked.

"I didn't mean to spy, but I couldn't help but see the message in your open telegram. I hope your mother isn't ill." Dahlia pressed her gnarled fingers over her heart.

Glancing down at the open telegram, I shook my head. "I'm sure it's nothing serious. She's probably heard most of Holland is out from under the Nazi's grip. She'll want me back under her wing as soon as possible."

"And is she in London?"

"Yes, ma'am." I sipped a little more. "I'll be working my way back when I'm able."

Mrs. Lundt bobbled her head. "I suppose I should go back home soon as well. Amsterdam is a good home when you have a family, but now I'm all alone—well, especially without you to look after." She picked up the plate with her frail, trembling hand. "Please, have one. It's still tulip flour, but the sugar is real. They're not too bad, if I say so myself."

"Thank you." The tea cake was the most indulgent thing I'd

tasted in a year—soft, sweet, and almost dangerous. The sugar erased the bland, grainy, non-flavor of ground tulip bulbs. "These are lovely, Mrs. Lundt."

"Oh, Penny. We shan't have many more afternoons together. Please call me Dahlia. Nobody ever calls me Dahlia anymore." She wrapped her fragile fingers around mine. "Please."

"It would be my honor, Dahlia."

After finishing our little celebration, Dahlia hopped to her feet in a sudden burst of energy. "I must be going now. So many things to do." Her silver-white hair rose into a neat little knot atop her head, and she patted the sides of her coif as though she'd lost something within it.

"Is there something I can help you with?"

"No, my dear." She rested her finger on her chin. "I have an idea, but I don't want to speak it before I'm sure." Her smile didn't quite reach her eyes. I'd seen that before, but never on Dahlia. My training told me it meant deceit, but surely Dahlia was only tired. She skittered to the door. "I'll talk to you about it tomorrow. You're not leaving tonight, are you?"

"Of course not. How could I?" I walked her to the front stoop, folding her towel and tucking it into her shaking hands. "I have to go to work tonight, and tomorrow I'll have to look into passage by train or boat or such."

Dahlia's face pinched. "Oh, please, not by boat if you can help it. I'd worry for you. My first husband died at sea."

"Not by boat, then." I squeezed her hand for assurance.

"And promise me you won't purchase tickets until after we speak again. Promise?"

I agreed and watched her walk across the narrow garden and back inside her home. "Now for tonight," I said to myself as I retreated to the meager warmth of my little hovel. I took my work dress from its peg and spread it across my cleared table. Covering the skirt with a tea towel, I used my kettle as an iron to press out the wrinkles around the hem. I had to look my best for Jack.

Pulling my house dress over my head and off, a flutter of white fell to the floor. The scrap of paper with the name. Kohler. I traced the ink with my fingertip. I hadn't thought I'd make it to the end. But now I had. And I didn't know what scared me more—finishing the list, or what came after.

The last one left to kill.

2

WEDNESDAY, MAY 2, 1945, EVENING

The walk from my home to the Afzijdig Club was merely a few blocks. The streets were pocked from mortars, and littered with glass, stone, and various personal items purged from destroyed houses and shops, necessitating careful navigation. Bombs and bullets had destroyed the main thoroughfares and many façades. Some of the canal bridges and walkways that spider-webbed out from the city's center were impassable, with some portions blocked by chunks of buildings and other parts missing altogether. Maintenance was not a priority anywhere unless it was a road or building regularly used by one of the high-ranking occupying officers.

My route took me past the Oude Kerk, or Old Church, with its towering stone gables and Gothic stained-glass windows. The fact that it sat in the center of the red-light district—restricted from most Nazi soldiers—made it a favorite place for dead drops and clandestine liaisons. Each time I passed the centuries-old chapel, I murmured a prayer of thanks that it had survived the ravages of this war and all the wars that had come before.

I stooped down to examine something leaning awkwardly against the curb. At first, I thought it was a tulip bulb, but when I nudged it with my toe, I realized it was the top of a child's leather shoe, curled from a fire's heat, but not burned to ash. My heart thumped hard and cold as I suppressed the image of a small boy or girl who'd once played along this road, but who no longer needed this or any other shoe.

A breeze swept through the street, carrying the scent of ash and rattling the shutters that hung from the windows nearby. I left the shoe in place, knowing someone would be along soon to pick up the scrap and put it to use somewhere in their meager home.

By the time I'd maneuvered between potholes and around debris piles, my feet were numb from the late spring cold.

Maddock, the club owner, shot me a disappointed glance as I hurried inside. He had the gruff build of a bulldog, with an under-bite and furrowed brow to match. I hung my coat and hat on the hook of the cloakroom door—hangers were for paying customers—before touching up my hair and pinching my wind-chilled cheeks. One more quick check in my compact mirror, and my purse went under the counter for the night.

The band in the dance hall warmed up with "Sweet Heartache," though there was some dispute as to who would sing up front tonight. I swayed with the melody as the trumpets practiced the lead-in a few times.

"Miss Tompkins, your lipstick," Maddock scolded. "I have a reputation to uphold."

"I'll share mine, Mr. Maddock," Vera, the club's cigarette girl, said as she set down her tray of Juno cigarettes and scurried to the counter opposite me. "Don't worry, kid." She worked her Dutch accent to mimic the American actresses she'd heard in the moving pictures. "I'll have you looking like a million bucks."

She was every man's ideal girl—a tiny frame with blonde curls and deep brown eyes. She wore her dresses a size small to accentuate her curves and lengthen her legs. Physically, I was her opposite. I stood a head taller than her, with dull, dark hair and grey eyes. My figure had gone from tennis-svelte to gaunt in the last few months. I no longer had the plump roundness in my cheeks, breasts, or hips, and my clothing puckered and hung loose from my shoulders.

Vera pulled a skinny brass tube from an old-fashioned black reticule, which always hung from her left elbow. "Here, Honey, bright Victory Red. You heard Herr Hitler is dead, right?"

I took the case from her open palm and applied the waxy crimson over my lips. "I heard. How long until Germany surrenders, do you think?" I kept my voice scant above a whisper.

"My brother says a week—maybe two." Vera glanced around the empty foyer. "I wonder what Maddock will do. All these Germans are his bread and butter. If they leave, who'll be left in town with enough money to drink and dance?"

I handed back her Victory Red lipstick and shrugged. "When the Germans roll out of Amsterdam, there'll be plenty of celebration. It may take a little time, but this place will be busier than ever."

"Lean here." Vera beckoned me over the counter between us. She passed her index finger over the end of the lipstick and dabbed at my cheeks. "See there? A million bucks. Honestly, Penny, why do you insist on staying in the cloakroom? You could make double the tips if you'd come out with me on the floor. Triple if you can dance."

I lowered my chin. "I know, but I like it back here. Nobody gets handsy, and I can stay covered up. I don't have the legs to do your job."

Vera pshawed and rolled her eyes. "Your legs are perfect. But you're right about the wandering hands."

"Besides." I leaned forward again. "Don't tell Maddock, but I'll be going back to London soon. My mum's sick or something and needs me home."

"Sorry about your mother, but good for you." She patted my cheek. "And my lips are sealed."

"Ladies?" Maddock boomed and cleared his throat. "We open in five minutes."

"Yes, Mr. Maddock," we said with one voice.

Soon, the club buzzed with patrons, all whispering about Hitler's death as if saying the words too loudly would bring fiery wrath down on their heads. Most of the officers scoffed at the idea of Germany's surrender, though they all wanted to settle debts between themselves discreetly amidst the fog of cigarette smoke and lulling melodies.

My job was simple. Take guests' coats, hats, and bags and tag them, giving each piece a claim check. Afterward, I carefully hung each jacket and shelved each hat and bag. When the guest was ready to leave, I retrieved their items, matching the check numbers.

I offered compliments, especially to the regulars, and thanked guests for their patronage. The guests who still had any money at the end of the night often offered a small tip.

It was, for me, the ideal job. I could be as visible or invisible as I liked.

"Good evening, Herr Schwartz. How good it is to see you tonight. And how well you look." A wool overcoat, scarf, and hat.

I slipped the coat over the wood hanger and wrapped the scarf over the shoulders, around the collar, and under the lapels. My fingers smoothed out the fabric to prevent creasing. Nothing in the outside coat pockets. A card or note in the inside breast pocket —I'd inspect it later. I used a stiff lint brush on the hat as I placed it over the mushroom stand inside the cubby. Nothing hidden in the outer hat band, crown, or inner band. Clean.

Next, I regarded the woman. "Lovely to see you again, miss. What a beautiful dress. And wherever did you find such a clever hat? Yes, it does flatter your eyes." One mohair coat with tortoise buttons. One hat. Cotton gloves in the coat pockets. Last week's claim check in the inner brim of the hat.

Maddock didn't abide laziness, and I became adept at looking busy. When I wasn't checking a coat or bag, I worked with the lint brush on the coats or pushed a lemon oil cloth over the shelves. I used my body to shield my true actions from the attention of the room.

Herr Schwartz had a meeting on Thursday morning, tomorrow, at eleven o'clock with someone named Brumstead. I had the information copied and the original note replaced in less than ten seconds. I slipped my copy into my bra and prayed it wouldn't fall out before I needed it.

I was tucking my fourth such note into my bosom when a familiar voice floated through the front door.

"See, Alice? We're not late." Jack Vogel strode into the room with his secretary on his elbow. "Let's get our things off and get inside. You can order whatever drink you like."

The couple might have stepped off the cover of *Photoplay Magazine*. Jack was the epitome of tall, dark, and handsome, and he carried himself with the poise of Cary Grant or Gary Cooper. Alice flaunted honey-gold hair, full, rosy lips, and an hourglass figure that seemed out of place in a city on the brink of starvation. I hated her and wanted to be her at the same time.

Jack was out of his overcoat and helping Alice out of hers within seconds. I flashed a smile as I took their coats and hung them up without small talk. I had their claim checks ready before Alice took off her hat. She was still checking her coral lipstick and stocking seams in the cheval mirror on the stand near the door when Jack took the check stubs and shoved them into his trouser pockets.

"Let's go." He nudged Alice. "I want to introduce you to a friend of mine." Jack had barely made eye contact before directing Alice into the main clubroom.

I reminded myself not to stare at the door too long. Not to wonder who the friend might be. Not to think about how close we'd once been, or how far apart we'd become.

Though I longed to exchange a meaningful glance with him, I knew it was a bad idea. His brown eyes mesmerized me, and I was sure he could read much more in my face than I wanted him to know.

Our interactions had been occasional at the start, once or twice a month. Lately, he'd come to the club almost nightly.

Wasting no time, I tucked all four copied notes into the hidden pocket beneath Jack's right lapel. This was our method. For over a year, we'd gleaned and shared information. In this way, we'd managed to stop multiple weapons shipments, foil more than a few meetings, identify half a dozen prime targets, and liberate a truckload of confiscated rations. Who knew what tonight's information might reveal?

My fingers slipped beneath his left lapel, and I found Jack's message with my instructions.

LE→15M-PAT-BAPI

I understood immediately. I must be in London, England, before May fifteenth—two weeks. PAT was me, Penelope Ann Tompkins, meaning I was on my own for travel. BAPI meant I was to belay all prior instructions.

That answered my questions. I was to let Herr Kohler live.

3

THURSDAY, MAY 3, 1945, MORNING

I woke the next day in a warmer world. Sun streamed through the window, leaving no room for the familiar chill that shook me from sleep for as long as I could remember. Vibrant blue replaced the aching grey that had dulled the sky for months. For a moment, I forgot about the war—but merely for a moment.

I rushed to dress and straighten my room, wondering how long it would take to find passage back to London. Would I be back in time for tea with Mrs. Lundt? I counted out the money I would need for a train ticket, plus a little more in case someone required extra incentive.

I opened the door and stood on the threshold to see if I needed my coat. I decided to leave it behind. But I hadn't stepped into my yard before I noticed my terra cotta pot, which typically stood empty beside my door, was now turned upside down. Strange.

I picked it up and found a folded slip of pale pink paper underneath, with my name scrawled across it. As discreetly as possible, I scooped it up and read.

I shan't be home for tea this afternoon, but we'll speak soon. -DL

I released an anxious breath. Dahlia. Now, I didn't have to worry or rush.

I decided the old bus station was the most efficient place to start because it had a working telephone. I headed north from my house. An hour and four phone calls later, I was no closer to London than before. By then, I understood it would take better connections than I had to find a car. The trains and buses were booked with waitlists for both. All ships were docked for anyone other than the German military. I'd called on several message board posts, but they had already filled their cars. Even the promise of more money couldn't get me squeezed into the backseat of anyone's private automobile.

I had to get back to London. I'd heard too many horror stories about how Mother dealt with agents who didn't obey orders. With my mission incomplete as it was, I might already be in line for Mother's wrath.

An idea flashed through my brain. Maybe I could get a ride on a grocer's truck. If it moved me only a hundred miles closer, it would be better than nothing.

"They're still a few hours away," I heard a voice murmuring behind me.

"What flag?" Another voice whispered.

I pretended to read an old train schedule while I listened to the men's conversation.

"Canadian, they say," the first man answered.

"With Americans?"

"I haven't heard anything but Canadian."

"Today or tomorrow?"

"Tomorrow, most likely. It's why we're in this pinch. Everyone with money is pulling it from their mattresses and either leaving for good or going to fetch their families."

The men took their conversation outside, and I followed. The first man wore a simple navy suit. The other wore a Dutch uniform; he was young and stocky, and his arm was in a sling. The fact that he dared to dress in uniform in a Nazi-occupied city spoke to his boldness and to the helplessness of the German plight. But when they turned away from the market, I continued on my way. Canadian forces were coming. The Nazis must be in a panic.

If they were scrambling, they wouldn't be watching for someone like me. There'd be no better time to slip from their grasp.

The grocer's shelves were as bare as ever, but he and his wife were busy tidying up the shop, anticipating a shipment of wares.

The wife nodded and trotted toward me. "Can I help you, miss?"

"Thank you." I tapped a finger to my chin. "I was wondering—if you had a truck going out soon—if I might pay you for a ride in it?"

The older woman frowned. "We don't have a truck, neither coming nor going." She shook her head. "Husband says soon. Says the troops are coming to free us. After that, we'll get trucks coming in. Can you wait for a week or so?"

I shrugged and said, "I'll check back if I can't find passage before then."

"You do that, miss. Is there anything I can get for you today?"

I scanned the shelves for anything I might use to buy her favor. There was a short stack of potted meat, probably ill-acquired, marked at twice the market value. I gestured to the tins and pulled out my small handbag. "Two of those, please."

She wrapped the small cans in old newspapers. "Anything else?" she asked as she made change.

"I may be back tomorrow if I need more tea."

The woman handed me my goods. "Yes, do. And I'll talk to my husband about when the trucks may run again. Perhaps I'll have better news for you then."

I thanked her and decided I might need to ask Jack for a lead on transportation.

"But he made it clear that part was up to me," I muttered as I walked toward the café a block away. "Either he believed it wouldn't be difficult for me to secure, or he needed me to keep my distance." I didn't want to keep my distance from Jack.

Jack and I had trained together, although he'd been in the SOE program for several months before I arrived at the country house. We got on right away and were paired for several small missions before being sent to Amsterdam. I had expected to be working closely with him—I think he did too, until we arrived and were split with two unrelated covers.

He had the posh job, if there was such a thing anymore, with a pretty secretary and a salary, which allowed him to make deals and rub elbows with all the German higher-ups.

I got the tiny townhouse and the barebones job. I was nothing and nobody—invisible to everyone. And I performed my job with finesse. Five men were dead, and officials only considered two of them murdered. Both of those were so well done, I'd never been a suspect. In fact, another German officer was rotting in a jail cell for one of the assassinations. That is, if he hadn't already been executed for it—two birds with one stone, as Mother would say.

The chairs outside the café sat empty, though a few people

bustled inside. I lingered beside the streetlight on the corner and kicked at the loose brick at its base. I bent down as if tying the shoelace on my brogues. I pulled the brick out and looked beneath. Nothing. No messages at all.

I hadn't used the drop in weeks. Hadn't needed to since Jack and Alice started their almost nightly visits to the club. But I'd hoped.

All my errands were finished, and I still had an hour before I had to be at work. "Maybe I'll go on in. The cloakroom could use a good polish, and perhaps someone up there has a lead for a car. Maddock knows everyone in the city," to myself again. But, besides Mrs. Lundt, who else did I have to talk to?

Sirens wailed ahead. A black pillar of smoke rose over the rooftops in front of me. I hurried, expecting Maddock and the others to be out, ready to help with a fire brigade. But when I reached the last block, I saw it was the club on fire. My heart lurched, and I ran toward the burning building.

The front doors stood open with employees rushing out and firefighters rushing in. Without thinking, I ran inside, too.

The dark interior was filled with smoke, and men yelled from every which way. I stumbled over something at the end of the counter at the cloakroom. It was a body.

I took a step back, pulled the collar of my dress over my mouth, and bent down to see who it was. Maddock. I gasped. He lay on the floor, gazing wide-eyed at the ceiling, with at least six bullet holes in his chest. No finesse, nothing but cold-blooded murder. It seemed someone wanted to settle his tab permanently.

I froze for several seconds and watched as the kitchen and wait staff rushed out, seeing nothing but the light coming through the open front doors. My eyes stung, and my lungs seized, trying to purge the burning air from them. I turned to the cloakroom to retrieve my cipher copy of *Twelfth Night*, and my gaze fell on two white legs sprawling from behind the coat rack. Blast. Training said I was to walk away, but my feet wouldn't go.

I dropped to my knees and crawled over to find Vera, sobbing and bleeding, clutching a blood-soaked handkerchief to her shoulder. Double blast. If I died trying to save Vera, Jack would kill me.

"What happened?" I asked, assessing her wounds. She'd been shot, too, but there was still time to get her to safety.

"That general came in. He and Maddock got into a fight. It was terrible. Before I knew what was happening, he started shooting." She coughed, and I pulled her up to her knees. "I screamed, and he shot me." Vera's voice sputtered. "Am I going to die?"

"No, I'll get you out. You'll be fine." I tried to stand us both up, but the smoke at eye level had become a black fog. With my arm wrapped tight around her waist and her good arm holding fast to my neck, I crawled out, dragging her over Maddock's body and through the entrance doors. Several neighbors descended and whisked Vera away to the hospital. I knew she would be all right now; I'd seen wounds much worse than hers.

"Is there anyone else inside?" A man's voice asked.

I gulped a chest full of fresh air and waved. "The owner is still inside. He's dead, but his body is through the door and to the left. Please don't leave him in there to burn."

The man marched back into the building.

A young woman in a nurse's uniform pulled me away from the crowd. "Where are you hurt?" She held my hands open, scanning for whatever injuries had coated my dress and arms in blood.

"I'm not hurt. I helped another woman out. It's not my blood. It's hers."

"Where is she?" The nurse scanned the area.

I motioned in the direction of the car that drove Vera away. "They already took her."

She examined me from head to toe. "All right, but you must get out of the smoke, away from this place. Do you have someone who can take you home?"

I cleared my throat. "I live a few blocks from here. I'll go home right away." I felt something damp on my face and scrubbed it away with the back of my hand. From the horrified look on the nurse's face, it had been blood and not tears. "Thank you," I said as she handed me a handkerchief.

She hurried to the men, dragging Maddock's body out, and was told to stay back. I looked around for anyone watching the scene. When I was satisfied the onlookers were merely concerned neighbors and those trying to help, I made a quiet exit.

The chaos settled once I was away from the fire. I took extra care walking home, watching for anyone following. Shifting window curtains. Slow-moving cars. Nothing.

Maddock was dead, and Vera was at the hospital. I tried to remember the face of the general who attacked them. There were a few generals who were regulars, but Vera called only one "that general." General Merkel. He was a pig—grabbing, making lewd comments, calling us whores. I was sure I had seen him a hundred times, but at that moment, all I could see was the description of Yann Kohler from his file. It wasn't him, of course, but what was the difference? They all left death and destruction in their wake.

I had orders not to kill him now, no matter how much I wanted to. But he'd already have been dead if I'd found him before the orders came. It was easy to justify, and I wouldn't feel any remorse. I wouldn't even hesitate. If I ran into Kohler—or any other Nazi officer—I'd kill him at the first opportunity. The one thing that would save him was my getting back to London without bumping into him first.

"My goodness gracious!" Dahlia cried when I hobbled through the gate in front of my home. She'd been standing in our front garden, peering at the smoke rising into the late afternoon sunlight.

I glanced at her worried expression.

"What in heaven happened to you? Are you hurt, dear?" She didn't wait for my answer. She rushed to my side, wringing her hands all the way.

"No, I'm fine. There was a fire at the club. It appears I won't have to give notice."

Dahlia wagged her head and clicked her tongue. "You're covered in blood and soot. Let's get you inside and cleaned up."

"You don't have to bother with me. I'm only tired. The blood isn't mine. I was trying to help, and…."

"Shush, dear." Dahlia clucked like a mother hen. "Let me take care of you. I'm sure you don't need my help, but you know I'll sit and worry if you make me go home. If I stay, at least I'll feel like I'm helping. And once you're settled, I'll bring over some dinner."

I tried to protest as I attempted to unlock my door, but my hands shook as the adrenaline wore off, and I couldn't slip the key into the slot. Dahlia pulled the key from my hand and opened my door in half a second. For as fragile and tiny as she was, she was quite strong as she pulled me into my little room.

"Thank you," I whispered, realizing how exhausted I was.

"Nonsense. You strip out of your soiled things while I heat some water for you. I'm happy to help."

I dropped my handbag onto the bed table and pulled off my dress, careful not to let the ash and blood spread to anything else in the room.

"I'll take those for you. I have a woman who launders all my things and never asks questions." Dahlia chuckled. "She can get any stain out of anything. One Christmas, I spilled raspberry preserves onto my lace tablecloth, and it's white as snow again. She's truly a wonder."

I had scant finished wiping the black and scarlet smears from my face when Dahlia chirped, "Water's ready!"

She moved my flimsy three-section screen around the small washbasin on my night table.

"You don't have to baby me, Dahlia. I can take care of myself." I finished my protest as my stomach growled loud enough for both of us to hear it.

"I know you can. But I want to help. You get your bath now, and I'll take your things to my laundry bag and whip up something to eat. I already started another kettle, and we can have some soothing tea with our meal."

There was no time to argue. She'd already scampered away.

The warm water felt good over the back of my neck. I sponged over my shoulders and arms, my body, my legs, and my feet. The water in the basin turned a dark purple as my skin returned to a pale, freckled peach. The heat from the water helped to sooth my muscles. My brain calmed. It was nice to have someone who cared. I'd almost forgotten.

The bathwater was exhausted; I slipped into my nightdress and put the screen back against the wall.

"Knock-knock!" Dahlia sang from the front stoop.

I opened the door, and she swished in with a plate of food. I looked around my kitchen counter and realized I had lost my expensive tins of meat somewhere in the smoke.

"Sit down and let me serve you, Penny. You always wait on me;

it's the least I can do." Dahlia poured the tea and floated into the chair next to me. "I have exciting news."

Once again, we were two friends sharing tea and an early supper. She seemed to have forgotten that I'd been blackened and bloodied half an hour before. And her forgetting seemed to wipe away my thoughts of it, too.

"And what is your news?" I asked, not hesitating before scooping up the sandwich she handed me.

"Well, my dear, I'm going to hire you as a ladies' companion." Dahlia settled back in her chair with a contented smile on her rosy, wrinkled face.

"What?" I didn't understand. Why did she need a companion?

"You know, I haven't felt very proper in years. Since my husband passed away— living alone. But I used to be quite the proper gentlewoman. And if I'm to go back to London, I want to be proper again. So, you see, I'll need a traveling companion."

My brain processed her proposal slowly but surely. "You're quite a dear," I started. "But you don't need to hire me. I'd be delighted to be your traveling companion, though I'm afraid we'll have to wait for things to settle down. I tried everything to get tickets back to England, but it seems everything is booked for now. There are rumors that Amsterdam will be liberated in a day or two. But it may mean more fighting—who knows." I sighed and prepared to take another bite, but Dahlia's pleased expression never flagged.

She blinked at me as if I should say more. "I know."

"You know what?" I sipped my tea.

"I know everything you told me. I spoke with my friends at the newspaper." She pursed her lips and blew over the top of her cup before sipping. "But I refuse to accept bad news."

She refuses. Hah! I wanted to be like Dahlia when I reached

her age—if I reached her age. "And what does that mean?" I chuckled.

Dahlia cocked her head to one side and, with a sly spark in her eye, said, "I booked us on the first train out for London, leaving Saturday morning. Of course, the train doesn't cross the channel. We'll have to take a ferry from Calais or some such, but then right into London."

I stared, dumbfounded. "But there were no more tickets available."

"Not after I purchased the last two. We leave Amsterdam in two days."

4

THURSDAY, MAY 3, 1945, EVENING

"I hope you don't think me rude for asking." I stared into Dahlia's liquid blue eyes. "But how in the world did you find tickets? I asked everywhere, and there were none to be had."

The silver-haired woman drew a long, tired breath. She beamed in my direction and then averted her gaze to her hands. Before she responded, she swallowed hard. "My husband—I don't remember if I've told you much about him—he was a hard man. A German." She shifted in her chair as if I were interrogating her. "I hesitate to speak ill of him. I don't want you to think all husbands are like him."

"You needn't worry about that. I know there are good men in the world."

"Yes. Well, my husband wasn't one of them. Perhaps I thought I might change him, though I should have known better at my age." Dahlia shook her head and wrung her hands. "We'd been married only a short time when he moved us to Amsterdam. And then the war started. And he seemed to bring it home." She released a long, low sigh. "He was very powerful—a colonel in the military. Before the war, I thought he was ambitious. But he turned into a tyrant."

Watching tears pool in her eyes, I leaned forward to take her frail fingers in my hands. "Oh, Dahlia." My heart lurched.

"His violence consumed him and affected everything he did. He was the perfect Nazi. And a demon of a husband."

"I'm sorry you had to live with a brutal man," I struggled to imagine anyone putting a hand on this gentle woman. "But I don't understand. What does your husband have to do with our train tickets?"

She looked up at me, and her lips pressed into a tight line before she began again. "You'll think I'm horrible. I suppose I am."

"Dahlia, I couldn't think a single bad thought about you."

"I miss my home in England. It's why I did it." She dropped her gaze back to her hands and squeezed mine. "How can I look to you for absolution?"

"I don't know what you may have done, but it can't possibly be so unbearable, can it?"

A tear fell from Dahlia's eyes, landing in my palm. The tiny splash seemed to cause her to clutch at my hands with all her strength, however feeble she was. "I used his name. I know how scared people still are, even all this time after his death. There were no tickets left, and I used Heinrich's name, and suddenly they had two seats for me. First-class, too." She hesitated. "Everyone believes I had—still have—connections with the Nazis."

I was sobered by her confession, and at that moment, I was glad she wasn't looking at my face. My thoughts flashed to all the times I'd bluffed with veiled threats and absolutely nothing with which to back them up. Part of me was impressed she had the cleverness to do it.

"It was a terrible thing to do. What if I've caused someone with a greater need to lose their seats on the train?" Dahlia's head rocked upright. "I'll take them back."

"No." My voice sounded sharper than I intended. I patted her hands to soften the tone. "You shouldn't try to return them. You need to go home at least as much as anyone else in this city. After what you've told me, you deserve to get back to your people."

She sniffed. "And I did so want to help you get home to your mother. I'm sure she misses you awfully. If you were my daughter—or granddaughter, I suppose—I would be on my knees every night praying for you to come home."

My heart punched at my throat with unexpected emotion. The poor woman had confessed her greatest sin, probably of her whole life, thinking I would be ashamed of her for it. If she knew the truth.

"We'll make good use of the tickets, and if all goes well and we get back to London safe and sound, let's wire fare back to the train station for another pair of travelers, all right?"

Dahlia's face brightened. "Oh, could we?"

I smiled at her improving mood. "Of course, we can."

"And you don't think ill of me for using Heinrich's name?"

I cinched her shoulders under my arm. "I should say not. I'm quite proud of you for using his name for a good cause. If you must bear the name anyway, you should get to use it however you like."

"My sweet Penny, I'm quite glad you never met Heinrich. His cruelty was infamous. People used to step out of my way when I walked down the street, whether he was with me or not." Dahlia shuddered. "I think you may be the one true friend I have."

"Well, we English must stick together." I reached out and

patted her back and moved for the kettle. "Would you like more tea?"

Dahlia paused. "Maybe half a cup more, dear. I should be getting home so you can rest. What an ordeal you've been through today." She held up her cup as I poured, and I noticed her hand shaking slightly. "Bless you, child. What was I thinking, talking about taking back the tickets? After the day you've had."

"I understand. You and I have seen such atrocities in Amsterdam in the last couple of years, and yet somehow, we're the lucky ones. We're still alive."

We sipped our tea until it was gone and the sky beyond the window started to purple, but neither made a move to end our little party. We sat in entranced silence, staring down at our empty cups as if reading our own tealeaves for what fortune tomorrow might bring.

Suddenly, Dahlia perked up and smiled. "I just thought of something. Your given name is Penelope, correct? As in the wife of Odysseus?"

"Yes," I answered, wondering where the odd question might lead.

Her eyes beamed. "My given name is Margaret Dahlia Helene. Helene after Helen of Troy." Her gaze rested upon me expectantly.

"It's lovely." I had no idea what else to say.

"You see? We're in the same story. Penelope was the long-suffering wife, defending the homefront, and Helen was the impetus for starting the wars."

Maybe it was the smoke I'd inhaled earlier or the gauntlet of emotions of the day, but my mind was slow to process her train of thought.

Dahlia persisted. "And so, as in *The Odyssey*, we are the anchors. The strong women, surviving the ravages of war."

I gave a half-smile. "Strong women, surviving men who don't deserve them."

Dahlia beamed. "Exactly."

A perfectly placed yawn pushed through, causing her to yawn as well. We both rose to our feet.

"Gracious! I'd better get home. We both need rest. Lots to do tomorrow, with packing and all." Her face turned sorrowful as she gazed at me. "Oh my. I got so excited about going back to London, I didn't think. How selfish I am."

"What do you mean?" I could never imagine a more kind or generous person.

She tilted her head and frowned. "Dear heart. Here I am, bossing you around. Making you my traveling companion without asking. And you, having to say goodbye to your beau."

I was still dragging behind, but this time I almost understood what she meant. I tucked my chin and cocked my head to match hers. "How many times do I have to tell you? I don't have a beau."

"But surely," she started. "I thought you were just a bit shy to say so." She clasped her hands together over her heart with a deep sigh.

I shook my head as I followed her to the door. "When would I have time for a man? I run errands all day, and I work all night. You know better than I do—men require a lot of care and attention. And that's the good ones, too."

"Perhaps there will be a nice gentleman on the train." Dahlia was relentless. "Though I hope you're better at choosing men than I was. I don't suppose you can be worse." She giggled like a schoolgirl. "Now, get some sleep. I'll be around tomorrow, but not too early."

I squeezed Dahlia's shoulders softly. "Thank you for taking care of me today. I don't know what I'd have done without you."

She looked up, and her gaze grew severe. "We take care of each other." Her voice had a razor-sharp edge.

Without another word, the little woman shifted back to Old Mother Hubbard, scurried around the short stone offset between our doors, and disappeared inside.

I closed my door and bolted it for the night. My mind raced through the day's events as if they had happened to somebody else. Images of Maddock's bloody body, of Vera's pale skin, of the black smoke—all fogged my brain and clouded my eyes.

Did Dahlia merely have to drop her dead husband's name to get passage to London? I'd known he was a Nazi officer, though Dahlia hadn't told me. I'd known Heinrich Lundt was a beast, but I had imagined the reports of him had to be exaggerated, at least after I met Dahlia. Had she done more than use his name? She seemed so meek and mild. He was known to uncover secrets and use them against people, both friends and enemies. My reports called him physically vicious. How could Dahlia be married to a monster like him? How could she share a home—a bed—with him, and still keep her honey-sweet disposition?

He was precisely the kind of man I would be sent to eliminate. Like all the other men on my list. But he hadn't been on my list. He'd died only a month before I arrived in Amsterdam.

I picked up the book from my bed table and opened it to the scrap of paper with the scrawled name. Yann Kohler. The palm of my right hand itched.

The palm of my right hand itched. Once, my mother would've said that meant I'd make a new friend. Now, I knew better.

Now, it meant blood.

I needed sleep. Craved it. But as desperately as my body desired rest, so my mind whirred with thoughts and plans and schemes.

I straightened up my room enough to settle myself. "I'll have to go through everything tomorrow, anyway," I rationalized, slipping into my bed.

Sleep clawed at my eyes, but guilt scratched harder. I'd judged Dahlia. For surviving. For adapting. For being clever. Who was I to judge?

Then the coughing began—sharp, choking, unstoppable.

I sat bolt upright, and I raced to my window, throwing open the sash to its extent and inhaling the cold, black night. Bile pushed up my throat and threatened to erupt if I didn't get air.

As a child, I remembered how much better I felt after I'd vomited from a sour stomach. It didn't work like that these days. The long, torturous moments, unable to breathe, were too much for me now. Merely the thought took me back to that day four years ago—no, five now—to the sour taste of memory and the burn of truths I wasn't ready to swallow.

5

APRIL 5, 1940, LONDON, AFTERNOON

ive years earlier...

Drizzle still clung to the awnings and gushed from the downspouts, pooling in the seams of London's cracked sidewalks. My friend Rebecca Smythe and I decided to finish putting up the last of our war effort posters in as many shop windows as possible and meet up again at the end of the block. She trotted down the east side of the road while I took the west.

This week's poster was a simple black and green drawing of a family spread out on their parlor rug, planning a vegetable garden. As the war ramped up, everyone in London was encouraged to plant their food rather than shop for it in hopes of keeping the kingdom from shortages—or worse, starvation. Rebecca's younger brothers had been distributing the posters until two months ago when they were evacuated to the countryside.

My mother, a schoolteacher, had gone with the droves of children to work as a governess in one of the make-shift schools. She'd wanted me to accompany her, but I loathed the idea of playing milkmaid to a gaggle of schoolchildren when I could better serve the effort in London. Rebecca's mother invited me to take the boys' bedroom in their flat, which satisfied my mother's insistence I have a chaperone.

"You're barely twenty-one years old," she reminded me one last time before she left. "Living alone is scandalous and dangerous. If you had a husband, it would be different."

"I won't be living alone. And I'll find a husband when the war ends; I promise." I kissed her forehead and then watched her go. Since that day, I'd spent every morning working in a factory and every afternoon putting up posters, collecting scraps for recycling, and whatever else the Women's Voluntary Service asked.

I hung my last poster and hurried to the corner, hoping to beat Rebecca. She raced as well and touched the lamppost a fraction of a second before me. She stood only five feet tall but had an athletic build and natural blonde curls. All the boys at school asked her out first, only turning to me after she'd been taken. We'd double-dated almost every Friday night of our eleventh year— which is to say Rebecca had two dates for the night while I served as the spare dance partner.

"That's twelve lemonades you owe me when the war is over." Rebecca cocked her head in a feigned gloat. "Face it. I'm just faster than you."

"At least that's what Harold Chapman says," I teased.

We giggled and joked as we marched toward the Smythe home.

"Excuse me, but are you ladies volunteers, perchance?" A man stepped out from an alleyway in front of us. He looked to be in his forties or even older, wide all over with an extra thick middle and sagging jowls.

Rebecca chirped, "Of course we are." She pointed to the juniper blue berets perched jauntily off-center on our heads.

He pitched a thumb over his shoulder. "I've been gathering some scrap metal for the boys that used to come 'round here. They've not been by in weeks. I thought maybe you two might want to take it in for me. I hurt m' back, and it's become quite a load now."

I exchanged a quick glance with Rebecca. "We can take it, certainly."

Rebecca gestured toward the next block. "It was probably my brothers who you're missing. I'll run home and fetch their wagon and be right back."

The poor man's grin sagged like an old clothesline. "You don't know how happy that would make me. I've been worried for the boys. They would always look through my salvage and help me find what's useful."

I waved Rebecca off. "You go get the wagon, and I'll help pick through the scraps with our friend here."

"Back before you can say *Jack Robinson*." And Rebecca skipped away.

I followed the old man into the alley toward a small stack of papers and other rubbish. "You've got a few things here that will be useful." I knelt to get a closer look. As I reached to lift the newspapers from the top of the pile, the man's legs bumped against my back, nudging me off balance. My hands flew forward to prevent myself from falling on my face.

"I've got an idea you can be useful, too." His graveled voice huffed behind me.

Before I knew it, he wrenched me backward, and I hit the ground hard. One hand yanked my hair; the other groped, tearing at my clothes.

I screamed, "No! Let go of me!" But the alley swallowed my voice. "Help!"

The man never slowed. He spun me around and pushed me to the ground, scrambling on top of me before I could crawl away. His thick hand squeezed my throat closed. His body crushed mine. His acrid breath huffed in my ear, saying words I didn't know but fully understood. My eyes bulged, but I couldn't see. I convulsed beneath his bulk, but all my desperation went unnoticed. Afterward, I felt nothing.

That wasn't entirely true. My flailing right hand searched for anything I might use to fend him off. Amid the trash, it found a discarded wine bottle. My grip closed around the cold, smooth neck of the bottle. I swung it with all my might.

A crack. A grunt. Air in my lungs again.

Pushing his hulking mass off and away, I clambered to my knees and dared to look at his face. I expected a groggy, bewildered expression, but that's not what I saw. His yellow-red eyes stared wildly up into nothingness. His mouth hung open as if still trying to speak. But whatever name he meant to call me—plea or curse—died unspoken.

Blood spread out from the back of his head and neck in a pool. Crimson fingers reached out to me. Pointing. Accusing. *Killer.*

I retched and vomited next to the man's body.

Clutching my shredded dress over my breasts, I ran, not stopping until I was home.

Rebecca's mother called a constable, and the matter was cleared up quickly.

"Poor bast—poor bloke had a rap sheet longer than my arm. No family. No one to fuss. You're lucky, miss," the police officer said. "I can take care of the whole affair tonight."

I was lucky?

"In fact, miss, you've done us a favor—getting him off the streets for us, you might say."

I didn't feel lucky.

I sat in my window, gulping the deep purple air and staring at my right hand for the rest of the night. It was as if I still held the broken bottle in my hand. My palm itched, and no matter how much or how hard I scratched it, the itch remained. I rubbed my palm until it was raw. I could still feel the bottle. Still feel him.

I wasn't a naive girl anymore. Killing had changed me. I vowed never to let my guard down—never to trust another person—again.

6

FRIDAY, MAY 4, 1945, MORNING

My mother advised me never to look a gift horse in the mouth, but my training with my Special Operations Executive Mother said I should check not only the teeth but also the tail and hooves, even if the horse were a gift from a kind old woman.

We couldn't be too careful if we were to complete our primary mission to *set Europe ablaze*.

Friday morning buzzed with an energy unlike anything Amsterdam had seen in years. The war still hummed from not so far away, but the sounds of the city were different. Excited voices chattered in the street, rousing me from the smoky fog of dreams and terror.

I hurried with my minor chores and dressed to face the news. The rumors predicted today, and this time they were right. Civilians stood in the streets, waving Dutch flags, as the German soldiers darted from one place to another in a collective panic.

Tanks and trucks marked with bright red maple leaves rolled through the main entrances to the city. Christmas in May.

In contrast to the celebrations rising from all around me, smoke billowed a few blocks away in all directions from me as I marched toward the train station. The occupation was ending, and the jailers were scrambling.

A short queue at the ticket desk kept me waiting for a moment. First in line was an older couple, gaunt with dark circles under their eyes. They whispered to each other in fitful hisses while the clerk explained something to them in a calm, hushed voice. The woman was a frightened mouse trapped in a maze, and the man and the clerk worked hard to keep her calm.

Behind them was a young woman whose wide, black eyes darted all around her. Her pale skin looked almost translucent in the sunlight. Had she been in hiding so long?

Beside a closed window at the other desk, a middle-aged man stood, checking his watch—too big on his thin wrist—as though he were waiting for someone. He looked up and then down the street, removing his dull blue fedora, scratching his bald head, and then studying his watch again. He shrugged and started to leave, then paced back. The person for whom he waited wasn't coming. Seconds ticked by before I stepped forward, and he gave up and walked away.

"Good morning, miss." The ticket master greeted me with a somber face once I'd reached the counter. The small storage building to the side of the station had been razed to charred rubble overnight. "I'm sorry. But like I told you yesterday, we don't have passage available for another week."

I responded with a hopeful expression. "I'm Frau Lundt's traveling companion. She has secured us tickets to London for tomorrow, I believe."

The older man straightened to attention. "Yes, miss. Your train leaves here at eleven o'clock in the morning. You'll go through Brussels and next Paris, with some minor stops between. Is there anything more Frau Lundt may need? I didn't know you were her companion, or I'd have mentioned it yesterday."

I shook my head. "No, thank you. You've answered my questions."

"God bless the Canadian soldiers," he said automatically. The man gestured out to the street with his chin as a slow convoy of Allied troops rolled past.

"Yes, God bless them all." I watched as a few soldiers jumped from the back of a truck and took up posts at the corner. "Oh, and how early tomorrow morning may we board?"

He dropped his gaze to the stack of papers in front of him. "Half an hour before departure. A porter will load your luggage as soon as you arrive. We can even send a truck to pick them up in the morning, if you like." Was this man scared of me?

"That would be lovely. Do you have the address?" I kept my expression placid.

"Yes, Miss."

I leaned closer to the man's face and whispered, "God bless you, too."

He flashed a nervous grin, looked up and over my shoulder, and motioned to the next person in line as I stepped away. He was most certainly afraid of something.

Seeing the Canadians standing alert at the street corners both comforted and concerned me. I'd intended to check the café dead drop one more time, but if there were something there—last-minute instructions from Jack—could I retrieve them without being noticed? If I were caught, I'd be taken into custody by whomever was in charge now, and it would be days before I'd be released, even if I could prove to their satisfaction I was on the right side. I'd have to be quick. And clever.

Walking the two blocks to the café brought more of the same. Troops posted at regular intervals, and war-worn citizens offering thanks, with Nazi storehouses looted and turned into pyres everywhere I looked.

The little café I'd passed a thousand times now overflowed with celebration, and three soldiers stood right over the loose bricks on the walk. They were young—still had bumps on their faces, though their eyes drooped from exhaustion. I could do this. I just needed to be perfect.

I stooped for a second and tugged at the back of my knee before I made my approach. When I got a little closer, I made eye contact with a ruddy-faced soldier and watched as he muttered something to the other two and gestured toward me with a nod. Once all three were watching, I flashed a smile and started my pass. Squarely in front of the middle one—likely the youngest, sporting a thick crop of bright auburn curls—I reached down to straighten my stocking seams. Pretending to lose my balance at precisely the right moment, I threw my arms out and grabbed for his hand. I made an exaggerated wobble, tugged on his uniform sleeve, and made a soft landing on my backside on top of the loose bricks.

"Whoa there, Miss," Red said. "These streets are a mess. You must be more careful."

His fellow soldiers scrambled to help me to my feet, and my fingers traced the edges of the bricks, finding a rolled scrap of paper in the drop. I feigned another bounce as I slipped the minia-ture scroll into my skirt pocket. All that was left was to draw their attention from my pocket by wiping the dirt from my backside.

"I shall try to be more careful in the future." Again, I made eye contact with Red. "I must have had something in my eye." I raised my brow and let my lashes rise and fall a few times, wishing I were wearing some of Vera's Victory Red lipstick. Not only fitting, but a nice match to the Canadian maple leaf flag. *Oh, well.* "Thank you, all three of you. I do feel quite safe with you strong men here."

"Happy to help, miss," the tallest of the three said. He tilted his chin toward me. "Just doing our duty."

Brushing away the last bit of dust from my pleated skirt, I continued my way down the street toward my home. At twenty paces, I paused and looked back over my shoulder with a contented-cat grin. They were all still watching. Good enough.

At the corner of my block, I pulled out the little note and scanned it. Even without my cipher book, I knew what the numbers meant. It was the standard code for the end of a mission. No more drops after midnight. Jack had found passage to London, too.

Finally reaching my front stoop, I heard the familiar chirp. "Good morning, Penny."

"Good morning, Dahlia." I leaned over the short wall between our doors. "Your news was right again. Canadian troops have rolled in—a handsome soldier on every corner, and the Nazis are running like rats abandoning a sinking ship."

Dahlia's chin wrinkled even more than usual. "The true believers will be going back to Germany for fortification." She spat out the words like they were bitter on her tongue. "The rest— the ones groping for power—will be heading for cover. Trying to escape the trials to come. I've seen it before. War always ends the same for the soldiers. And the people...." The woman's face became still as she looked past me. I couldn't see her lips move for a moment, but her voice continued. "The people are left in tatters, trying to put back the pieces of their homes and families. Of their own bodies."

A shiver shot down my spine when her gaze floated back to meet mine.

"Listen to me," she said, returning to her ever-cheerful self. "Rattling on like an old woman. I am an old woman, though." Dahlia patted the sides of her silver updo, smoothing a stray wisp of hair behind her ear. "Are you already done with errands?"

"I went to the station to see how early we could board in the morning. Half-past ten, by the way. And I started to run to the market for a few things for the trip, but when I saw the troops taking posts all over town, I thought I should come back and see what you might need. No reason for us both to get out."

Dahlia cocked her head and clutched her hands together. "How thoughtful you are, dear. I do have a short list if you don't mind." She handed me a folded scrap of paper from her apron pocket. "And while you're out, I'll make us up something sweet with the last of my sugar. We can enjoy one last afternoon before our journey."

"That would be lovely."

I examined her list as I walked to the general store. She'd written it on the back of a wrapper from a can of beans. She wanted a small package of notepaper, six envelopes, and two fresh pencils. She had mentioned she needed to write to her people to let them know she was safe. She planned to mail the letters as soon as we reached England. "I shall want a London stamp on it for proof," she'd said. I wondered if the proof was for her relatives or herself.

A little bell chimed when I pushed through the door, and the man at the main counter stiffened.

"Good morning," the clerk said with a clipped tone. His eyes shifted from side to side. "We're out of most everything, food-wise, but we've got a few house goods. And more to come soon, I expect. Come back tomorrow."

His voice tremored in such an odd way, I couldn't help but wonder what fear had him so paralyzed. Taking a step closer to the man, I noticed a bead of sweat on his upper lip. His arms were straight, tight against his sides. My senses tingled at the nervous atmosphere in the room. Something was very wrong.

"I have a list," I said, keeping my voice breezy as I scanned the place. "But I'd like to look 'round first if you don't mind." I made a slow twirl in place, looking for anything amiss.

"Erhm, well." His eyes shot a quick glance down behind the counter where he stood. "I have to close up in a few minutes." He kept drawing short breaths, but he never exhaled. "Maybe you should come back tomorrow?"

The cash register drawer yawned open and empty. At the end of the counter lay a German field cap without its soldier. The clerk moved his head a fraction of an inch and swallowed hard when he saw that I noticed it.

I searched my immediate surroundings for anything that might be used as a weapon. I was sure someone was hiding behind the counter, probably holding a pistol on the poor man.

"I think you should be going, miss." His face drained to a wan grey when I didn't move.

"I came for a few paper goods." In that second, I saw the fat roll of brown paper in its heavy iron holder on the cabinet above where I surmised the soldier hid. I knew it wasn't screwed down, and I wondered if I could move the heavy thing. I only had one chance, and both our lives were forfeit if I was wrong.

Without a word, I lunged forward and, with all my strength, pushed the wrought iron contraption over the edge. A yelp, a crunch, and a hissing gasp, and I watched a black pistol skitter from behind the display case.

The clerk tottered back in a heap against the shelves. "What have you done?" His voice trembled more than his hands.

"Are there any more of them? Soldiers? Was he the only one?" I grabbed the field cap and handgun and rounded the end of the case.

The clerk shook his head. "No. Not here. But others will find him. They'll find out. They'll kill me." His eyes widened, and his head swiveled in every direction.

I grabbed his hands in mine to ground him, if only for a moment. "No, they won't. You didn't do anything. And you didn't see anything. Go find a chair." I pushed the man toward the step ladder at the opposite end of the counter. "Sit down and take a deep breath. I'll take care of this."

The heavy end of the paper roller had hit the young Nazi square in the head and crushed his skull enough to cause a mess. He was of slight build, but that wouldn't make the clean-up more manageable.

I grabbed a spare apron from the hook on the side of the cabinet and prepared for the job at hand. "Put your CLOSED sign out," I ordered the shopkeeper.

"Yes." He nodded and stood, meandering toward the door as he emerged from his stupor. He pulled down the Roman shade over the glass and took several deep breaths. "What are we going to do with him?" Another breath. "He's dead? You're sure?"

"Yes, I'm sure." I forced a smile. "*We* are not doing anything. *I* am going to take care of this. It's my mess to clean up."

After spreading the heavy brown wrapping paper on the floor, overlapping the edges, I went through the soldier's pockets, returning the stolen money to the shop owner. I tugged and hoisted and finally rolled the body into a tight mummy package. I yanked a dozen yards of twine from the nearby mounted spool and tied him securely. With not a little trouble, I dragged the bundle to the alley behind the shop. Due to the numerous fires, there were heaps of burnt garbage everywhere.

Within half an hour, I had dragged and hidden the body under a pile of smoldering rubble from a storehouse halfway down the block. Though I was panting from the physical exertion, I had to keep a clear mind. I scanned the alleyway in every direction, then used my pocket lighter to kindle another fire with my mummy. I covered him with more garbage and included the ruined apron in the fire. I didn't want the store clerk to be incriminated if the body was found too soon. I had to get back to him.

To my surprise, I wasn't nearly as filthy as I expected. Almost no blood and less soot and ash on my clothes than I'd had yesterday.

When I returned to the shop, the clerk nearly jumped out of his skin.

"Is he dead?" he asked again. He was mopping up blood and brains from the floor.

"He won't be back. And neither will anyone else." I took the dust towel he handed me. "What did he want?" I asked, wiping my hands to an acceptable shade of dirty.

The man clung to the mop as if it were a rifle. "He wanted me to drive him out of Amsterdam in my truck. He said he would kill me if I didn't. But I don't have any petrol. Not enough to get anywhere."

"Why didn't you give him your keys?"

"I tried. He said I had to drive him. He wouldn't make it past the checkpoints. He wouldn't take them." The man's face began to crumble. "He'd have killed me, wouldn't he?"

"As soon as you got him past the Canadians, yes." I patted his shoulder. "You're going to be all right now."

"Thank you," he mumbled. "I have children." He looked around the shop and shook his head. "Take whatever you need."

"Let me help you finish cleaning. Then we can sort it all out." In another forty minutes, the floor was mopped and the shelves were washed clean. They had been mostly bare, anyway, so the damage was minimal.

The man went back to the store sign and flipped it to OPEN. "You should take whatever you need and go. I can straighten up whatever is left. You saved my life. You shouldn't have to clean my shop, too." A weak smile returned to his face, reaching the corners of his sad eyes. "What would have happened to my children?" came in an almost-silent whisper.

I found the package of paper and envelopes quickly, and he handed me a box of pencils. I waved him away. "I only need a few."

"Take them all." He reached down beneath the cash register and brought up another wrapped package from the bottom shelf. "I was saving these for my wife, but she died last month." Tears flooded over his hollowed cheeks. "This is for you."

I reached into my handbag and started counting out the payment.

"No, you owe nothing."

"For the paper I ruined, then," I said, pushing the money into his hand.

"Nothing," he sobbed.

Gathering the stationery paper and the package of gifts. I leaned close to his ear. "For your children. Keep the money for your children."

I hurried out before he could protest again, rushing home to clean up before my visit with Dahlia.

~

"THANK you for being such a dear and for picking these up for me." Dahlia hummed over her teacup. "Train trips are quite relaxing; I find them the perfect time to catch up on my correspondence." She nibbled on a sweet biscuit. "And what did you find at the shop?"

I swallowed hard at her question. "We needed a few things for the trip." I patted the still-wrapped bundle.

"Oh! Well, let's see. I love to see what people take with them on travels." She dabbed at her mouth with a napkin, then snapped straight-spined and clapped her hands to her cheeks. "My dear, how rude of me. Only if you want to share, of course."

"Of course." Let's see what the poor bereaved soul was saving for his dead wife.

Anticipation danced over Dahlia's cheeks as I placed the bundle onto the table and loosened the twine holding the brown paper—*the brown paper*—closed. A pair of beige spring gloves topped the small stack of folded items.

"How nice!" Dahlia said when I held them up to examine. The fingers were slim but short. Too short for my long hands.

"I'm glad you like them." I gave them to Dahlia, and her face beamed.

"No, dear, this is too much."

"Nonsense," I insisted. "How long has it been since you had new gloves?"

She slipped her hand into one, and it fit perfectly. "It has been a while."

The next item in the package was a matching set of handkerchiefs, each embroidered with a tulip in one corner. I picked them up and handed Dahlia one. "One for you and one for me."

Again, Dahlia glowed. "I feel as though it's Christmas. You're spoiling me."

When I saw the last two items in the package, I burst out laughing. "Well, the rest is for me." I picked up a small silver tube of ruby red—*Victory Red*—lipstick and a pair of real silk stockings.

My elderly friend gasped when she saw the hosiery and the lipstick. "My dear! You're lucky to find those things. Most women I know would kill for luxuries like these."

"Who says I didn't?" My mind flipped between heavy guilt and the lightness of a job well done.

We spent the rest of the afternoon laughing and packing away our belongings. Once Dahlia's things were secure in her trunk, I left her to rest before our journey home.

Back in my room, I spent the night turning all my paper scraps into ash. The little fire danced in my dustbin while outside my window, the glow of bonfires reached up to the stars. It was my last night under the stranglehold of Nazis.

I thought.

7

SATURDAY, MAY 5, 1945, MORNING

We spent the morning checking and rechecking through each of our homes for anything we might have forgotten, and afterward, Dahlia and I walked the short distance to the train station. We'd had our bags picked up, and the cabman offered to take us as well, but Dahlia insisted on walking.

"We've plenty of time. It will be our last outing in the city, and then we'll spend the next two days on the train." She drew a deep breath. "Fresh air will do us good before our journey."

The Dutch tricolor flag, red over white over blue, fluttered defiantly from windows and lampposts in front of every home or business we passed. The Dutch were proud, unwilling to cede their colors to the Nazi pyres, no matter the cost. More Canadian troops had arrived, and smiling young men stood at every corner. The Germans were nowhere to be seen.

Arriving at the station a few minutes early, the porter greeted us with a nervous smile. "Mrs. Lundt, I've already loaded your things. I can show you to your compartment as soon as you're ready."

I blinked. There were still people disembarking our train. "We're a little early for boarding, but we don't mind waiting until the train is ready."

"Yes, miss, but your compartment is prepared now. No need to wait," the tall, middle-aged man said. "Unless you'd prefer to wait," the tall porter said, his wrinkled brow and twitching moustache betraying nerves.

Dahlia's lips quivered as though she stifled a smirk. "We'll board now, thank you."

The man stooped to offer his elbow to the old woman. What sort of person was she that everyone seemed so nervous? Or was it fear? Perhaps it wasn't fear of her but of her late husband. But why? He'd been dead for a while. Did his cruelty cast so long a shadow?

The porter helped Dahlia up the grated steps onto the once opulent rail car, and I followed down the passage to our small compartment. Number four. Even our first-class room was tired and war-worn. The seat cushions had frayed edges, and the maroon floral pattern was faded to almost the same dingy grey as the trim.

"Thank you, porter," Dahlia said once the man showed us the amenities. He handed her a card, and she pressed a tip into his palm.

"Thank you, Madam. This is the menu for dinner tonight, and you're welcome to dine here or in the next car at your pleasure."

"We'll eat with the other guests." Dahlia's chin rose with a gesture of appreciation and dismissal, and the porter disappeared down the hall.

Our room was in the center of the car, where we could watch

the other travelers board at either end. I took up my post in the hall at our door. Watching for trouble. Amsterdam overflowed with trouble, and I didn't let my guard down simply because I was leaving. Would there ever come a day when I could let my guard down? The war was over, unofficially. But, of course, there would always be another war. Always a reason to kill or be killed.

An older couple approached the train, and I could see right away they didn't know where to go. Looking more closely, I saw that it was the same couple that had been in line ahead of me yesterday. They stood, swaying over their trunk, looking for someone to direct them. After a minute, our porter strode to their side, appearing much more relaxed with them than he was with us.

The man and woman flinched at every sound booming in the noisy station. Was it shell shock? What had they lost? Their home, maybe? Their business? Their family? Probably everything. And now they hovered over the little green steamer trunk as though it was their last possession—because it most certainly was. The porter pointed to our car, picked up the luggage, and led them to the door where we had boarded.

Travelers filled the station now, and I checked over my shoulder to see if Dahlia needed me. She dropped her wristlet purse onto the seat and stationed herself beside me at the compartment door.

"I like to watch the people, too." She motioned through the window to the travelers gathering on the platform. "I think it's interesting to guess about them."

The weary couple followed the porter into compartment one in our car. The husband kept his hand planted in the small of his wife's back. His head swiveled to and fro, alert to whatever threat lurked in the next shadow. I wasn't the only one.

I nodded in his direction, and again, he flinched, ducking into his compartment.

"Scared to death," Dahlia whispered, her voice forming the words pounding in my mind.

"Quite."

"Now, he's a bit more confident, don't you think?" Dahlia's wrinkled hand pointed toward a gentleman in a suit carrying a valise under his arm. "Perhaps a salesman before the war." Another porter stopped him for a moment before directing him to the other end of our car.

The man appeared to be about forty years old, give or take a year. Average height and a little heavy around the middle. He wore steel blue flannel with a paisley pocket square. The suit seemed to be a few years old, though well-kept. His black shoes were freshly polished, but maybe of a style older than the suit. He had a dark grey hat with a blunt blue feather tucked in the band.

The hat. I'd seen it before. It was the man who'd been waiting for someone. I looked around for a companion, but there was no one. Apparently, he was destined to travel alone.

The man took the second compartment from the end—number six—and as he opened the door, he shot a glance toward us. He went inside for a moment, then poked his head out again and tipped his hat to reveal his bald head with a short grey fringe of hair around the edges. "Goedemorgen," he said with a bow.

"Good morning," Dahlia and I answered together.

His eye lit from within. "Ah! Fellow Brits. Perhaps we can visit over supper if I'm not too forward." His accent was as posh as Dahlia's. Certainly from a higher class than me.

"Perhaps," Dahlia said with an almost imperceptible shrug.

The man tilted his forehead toward me as if I might give him a more definite answer. But, considering Dahlia had already spoken, I didn't respond. He made another run at it. "Have we met before?"

"You might have seen me here at the station yesterday. I think I saw you." I didn't add anything, not wanting to embarrass the man.

"Yes, perhaps that's it." He looked as if he might add something but changed his mind. Instead, he bowed again and retreated to his room.

"Definitely more confident," I said under my breath.

"And that poor soul," Dahlia murmured as a younger man with his arm in a sling hobbled down the platform toward our car.

He reminded me of the young man I'd overheard two days before talking about the Canadian troops coming in. I couldn't be sure, but he certainly looked like the man. I must pay more attention.

Our porter followed with his duffle to the first door.

"God bless him." I studied him as he took compartment two. At closer inspection, I was sure it was the soldier I'd seen the day before. "How do you think he has a compartment in a first-class car?" I whispered.

Discreetly, Dahlia scratched at the tip of her nose to conceal her reply. "Maybe God *did* bless him."

With one more room to our left and two still open on our right, we watched the platform for others, anticipating who else would join us.

Two nuns escorted three children toward the right door but were redirected to a car farther down the platform. We both released a quick sigh of relief.

"Someone is getting their children out at the first opportunity." My voice was still low.

"Expecting more violence." Dahlia nodded. "Likely, they have family in Paris or London."

I glanced up to see a blonde woman in a smart forest-green skirt suit and a black, wide-brimmed hat marching in our direction. Before boarding, she stopped and turned back, looking for someone. At that point, pausing, she stepped to the side of the door and pulled a lipstick and mirror from her purse, tucking the black clutch under her arm. I watched her dab at her lips with the flame-red balm and check her whole face in the reflection. I swallowed hard, recognizing the face in the little mirror. It was Alice, Jack's secretary.

"She's a beauty," Dahlia said, no longer whispering.

Without responding, I scanned the platform for Jack. If Alice was here, so was he.

"She's probably escaping with a German officer, maybe heading for South America. Notice how she's not gaunt and pale like the other women." Dahlia sighed. "I used to have looks like hers."

The crowds on the platform tapered off, with travelers boarding the train and others leaving the station. Still no sign.

But at that moment, from the corner of my eye, I saw him. Tall, with dark features, wearing the charcoal tweed suit I preferred. His red and gold tie hung in a crooked knot at his throat, begging me to straighten it. Jack joined Alice, and they climbed the steps into the car. He escorted her to number three to our left. As was typical, his eyes met mine only for a split second before he followed her inside.

Dahlia released a long gasp, and when I looked down to meet her gaze, she had one silvery brow arched high.

"Oh, so *he's* your young man?" Her tone was back to a whisper.

"Good morning, ladies," Jack said in his low-end tenor when

he returned to the hall. He tipped his black fedora toward us as he passed and went to the number five compartment on the other side of ours.

I held my breath and waited as the door closed and clicked behind him. "Why would you say such a thing?" I asked. "How could you guess something like that from looking at him?"

"I wasn't looking at him, Penny. I was looking at you. Your eyes have a sudden glow to them. No one else has caused such a reaction." Dahlia's lips curled up, and her eyes sparkled. "I'm right, aren't I?"

I didn't answer. My face already had. My cheeks flushed a deep pink that I could see in my reflection in the window.

But when my eyes focused back on the platform, my gaze landed on someone else. A man with sandy brown hair stood alone, finishing a cigarette. After stamping it out, he held up his hand and snapped his fingers. That's when I saw it.

"Boy!" the man barked.

Ironically, our middle-aged porter responded. "Yes, sir?"

They spoke for a moment, and the porter gestured to the door at the end of the car. My heart pounded. I knew this man, though I'd never seen him. But, no, it was my imagination. I was seeing what I wanted to see. My stare bored into him, and I knew. My blood turned to glass. A year of dossiers and dead ends—and here he was, boarding my train.

He climbed the steps and took the last open compartment in our car. Number seven. He reached up and touched the brim of his hat without tipping it to us. I didn't imagine it.

Running down the side of his left wrist was a dark burn scar in the shape of a thunderbolt. The exact identifying mark for which I'd spent the last year searching.

I steeled my expression, desperate not to betray my feelings as

I had at the sight of Jack. Dahlia didn't notice, or didn't comment. For that, I was grateful.

Yann Kohler stood little more than a dozen feet from me. He blinked without smiling and disappeared behind his door. He was leaving Amsterdam on the same train as me. If I had found him five days ago, he'd already be dead. It's what he deserved.

But I was under orders not to touch him.

For now.

8

SEPTEMBER 21, 1944, AMSTERDAM, MORNING

*N**ine months earlier...*

Dull grey fingers of morning pushed through the blanket of fog lingering over the city's canals. I tugged the gap in my coat closed and realized I'd lost a button. Just one more thing I'd lost.

I had worked through the first three names on my list when Willem and Harriet arrived on my doorstep last July. They were young couriers for Mother, delivering information and a few luxuries from home. They'd been confident. Too confident, I'd warned them.

"I'll face the whole Nazi army alone," Willem boasted that night. And within a week, he was gone.

A German soldier had caught him stealing guns from a truck. The soldier made an example of Willem. His body hung from a lamppost for days before someone had the compassion—and courage—to cut it down.

And now Harriet.

Harriet glowed with fresh stubbornness. Her bronze hair shone and curled around her pink face, imbuing her with unnatural youth. The effect was made even more striking by the backdrop of the rubble of Amsterdam.

I remembered her primping in the clouded mirror over my washstand. "I'll find your targets and draw them out for you." She pinched her cheeks as she boasted. "That's never been a problem for me."

"You'll be working for a small laundry. They often take in soldiers' garments." I passed on her assignment details as I put away the new box of ammunition for my pistol and admired the boot knife and wrist dagger she'd brought. "You must search through everything thoroughly and keep a piece or two when possible. We almost have a complete uniform."

"Understood." She tilted her chin toward me and beamed. "And I'm happy to help you with your assignments whenever you need me."

I slipped the envelope for Jack under my mattress and turned to face the girl. "I don't think you do understand. You and I are not friends here. Willem, either. After tonight we will not communicate with each other directly. Instead, we will leave messages at the drop. The directions are in your packet, and you'll use your book for deciphering."

"What about emergencies?" she asked.

"We handle our own emergencies." I narrowed my gaze into a cold stare. "And dirty yourself up. You'll stand out like a sore thumb looking like that."

She blinked back as though she were bored. "But I want to stand out. The better bait catches the bigger fish."

I grabbed her shoulders, tempted to shake some sense into her. What was Mother thinking, sending a girl like this?

"In this city, you don't want to stand out. Fresh new faces telegraph resistance to everyone around you." I released an exasperated sigh. "The Nazis know we're here but can't find us. If you prance around Amsterdam like this—if you speak to Willem or me or anyone you think might be an ally—you'll get yourself killed. Along with all of us."

Her bottom lip shot out in a pout.

"Stop that now." I glared. "You're not a child, no matter how much you look like one. Mother wouldn't have sent you if you were stupid, so smarten up and listen to me." I hated her pride, but I'd seen her file. She was top of her training class; she simply had no experience. I relaxed my grip on her. "You need to dull your appearance. Look war-weary, shabby. Do your job, and I'll do mine. It's the way we survive here."

That night in July was the last time we'd spoken, though I received several messages from her in August. Her first message clearly showed she wasn't heeding my advice. At first, I dismissed her enthusiasm as naïveté. But by the third note, I feared she was in over her head. Then suddenly, her messages stopped.

In mid-September, I let Jack know I was worried, for all of us, and he indicated that he had a lead on what had happened to Harriet.

A chill crept down my spine as I approached the dead drop. The corner café owner swept his sidewalk next to the loose cobblestone. I needed to be quick and smooth.

I pulled my tattered handkerchief from my coat pocket and dabbed at my nose. The gaunt man averted his eyes as usual. One step short of my goal, I pretended to stumble and drop my hankie.

The man didn't turn to look. Good little Dutchman.

I bent to pick up the fabric square, gathered the folded paper from between the stones simultaneously, and shoved them both into my pocket.

I walked on, and he never paused his sweeping.

To be sure my outing appeared incidental, I continued to the grocer, who was unlocking his door as I arrived.

"May I help you this morning?" He held open his door.

I stepped inside. "Anything new today? A tin of fish, maybe?"

The man's head dropped to his chest. "I'm sorry, no. Perhaps tomorrow." The words were so common they'd possessed his whole person.

I grimaced, pretended to look for something else, then left the shop, heading back to my tiny flat.

My fingers itched to read Jack's words. When I settled at my table with my book and pencil, I went right to work on the note. Unlike most of our missives, this one filled the page. I decrypted the codes quickly and cried at what I had learned.

Harriet had started going out with a young soldier, and soon after, promoted herself to his commanding officer, Yann Kohler.

My heart pounded as I read what he'd done to her. She'd underestimated his cunning, becoming his toy. Jack reported several of his resistance contacts had seen her on Kohler's arm, acting like a whore. Her poor, innocent mind had no idea what a monster the man was.

I gulped a deep breath. She might not have known, but I did. My heart slammed against my ribs as I read on.

He had taken her to a camp to show her the power he wielded. He allowed her to watch him execute a dozen prisoners and then offered her to the soldiers in charge. After they'd each had a turn, Kohler took her aside, pretended to offer comfort, and raped her to death.

The message said that striking rail workers found her nude

body a few days later. She had a swastika carved between her breasts.

Kohler wasn't just a monster. He was the devil himself.

My eyes burned while I reread the message. Jack had delayed sending it. Harriet had been murdered last week; the message arrived today.

I rarely cried—there was no time for such luxuries. I wiped a tear from my cheek while I watched the message burn on my stove. Fury burned in my gut. Harriet had defied her assignment and paid the price.

That devil was on my list, not hers, and I was going to kill him.

9

SATURDAY, MAY 5, 1945, AFTERNOON

The train rumbled over the tracks slower than I expected. The damage of war wasn't limited to the city streets and buildings. Fallen trees and scorched countryside marred the once scenic views from the train windows.

We'd barely begun the journey when Dahlia heaved a burdened sigh. "Oh my," she murmured, touching a fingertip to her forehead.

"Are you all right?" I hoped the rhythmic sway of the rails wasn't making her motion sick already.

"I'm more tired than I thought." Her hands trembled as she folded them together and settled them in her lap.

"Why don't I have the porter make up your bed so you can nap?" I patted her bony knee. "A little rest will have you ready for supper."

She shook her head, and the silvery wisps of hair straying from her top knot caught the sunlight, creating a halo around her face.

"Oh, no! I couldn't do that. Where would you sit? I don't want to displace you."

I glanced around our tiny cabin. The tufted bench where we sat converted into a bed with a smaller berth above. Across from the seat was a shelf cabinet for luggage and other belongings, and beside it was the narrow door that led to a cramped washroom. We didn't have many options.

"Nonsense," I told her. "You can rest, and I'll do a bit of reading in the dining car." Before she could argue, I saw the porter in the hall and hopped up to catch him.

"Yes, miss?"

"Could you please make up the bed for Mrs. Lundt when you're free? She's quite tired."

"Of course." He bowed to the tray he carried. "I'll take this to the last cabin and be right back."

As he left, I found Dahlia's face screwed into a knot. "Such a fuss. I'd be fine resting here on the seat."

I shook my head and clicked my tongue. "And if the train bumps or lurches, you'd find yourself on the floor. I don't want you to get hurt."

The old woman sighed again. "Penny, you're the daughter—the granddaughter, rather—I wish I'd had." Her smile grew wan. "I suppose I do need a little sleep."

"Of course you do. All the excitement of this last week has caught up with you."

The porter returned, and in moments he had Dahlia's bed set up.

"Is there anything more I can do for you?"

"Miss Tompkins would like to do some reading in the dining car. Would you mind escorting her there?"

Lowering my gaze to meet Dahlia's, I asked, "Are you sure you don't need my help?"

"My dear, if I can't get myself into bed, what good am I?"

"I'd be pleased to show you the way." He made a grand gesture through the doorway. "Do you have your own book? If not, we have a nice selection on the shelf."

"Hmm." I blinked an unspoken enjoy-your-nap to Dahlia. "I think I'll see what you have."

The thin man directed me toward the rear of the train, past the cabins of Jack and the two other single men in our car. From the corner of my eye, I glanced into their rooms. All three sat reading newspapers.

The sounds of the tracks grew louder as we moved through the transition hall from one car to the next. The dining car was empty, save the steward at the far end behind a counter, polishing glasses and serving ware. The porter gestured to a comfortable-looking wing chair on the sunnier side of the car. "May I bring you some tea?"

"That would be lovely."

"The bookshelf is there." He pointed to a glass-front cabinet on the opposite side of the room. "Choose whatever you like."

As he continued back to the steward, I crossed to peruse the books in the small library, keenly aware that the men could be watching me.

There was a poetry book by Shelley, a volume of *Grimm's Fairy Tales*, *The Hound of the Baskervilles*, and an old Bible on the top shelf. The last book on the shelf, placed upside down from the others, was Shakespeare's *The Tempest*. I scanned the room before making a move. No one else had entered, and neither the porter nor the steward paid attention to me.

I pulled *The Tempest* out and flipped it open. Tucked behind the last page was a scrap of paper, which I removed and slipped into my pocket before righting the book and sliding it back into place. Next, I plucked the leather-bound, well-worn copy of *Tarzan of the Apes* from the shelf below and returned to my seat as the steward brought a cup and a teapot to my table.

"If you'd like anything else, please let me know." He bowed forward, shooting me a pleasant expression. His light hair and pale eyes reflected the sunlight that flooded in from both sides of the train car.

"Thank you."

Waiting until the steward returned to his post, I sipped my tea and stroked the gilded title and embossed silhouette of a man standing on a tree branch, surrounded by jungle. When I was sure I wasn't being watched, I moved the scrap of paper from my pocket to the pages of Tarzan with the same regard as a bookmark.

Across the torn strip was scrawled: PAT 1800 JCV #5. I took a moment to ponder the meaning. A flutter lifted my stomach with the bounce of the train.

So I was to meet Jack in his cabin at six o'clock. For what, exactly? Were we regrouping? Was he going to reinstate my original mission? And how was I to meet him without raising Dahlia's suspicions?

Having or being a lady's companion was a mutually beneficial arrangement, common after the First World War, which left Europe with millions more women than men. The older woman received all the help she needed to make a journey comfortable, and the younger woman had the necessary chaperone to keep her reputation above reproach.

Dipping into a single man's cabin all alone was anything but above reproach. Especially when the single man was six-foot-tall with dark brown hair, a cleft chin, and brown eyes flecked with green and gold when the sun danced in them. I would have to be creative.

I spent the rest of the hour sipping tea and staring at the jumble of words in front of me, turning the pages every few minutes whenever the steward looked my way. I was on page seventy before I realized I hadn't read a single word.

A quiet crack split the silence as the door behind me opened. I pushed the paper scrap into my pocket before the enthusiastic British man in the blue suit walked past me on his way to speak to the steward.

"I say, good man, might I trouble you for a cup of tea?"

The man saluted. "Yes, sir. It won't take a moment. If you'd like to take a seat, I'll bring it right out when it's ready."

"Thank you." The Britt turned back toward the room and flinched when he noticed me.

I dipped my chin and flashed my most polite expression. My mind went to work, automatically assessing the man. He had narrow shoulders and a slight paunch, giving him the overall look of a pear. Adding to that, his light, almost golden eyes smiled before his lips moved.

He was at my side in three stiff strides, offering his hand. "I'm Collin Graves. Please accept my apologies for interrupting your solitude. I didn't even notice you sitting here. I tend to be a bit single-minded at times. I'm afraid my focus was on procuring a good cuppa."

I gestured to my own cup and teapot. "I do understand." I shook his hand. "I am Miss Tompkins."

"A pleasure to meet you." He angled his bare forehead to my book. "Tarzan, eh?"

"Have you read it?" I closed the book over the corner of my napkin.

"Certainly," Graves said. "But it's unusual reading for a young woman."

"Is it?" I tried to keep my expression placid.

He tapped the corner of my table. "Burroughs is an excellent writer, but for adventure, I prefer Jules Verne."

"I like all kinds of books." The statement was true and might be vague enough to keep me from having to discuss too much of the book in my hand.

"My sister is a devotee of Jane Austen and the Bronte sisters." Graves arched his salt and peppered brows, raising them up into his bald head.

Before he could continue, I interrupted. "More suitable for a young woman?" My voice dripped with indignation—almost in a challenge.

Graves looked as though I might have slapped him in the face. "Yes, erhm. No." He fumbled. "Please allow me to start again." He put his fisted hands on his hips and lowered them again as if he didn't know what to do with them. He looked a bit lost and befuddled.

I smiled and gestured to the chair across from me. "Please sit down, Mr. Graves."

He loosed a tense sigh and lowered himself into the chair. "Forgive me, Miss Tompkins. I didn't mean to make assumptions. The truth is, my wife read the Tarzan books to our son. All of Burroughs's series, actually." He choked out a weak laugh. "Donald used to call his mother *The Princess of Mars*." He straightened in the chair as the steward delivered his cup of steaming tea and replaced my cooled teapot with a hot one.

"If you don't mind sharing," the steward said without making eye contact with either of us.

"Thank you," Graves and I said together.

Graves continued. "These days, I think of the books as bedtime stories for little boys, I suppose."

"I see."

Graves lifted the pot and poured tea into my empty cup first. "I hope I didn't insult you too much."

"Not at all." I thanked him and took a sip. "And I suppose you're looking forward to seeing your wife and son again?"

His gaze lowered to his cup. "They were killed two years ago."

"Oh." I wasn't quite sure what to say. "I'm so sorry."

"No need to apologize, my dear." Graves's voice bolstered, and he fixed a brave visage. "I'm quite sure you haven't killed anyone in this bloody war."

I swallowed my guilt and conjured a smile. Graves had no idea. Nobody did, thank God. We chatted for another half hour, emptying the teapot between us. Finally, I glanced at my wristwatch, noticing the second hand had stopped. "I should check on…."

"Is it your mother?" he asked. "Or grandmother?"

"Actually, Mrs. Lundt is a good friend. A fellow citizen of the crown. We're traveling home together." I stood, closed the Tarzan book, and moved back to the shelf to replace it. I tapped on the crystal of my watch and held it to my ear.

"Here you go." He stood and held out his watch. The extra-wide black chronograph face was secured to his arm with a worn clunky leather strap. Like the rest of his things, nice at one time, but utilitarian now.

"Thank you." I corrected my minute hand and turned the crown a few times.

"What a good heart you have, Miss Tompkins." He offered a slight bow. "I hope to see you at supper tonight. And if there is any service I might provide for you or Mrs. Lundt, please don't hesitate to ask. I believe I'm two compartments down from yours."

"Thank you, Mr. Graves."

I hurried back to my cabin to find Dahlia sitting up on the side of the bed, stretching her arms wide.

"What a pleasant rest." She patted her cheeks and looked up at me. "Oh, Penny! Did you have a visit with your young man?"

Blinking away whatever expression I might have on my face, I shook my head. "No, why do you ask?"

She swatted away her words with a swish of her hand. "Your eyes looked—bother, now I suppose I'm turning senile. Well, I'm old enough. I'll turn senile if I want."

I laughed aloud. "Sweet Dahlia, you're not senile at all. On the contrary, you're a very perceptive woman. In fact, I did have a visit with a man, but not the one you think. I met the friendly British man in the dining car and shared a pot of tea."

"Ooh." She almost cooed. "The older gentleman? Is he very interesting, then?"

"Isn't everyone interesting when you're on a journey?" I deflected with a question.

"They can be." Dahlia blushed and hurried into the washroom.

I tidied up the room and took my turn in the water closet when she came out. Looking into the small oval mirror, I pinched my cheeks and smoothed my dark waves. I suddenly remembered the gift from the store clerk and dabbed my lips with the bright red rouge. Was Collin Graves interesting? Maybe not as handsome as Jack, but interesting all the same.

The train lurched as it made its first stop in Brussels. I wanted to see who might be getting on or off, so I hurried out and into the hall. The platform was almost empty. A porter met a man with a bag of mail, and the nun and children left the train. No one boarded—at least not that I could see—and the train resumed its rumble over the rails.

When I rejoined Dahlia in the main room, she looked like the cat that ate the canary.

"What?"

"Are you going to have supper with your new man and a midnight rendezvous with the other?" Dahlia's feisty smile curled at the corners.

"Absolutely not!" I could feel my face flushing as red as my lipstick.

Dahlia frowned with her mouth, though her eyes gleamed. "And why not? If I were your age—honestly, if I looked like you, no matter what age I was, I would do it."

"And what do you think I *should* be doing?" I asked the question before I realized how little I knew of Dahlia Lundt. "Wait. Don't answer." I gave her a scolding look from the corner of my eye. "You're supposed to be keeping me virtuous, not getting me into trouble."

The woman sighed and feigned frustration. "No, I'm supposed to give you the *appearance* of virtue." All at once, her expression changed almost to disappointment. "Listen to me, Penny. In the last forty years, I've been married and widowed four times. At this point, I must live vicariously through you. My advice is to live life while you're young. It gets harder as you get older. Get out there and sow your wild oats, and I'll make whatever excuses you need me to make for you."

My jaw must have dropped to my chest, and Dahlia giggled like a child. I didn't know what to say. Dahlia was going to be a handful. Of what, I couldn't be sure.

10

SATURDAY, MAY 5, 1945, EVENING

The cocktail hour approached. I hadn't observed the tradition in the last year and a half, which probably saved my life, considering how malnourished I'd become. From the nightclub counter, I'd watched people go from thin but healthy to deathly gaunt as they drank away their sorrows, fears, and anxieties until they disappeared altogether.

I glanced down at my watch—five-twenty. Then, pressing the crystal to my ear, I held my breath to listen for the faint tick-tick-tick. It was there, but I gave the crown a few good turns to ensure it didn't wind down again. I couldn't be late to meet Jack.

Five minutes ticked by, and the couple from the first compartment walked past our room arm in arm. They both appeared more relaxed than they'd been at the station two days ago or this morning. The woman gazed at her husband as if he were the most handsome man she'd ever seen. His eyes focused on the door at the other end of the car.

"She probably thinks he's saved her life. Maybe he has." Dahlia's voice startled me to attention.

"Maybe he thinks she's slowing him down. His expression certainly doesn't match hers."

Dahlia chuckled. "My dear, all men think women are slowing them down. I always slowed my husband."

"Which one?" I turned to study her face.

"All of them, I suppose." She smiled. "Not Theodore, though. My first husband died in the Great War. We were both so young. I couldn't have stopped him from doing anything, even if I had wanted to. Oh, how I loved him." Her face beamed and transformed with a blink.

"The others?"

"Yes, the others I held back. Every chance I got. Perhaps I was trying to keep them with me longer. Or change them. Maybe even save them." A shadow crossed her eyes, and she drew a deep breath. "It is the Lord's to save or not; I could merely point the way."

I had heard her utter prayers and sing hymns before, but this was the first time I'd heard Dahlia speak directly of God. My surprise must have been apparent.

"Oh yes, my dear," she continued. "The late Herr Lundt could not be saved, I'm afraid. He was a dreadful man and a terror of a husband."

"I'm so sorry to hear it. You deserve so much better." I patted her hand.

"Who's to say?" Her words faded and suddenly returned. "He found out things about people—the worst kinds of things. And he used their secrets against them whenever he could. He led the most despicable lifestyle." She blinked away whatever memories might have flashed in her mind. "This is why people fear me, I think."

"They're afraid you may know their secrets, too?"

"Very likely. I don't, and even if I did, I wouldn't use the knowledge for profit. But I cannot change what other people believe." Dahlia's eyes misted. "The best I can do is leave them alone."

The word echoed in the back of my mind. Alone. I didn't want to think about it. But I didn't have to—I wasn't alone.

The sound of a door latch snapped my attention back to the hallway. I watched Jack pass our windows without so much as a side glance into our cabin. His knuckles tapped on Alice's door.

"I'm almost ready," Alice's alto voice lilted above the ambient rumble of the train's song.

Jack must have said something charming because a few seconds later, she laughed. I imagined her throwing her head back as she draped herself over his arm. I ground my molars.

Next, the soldier limped past our room, cradling his injured arm. Unlike Jack, his grey eyes roamed over our cabin until his gaze met mine. I smiled, but he looked away and shuffled toward the dining car. Close behind the man strode Jack and Alice, still laughing at whatever witty thing was said before.

"We should join them all, don't you think?" Dahlia fluffed her hair and smoothed her hands over her skirt. "We should at least try to be social. Find out who these people are. Can't get all the way to London without at least knowing their names."

I cocked my head and grinned. "And what if I want to sow my wild oats, as you said? How should I go about it?" If she wanted to be an accomplice, we might as well be organized about it.

Dahlia hopped to her feet and clapped as if I'd given her a gift. "Well, I think we should have some sort of plan, don't you?" She didn't wait for my reply. "If you wish to slip away for a bit, simply ask me how I'm feeling, and I'll suggest you take me back to get some rest. It seems simplest."

Her eyes sparked again, and I thought I should tease her a little more.

"And what if I'd like to slip away alone, perhaps to meet my young man?"

She thought for a moment with her brows furrowed and her face beaming with a devious strategy. "I've got it! You tell me you have a headache, and I'll send you off for one of my powders. See? No trouble at all. Really, Penny, you should try to expand your imagination."

"What a dear you are," I said. "Though I doubt we'll have to employ your plans tonight."

"Don't fret that your friend has another on his arm. My last three husbands were with someone else when I met them."

"Dahlia!" I chided. The woman's history was far more complex than I expected. Perhaps one day she'd tell me all about it.

She pretended to hide a blush. "Well, I'm afraid all the men in this car are too young for me. Otherwise, I might be looking for husband number five. Unless you think your Mr. Graves might be interested?"

I chuffed, opened our cabin door, and waited for her to step into the hall. The steady bounce of the train caused Dahlia to reach for my arm to keep her balance. "I'm here."

"I'm not as agile as I used to be."

I rested my hand on the rail under the hall window. "I don't think any of us are, you know?"

We ambled by the empty rear cabins and through the transition to the dining car. Our fellow passengers mingled around the room, at tables, and the bar counter, sipping aperitifs and talking about the weather and war. I settled Dahlia into a chair and went to the bar for our drinks. The steward served them in a mere second, and as I walked our cocktails back to our table, I took stock of the room. It was nearly six o'clock.

The married couple sat huddled over their drinks as though someone would come and snatch them away. The husband cupped his hands around his glass while his wife stirred hers with her ungloved fingertip. She stared into the mixture as if it were a potion to reveal the future.

The soldier and Graves stood talking beside the next table. The soldier's good arm gestured wildly with a war story, and Graves crossed his arms above his belly. His right index finger and thumb stroked his grey moustache as he listened to the younger man's adventure.

Yann Kohler sat alone at the table beside the bookshelves, staring out the window into the twilight, and Alice sat by herself at the table across the car from Dahlia. Jack wasn't in the room.

As I placed the drinks on our table, I feigned a shiver. "Dahlia, I'm a little chilled. I think I'll run back to the room for my sweater. Would you like me to bring your wrap?"

She looked at me with one brow arched. "Not a headache?"

"Oh, no, merely a chill." I didn't want to be obvious, not even to Dahlia.

Alice leaned toward us. "I was cold, too. Jack—my fiancé, well —he went to get my sweater."

Fiancé? When did this happen? When was Jack going to tell me this *happy* news?

Dahlia didn't allow me time to dwell on what Alice had called Jack. Instead, she stared straight into my eyes and chirped, "Yes, dear. That would be nice. But I can't remember if I unpacked my wrap or not. I hope it doesn't take you too long to find it."

Clever woman. Maybe it wasn't so bad having an accomplice.

"I'll be right back," I assured her with a wink.

As I turned to leave, Dahlia faced Alice, and her honey-sweet voice said, "Well, felicitations to you, dear girl!"

The woman could think on her feet.

I rushed back to our cabin and pulled out my sweater and Dahlia's shawl, leaving them on the shelf within reach of the door. Now all I had to do was wait.

I peeked into Jack's room. The blinds were up on one window and the door. Where was he? I shifted to the outside window to look down the tracks, but the trees lining the rails kept me from seeing very far ahead or behind.

"Not a word." His arms circled my waist and waltzed me into his cabin.

We had danced this way before, and within a second—maybe two—he whirled me into his washroom without a sound.

As the door latched behind Jack, I found myself snugged between the side of the washbasin and his body.

"Hello, Penny." His deep, graveled voice conjured images of a storm coming in from over the ocean.

I longed to be drenched in his storm. "Hello, Jack. It's good to see you." My backside pinched against the cold ceramic sink, but the rest of me melted in the heat of his body.

"Hah! Seeing you is all I've done for far too long." His arms cinched me gratuitously close. "It's nice to have you back in my embrace."

"Congratulations," I said. My voice was as flat as I could make it, though my heart pounded in my chest.

"For what am I to be congratulated?" His warm, dark eyes bored deep into mine.

"I heard you were getting married. Is that why you summoned

me? One last fling in the closet before you resign yourself to husbandry?"

He chuffed. "You were talking to Alice?"

"She was talking to us."

"What's the first thing we learned in training?" He smelled like expensive pipe tobacco and fresh laundry. I had to focus on the job.

My arms draped over his shoulders out of necessity, so my fingers danced through the short hair at the nape of his neck.

"Don't believe everything you're told," I answered. "So, you're not marrying Alice?"

He smirked.

"Does she know this?"

"I won't leave her waiting at the altar if that's what you're asking."

I wasn't sure what I was asking. I wasn't sure of anything. "Why did you want me to meet you?"

His back straightened. "I thought you needed some information."

"You wanted to tell me Yann Kohler is on the train with us? Two doors down from you?"

"Of course, you know. How could I have doubted?" His hands squeezed at my ribcage.

The flutters in my stomach intensified. "I'm very good at what I do."

His lips grazed my neck. "I know."

"And it would be so easy to kill him...."

Jack straightened again, and his eyes stared into mine with an edge. "No. We have orders to let him live." He was my superior officer again. He'd repeat orders and expect me to follow them.

It was my turn to tempt. I pulled his face down over mine and kissed him full on the mouth. When we parted, I whispered, "Maybe it was because we had to get back to London, and we couldn't stay in Amsterdam to kill him. But now, we don't have to. Please let me take care of him. You know I can do it without any suspicion."

Jack laughed. "That's what I'm afraid of. No. The orders were clear. We don't touch him." He sighed a hot breath on my shoulder. "Look, I don't know what they have in mind for Kohler. He's not our job until they tell us." He gulped hot kisses over my neck. "When I messaged you to belay all prior orders, it may have seemed ambiguous. But my orders were not up for debate. We steer clear of him for now."

I let my fingernails trail down the top of his spine and back up into his hair. "I could give him a shot of adrenaline, like the first one in Amsterdam." My lips curved into the mischievous smile I knew Jack couldn't resist.

"How did you do it without leaving a puncture wound? They said they couldn't find any sign of an injection."

My fingers curled and flexed around the back of his neck. "We were standing together, quite like we are now, actually. Doctors sometimes forget to look in the hairline." I tickled the soft, short hairs on each side. "Right here, behind the ear."

Jack moved his hand up to his neck.

"Let's say, if I had an order on you, you'd already be dead." I let a smirk settle on my mouth. I knew what came next—he called it debriefing. Though I'd given him all the details before, he insisted we talk through my jobs whenever we had the opportunity. Maybe it was standard operating procedure. Maybe it was something else.

"And the two you poisoned? What was it you used?" His fingers walked down my back.

"I have a travel sachet of lavender and oleander. I mix a little in some tea or soup." I shrugged. "Men will take anything handed to them by a pretty face."

"Mm, you do have a pretty face." He shifted his lips to the other side of my neck. "But the one you shot? Now, that was artistry," he said between kisses.

"It took a little more work," I explained in a breathy cadence. "I got him to loosen his tie and undo a few shirt buttons."

"And what did you have to promise him?"

"Not as much as you might think."

"But the bullet went right through his heart. Just a drop or two of blood. I'll bet he never felt a thing. He still had a smile on his face."

"I always try to leave them with a smile." My lips sizzled over his.

"Well, except for Herr Walter. He wasn't smiling."

My blood went cold at the name. I pulled both my arms between us and pushed Jack as far from me as the tiny closet allowed. "I don't want to talk about Walter."

Jack held up his arms. "Why not? You did everything you were told to do. It was perfect."

I buried my face into his shoulder. "It was a mess."

"As per the assignment. And then his partner took the blame—precisely as planned. You single-handedly took out two Nazi terrors with one slice of the blade."

I trembled and shook my head. "Was there anything else you needed to tell me?"

"No, I wanted to tell you about Kohler. To make sure—"

"As we've established, I can follow orders, even when I don't want to." I glanced at my watch. "Now I must get back to Dahlia, and you must get back to Alice. We've both been gone too long as it is."

He gasped and dropped his arms to his side. The mood was lost. "I'm sorry, Penny."

I didn't want to play anymore. "If you look and ensure the hall is clear, I'll get our things and head back to the dining room. You should wait another minute before following me."

"Yes, of course."

Jack muttered something else, but I couldn't hear anything over the pounding of my heart. He signaled I was clear, and I hurried past him to my cabin. I wanted nothing more than to stay holed up there, but I couldn't.

I touched up my smudged lipstick, pulled my sweater over my shivering arms, and hugged Dahlia's shawl to my chest for a little extra comfort. As I passed his compartment again, I saw him standing on the far side, with his back to the door, his arms braced on either side of the center window, staring out to the trees beyond the rails.

Sitting down across from Dahlia, I handed her the wrap. "It took longer than I expected to find the shawl."

The old woman bobbed. "This delightful young woman kept me company while you were away." She regarded Alice. "Miss Fairchild, this is my dear companion, Miss Tompkins."

I offered my hand and smiled. "My pleasure, Miss Fairchild."

"Please call me Alice." She tilted her head to one side and squinted her eyes. "I know you, don't I? Didn't you work at the nightclub?"

"Yes, I was the hat-check girl. Call me Penny, please."

At that moment, Jack returned with a sweater for Alice. "Darling, how many sweaters do you have? I had a dickens of a time trying to decide which one went best with your outfit. Finally, I decided to go with this one because it matched your lovely blue eyes."

Alice laughed and leaned forward to let Jack slip the sweater around her shoulders. "Silly, my eyes are green."

"Well, there you have it. Next time I'll take you back with me." Jack looked back at the bar. "I'll have my drink now."

Alice caught his arm. "Jack, dear, before you go, look who's here. This is Penny, the hat-check girl from your club. Remember?"

Jack turned and looked at me as if it was the first time. "How do you do? Penny, is it?"

I offered my hand and a placid grin. "Miss Tompkins. And this is my friend, Mrs. Lundt."

"Miss Tompkins, Mrs. Lundt, it's very nice to meet you both. I'm Jack Vogel." He glanced back to his table. "And I don't mean to be rude, but I'm parched. Can I bring either of you a drink? We can have a nice little chat afterward."

Dahlia seemed to read my face like a book. "No, thank you, Mr. Vogel. I'm feeling a bit tired. Penny, I don't want to spoil your evening, but I think I need more rest. Can you take me back to the cabin, please?"

"Certainly."

Alice knit her brows in sympathy. "Mrs. Lundt, I hope you feel better soon. And Penny, if you're able, we'd love to have you join us for dinner later, wouldn't we, Jack?"

Before he could answer, I shook my head. "Thank you, but I feel a headache coming on. I may take dinner in our room. Perhaps we can visit tomorrow."

"Good night," Jack said, waiting for us to reach the door before leaving Alice's side.

We bustled through the transition and to our compartment

without a word. Once inside, I latched the door and lowered our shades for privacy.

Dahlia settled on the side of her bed and unwound the wrap from her shoulders. "And while you and Jack searched the whole train for our sweaters, did you happen to bump into each other?"

"Dahlia! How could you say such a thing?"

She dipped her chin and stared. "I ask because Mr. Vogel had your Victory Red shade of lipstick on the inside of his shirt collar and *not* Miss Fairchild's."

11

JUNE 1941, THE COUNTRY HOUSE, MORNING

our years earlier...

I shivered in the cool interview room, dressed in my brown tweed skirt and Fair Isle jumper. The wall of windows behind me washed the room in blue-white sunlight. The pair of uniformed officers sitting at the table, studying my appearance, grimaced as though my reaction to the chill had been a breach of etiquette.

"In what languages are you fluent?" the male officer asked.

"Besides English, I speak a little French—from school—and a bit of Dutch. I had dreamed of studying art. Before the war."

The man revealed the slightest curve of his mouth before immediately quashing his expression of pleasure. "Miss Tompkins," he said. It was the name assigned to me when I arrived. "The truth is, you'll very likely go back to your home next week. Most recruits stay here about eight days before discovering they don't have the aptitude or the natural skills required for this work."

I tipped my head down for a second, then raised it with as

fierce an expression as I could muster. "I'll learn whatever I need to learn. I'll do whatever you ask of me." I paused for a hard swallow. "The family I was staying with was killed. Their building was destroyed in the Blitz while I was safe in a tube station. I—I don't have a home to return to."

The auburn-haired woman at the man's elbow tapped on a folder. "We understand, and we're sorry for that." She straightened her lip as she finished. "But we must think of your safety. Not only yours but also that of the other agents in the field. Carrying messages may seem easy enough, but being searched is not a comfortable experience. Avoiding being suspected—and, in turn, being searched is almost impossible."

The tall, dark-haired man standing arms-crossed in the corner shifted his weight in a subtle gesture to join the conversation. "A pretty girl such as you may encourage someone to instigate a search even without suspicion."

The woman tilted her head in reluctant agreement. "Mr. Vogel has a fair point."

I again swallowed hard before I spoke. "Then I won't be pretty. I'll appear however you say I should. I can learn to be a courier or whatever you need. Give me whatever job you like. I'm not afraid."

Before the last word left my lips, Vogel charged toward me.

I didn't have time to think. Fear-fueled adrenaline competed for control of my mind in a fight-or-flight reaction, and thankfully, the fight won out. I'd spent months reliving the nightmare of being attacked in the alley, planning how to defend myself if another attack occurred. Planning how to never be that helpless again. No one was going to hurt me like that again. My heart slammed against my ribcage as my body engaged.

I spun away from him and retrieved the dagger-point chignon pin from my hair. His long arm reached out and gripped my waist, pulling me back. He turned me to face him and trapped me against his body, but I held my pin at his throat, under his ear.

The two at the desk hopped to their feet with their hands up. "Stop," they said with one voice.

Mr. Vogel loosened his grip and chuffed. "Outstanding, Miss Tompkins."

The officers exhaled loudly as they reclaimed their chairs.

"You underestimate me." I turned to direct the statement to all three of them. "You shouldn't do that."

Vogel bent slightly at the waist in an almost indiscernible bow toward his superiors. "If I may make a request." He straightened. "I'd like to take Miss Tompkins under wing."

They exchanged a glance and whispered a syllable or two.

The woman regarded Vogel with a stern expression. She flashed me a matching look before handing a file to the man. "You think you'll survive?"

He cut his eyes toward me and back. "I won't underestimate her again."

The superior officer swept his hand from me to Vogel as if offering a gift. "Penelope Tompkins, Jack Vogel will be training you. He's our best man; try not to kill him."

THE NEXT DAY, I began instruction in first aid, dead drops, coded messages, and parachuting. Most of the other trainees, men and women ranging in age from late teens to early fifties, went home after only a week or two. They hesitated, expressed fear, or simply couldn't grasp their assigned task.

The following month, I learned to shoot every pistol and long gun available, as well as up-close and personal hand-to-hand combat under the close supervision of Jack Vogel. After our third week, both of us covered in bruises, we began to anticipate each other's moves. We shared a chemistry neither could deny.

One evening, after an especially grueling training session, Jack blindfolded me, drove me to a wooded area some distance from the country house, and told me to get out of the car. When I stepped out, he spun me around a few times before he loosened the blindfold, letting it fall to my shoulders.

The trees hemmed us in all around, and I wondered how he got the car this deep into the forest. I wondered, too, how he'd get it out.

He glanced at his watch. "You have thirty-six hours to get back to the house."

"And you're leaving me with nothing?" I pursed my lips and shivered as I pulled the scarf from my neck, hoping to appear pitiful.

"You can keep the blindfold if you like."

I sniffed and shivered again, hugging my bosom inward and upward. Both my Cardigan and my cotton blouse were unbuttoned enough to tempt him. "Maybe one kiss to keep me warm?"

Jack's dark eyes sparked, and he slid his body against mine. "I suppose we can get a jump on next week's seduction training."

I wrapped my arms around his waist beneath his jacket, my fingers crawling over his muscular back and then dipping into his back trouser pockets.

His fingers played with the waves of hair around my face. Lifting one curl, he seemed to measure it in his hand. "This is a problem, you know."

"My hair?"

"All of you. You're too pretty. We are supposed to blend in—be invisible." He nuzzled my forehead.

I leaned into his warmth. "I've spent my whole life being invisible."

"Impossible." His lips brushed my ear.

My fingers roamed a little more. "It isn't difficult. You simply put yourself next to someone more appealing."

His arms wrapped tightly around me. "Who could be more appealing than you?"

"I appeal to you because I'm here, and I suspect I complement your skills." I gazed into his eyes while he focused on my lips. "But I think you'd be more inclined toward a blonde or redhead under normal circumstances."

Before I could read his response to my supposition, his lips covered mine for several warm seconds. When we parted, we each rocked back with unsteady steps. Perhaps I was wrong.

"I have to get back." He sucked in his lips as if he was savoring the taste of me. "And don't bother trying to follow the car. I'll be circling around here for a while—orders, you know."

"Well, that kiss will surely keep me warm long after you leave." I pushed my hands into my Cardigan pockets.

Jack stepped toward the car and turned back with a snap of his fingers. "One more thing." He held out his palm to me. "I will need my knife back."

I dropped my head and reluctantly handed back the pocketknife I'd pinched from his pocket. It was a risk, but I figured it was worth trying.

"Be honest," I said. "Did you feel it when I took it from you, or did you only notice it after?"

He returned the knife to his pocket. "I shouldn't tell you. Don't want you getting a big head about it." Jack looked me over from head to toe and back. "I didn't feel a thing. You're good."

"Yes, I am." I hugged myself against the cold as he slipped back into the car.

I watched him drive away through the trees. Once he was out of sight, I pulled his silver lighter from my pocket and my knife from my handmade sheath beneath my skirt.

I had a lean-to shelter built, a small meal of mushrooms and wild currants, and a tidy pile of firewood gathered in only a few hours. Jack's training had armed me with efficiency and skills I'd never dreamed of as a youth. And so much more.

The sun dropped out of sight as I huddled inside my shelter. My small campfire blazed beyond the little doorway.

"Seduction training?" I whispered to the firelight. "I can't wait."

12

SATURDAY, MAY 5, 1945, LATE EVENING

Dahlia settled in her seat and folded her hands in her lap. "Your young man should be more careful."

I ignored her comment. "I'll find the porter and order your dinner in here."

"I'm not so hungry as tired. And not a little irritated."

"With me?" My expression sagged with contrition, but my voice didn't quite match.

"Of course, not with you, dear." She released a cute huff. "With Miss Fairchild." She spat Alice's name as a curse.

"Well, we shan't worry about her for the rest of the evening." I stood at our cabin door and looked down the hall. "There's the porter now."

I stepped out and closed the door behind me without making a sound. The man was at the far end of the corridor, staring out the window with his arms at his side. His hands fisted and flexed alternately. As I approached, he straightened and blinked away a fiery visage.

By the time I was in arm's reach, he wore a cheerful smile, though his eyes were still red-rimmed.

"How may I serve you, miss?"

This was a chance to work—and to recover from my recent loss of control. I drew a deep breath. "Are you all right?"

"Yes, miss." Now he took a deep breath and exhaled.

"It must be difficult to be back on a train after so many months on strike." It wasn't a question. It didn't require a response. But I hoped.

"Months in hiding," he murmured.

I was in. I spread my warmest smile over my lips. "What's your name?"

He stared at me for a long beat—almost as if I was interrogating him. "Miss?"

I offered my hand. "I'm Penelope Tompkins—Penny."

He took my hand and squeezed gently. His palm was warm, but his fingers were like ice. "I'm Van Dyke. Carl Van Dyke."

"It's a pleasure to meet you." I tilted my forehead a fraction of an inch.

He stiffened again and twitched his moustache. "I'm afraid I shouldn't be so informal. Not appropriate, you know." His English was perfect, though his Dutch accent clipped the end of each word.

The poor man had been raised in proper society only to be engulfed by the most improper atrocities known to man. He reminded me of a beached herring, desperate to breathe or swim, unable to twitch a tail or fin, watching with bulging eyes as death descended.

I shook away the notion from my mind. "We're simply making new friends. There's nothing wrong with that." I smiled until his bloodshot eyes met mine. "The war is very nearly over, and we all need more friends."

"The war," his baritone voice crackled. "It won't be over for a long time. Maybe never."

"It will take time, but we'll all have to let it go." I put a cautious hand on his arm and chose my words. "And after all, we won."

"Nobody won." He spat out the words like rancid milk. "And nobody will pay."

I softened my voice. "Judgment comes to everyone."

He pulled away and worked his hands into each other, kneading invisible dough. "Not enough."

I cocked my head in his direction, asking an unspoken question.

He nodded. "At first, we thought we were helping. Even the Rabbis said it was best to take them to a safe place. Keep them together. Keep them out of the way and safe." He rattled out the mantras he'd heard a thousand times. "We thought we were doing the best thing."

He turned his eyes back to the countryside racing past the window in the dimming sunlight. I matched his stance and watched his reflection in the glass, allowing him to continue.

"Hundreds, and before long thousands. Many times what the trains should hold. Clinging to their last, most valued treasures. I watched—most didn't, but I did. First, they took their belongings. They separated the men and women. Husbands from wives as the children screamed. I can still hear." His voice floated away on a ragged breath.

"And you took a stand with a rail strike."

"Too late. How many months? We all knew there were far too many people going into the camps. Too many for the camps to hold. We couldn't ask questions. We weren't allowed to show them even the most minimal kindness." He gulped for breath. "And all along, the Germans barked, 'Don't treat them like people. They are not people. Jews are sub-human,' he told us."

He told us. I waited for Carl to say the name.

"I wonder." His voice calmed and rolled with the sounds of the train.

"What do you wonder, Mr. Van Dyke?"

He held his hands out and upward as if he were showing me something. "When you have the blood of so many on your hands, what difference does one more make?"

I knew who his *one more* was. All of Amsterdam knew the names of the Nazis who had herded the Jewish residents onto the trains. Kohler's hate for the Jews was infamous, "matched solely by Hitler himself," he often boasted.

No, I wasn't the only one with a bloodlust for Kohler on this train. I rested my hand on his wrist with a careful squeeze. "One more might not seem like it could hurt. Particularly if it is so well deserved. But you are a good man, Mr. Van Dyke. Much too good for such a thing."

"But what he did." His voice pleaded with an anguished rationalization.

"Was unthinkable." I finished his thought. "The whole lot deserves God's full and infinite wrath unleashed upon them. You could kill him. Perhaps even torture him first. But whatever you did, it wouldn't balance the scales, and the pain it would bring would destroy you, not him."

He raised a shimmering gaze to meet mine. His lips quivered but made no sound.

"Because you're a good man," I reminded.

His jaw tightened, and the clouds in his eyes cleared. "You and Mrs. Lundt are missing your supper."

I straightened my back and raised my chin, causing him to match my posture. "Yes, I came to ask if you might bring a meal for her to our cabin. She's still quite tired."

"Of course," he said. His eyes flickered to life, and he was back to work. "And you?"

I shook my head and shot a glance at my Lady Macbeth hands, covered in blood that only I could see. "I believe I shall try the dining car again."

"Very good, miss."

Van Dyke bent in a quick bow and marched away while I considered the idea of killing again. I'd never disobeyed orders before. In fact, I'd followed them to the letter even when the result had made me violently ill. To the point of hellish nightmares and a near-dead conscience.

I walked back to our cabin and explained to Dahlia that the porter would bring her meal shortly, and I would return to the dining car. I'm sure she and I had a whole conversation about everything, but I was barely present. My mind reeled and jolted, already intoxicated with the process of making the plan. I touched up my lipstick, pinched my cheeks, and discarded my sweater. I worked out the choreography in my mind's eye as I undid the top two buttons on my shirtdress.

The wrath of God was coming.

At the threshold of the dining car, I paused. Everyone was exactly as we'd left them. *Had it been only ten minutes? Maybe fifteen.* Every eye in the room looked up to my focused gaze. But I had only one man in my crosshairs.

Kohler's lips curled when he saw that my attention was on his face. I raised a brow, and he cut his amber eyes to the empty chair across the small table from him. I was already striding in his direction when he made eye contact again.

I ignored Jack and Alice, the wounded soldier, Mr. Graves, and the poor couple opposite Kohler. As I took a seat with the Nazi officer, the couple hmphed and stood, making it quite clear how they felt about my choice of dinner partners. I was no better than the prostitutes who traded favors for ration cards.

Maybe they were right; I wasn't. Let them think what they may.

Van Dyke was at the serving counter with the other attendant, and his brows wrinkled when he saw where I sat. I blinked a placid it-will-be-all-right to the porter and turned my wicked grin to the Nazi.

The wrath of God had come.

13

APRIL 14, 1945, AMSTERDAM, AFTERNOON

One month earlier...

A chill prickled across my shoulders, and I stepped out of the rain and under the awning of the café. From the cover of the green and white striped canvas, I could see the loose brick on the corner walkway—my regular dead drop.

Jack's message was clear. This was where my next German officer enjoyed his afternoon breaks. My watch showed four-twenty-six; he should arrive any moment.

"Ben je hier voor koffie?" a young server asked. He pulled out a chair for me at the nearest table. From inside, a violin played a Dutch folk song.

"Ja, een kopje. Dank je." When the man went inside for my coffee, I shifted my seat for a better view of anyone approaching. I didn't have to wait long.

He strolled up to me exactly as Jack had anticipated. *"Entschuldigung. Sie sind auf meinem Platz."* He politely explained I had taken his seat.

I glanced around and started to stand. "I'm so sorry. I just came out of the rain. I didn't know this seat was taken."

"You are English?" He gestured for me to stay in the chair. "What are you doing in Amsterdam?" Without asking, he took the seat facing me. He doffed his peaked cap and set it on the table between us. He raked his fingers through his chestnut hair to fluff what the hat and the rain had deflated.

The server returned, bowed to the Nazi, and set my cup of coffee in front of me and the German's in front of him. "*Sonst noch etwas für Sie, Oberstleutnant?*" he asked the officer. Did he wish for anything else?

"*Nein danke.*" The German shooed the server away with a turn of his wrist. He raised his cup and directed me to do the same.

We sipped our drinks together.

I finally had the chance to answer his question. "I was an artist in London. I came here after the Blitz."

"An artist, eh? I have some paintings at my home. You would enjoy to see them, I think." He tipped his forehead toward me. "Perhaps after this?"

Jack's intelligence was spot on. It was too easy.

I didn't want to appear overly eager. I forced a blush. "I shouldn't. I don't even know your name."

"Nor I yours, but should that matter, my dear? You are an artist, and I have paintings. I am sure you could tell me about them if you have studied. I know so little of art." He took another sip without breaking eye contact. "You would be doing me a favor. You would tell me what they are worth, no?"

"Then perhaps." I warmed my fingers around the hot mug. "How did you come by the paintings? Did the previous owners have no information for you?"

"Unfortunately, no. They could tell me nothing." His green eyes matched the green braids on his epaulets.

He didn't know a brushstroke from a blot. Just knew they were valuable. The owners? Gone, of course. Exterminated. That was how it worked. Take and kill. It was common practice for the Nazis.

"Then I would be happy to help." I gulped my coffee quickly, anxious to be done with the man.

We walked a few blocks in the opposite direction from my home. As we climbed the steps to his door, my hand began to itch with anticipation.

The building was ancient but well-kept, with dark brown brick arches over the doors and windows. "Quite lovely," I said.

"Rank has its privileges, as they say." He held the door open for me and gestured to the doorway on the right. "Through there. The first painting is over the fireplace."

I stepped around an overstuffed velvet sofa to study the piece. I stared into the dark brown eyes of a young woman clutching a nosegay of white jasmine or possibly orange blossoms to her breast. The oil painting was undoubtedly a Caravaggio; I recognized the model from a few of the baroque master's other works. I studied the form, the lighting, and the gentle brush strokes of the painting while the Nazi started a German version of "Lili Marleen" playing on the gramophone.

"Stunning." I released an awed sigh. "Italian baroque. You can tell by the luminous face and figure contrasting against the almost black background. It's worth a fortune."

"Ah, you do know your art." He beckoned me to follow him down a hall. "I have another more contemporary piece in my bed chamber."

The back of my neck grew warm. I could not let my guard

down for one moment. My fingers dipped into my pocket for assurance. Everything was in place.

"I think you will like this one, too." He made a grand sweeping gesture to the painting above the bed. "Quite appropriate to Amsterdam, don't you think?"

I sidled up to the bed and propped my knee onto the mattress to examine the piece. The main subject was the prow of a bright blue boat and its reflection in the water. "Very nice." I turned coyly to face him. "I think this one is by an Austrian artist called Schiele. He's more commonly known for his nudes." I settled onto the side of the bed. "They are more valuable. It's too bad you don't have one of those."

My German took slow steps toward me. "It is too bad." He took off his jacket and loosened his tie. The music from the other room echoed down the hall. "Perhaps you can educate me more on this artist."

I kicked out of my shoes, letting them hit the wood floor loudly, and scrambled up on my knees. I patted the bed in front of me. "Why don't you sit down here? I can rub your shoulders while we talk."

He grinned like a schoolboy, pulled off his belt and holster, and put everything away neatly while I waited.

"What shall we talk about first?" I unfastened a few buttons on my blouse.

He sat on the bed with his back toward me. "Tell me about the nudes. How would he paint them?"

It was time to move. With my left hand, I pinched deep into his shoulder, and he rested the back of his head against my chest. With my right hand, I loosened his tie a little more and unfastened his top four buttons. His shirt stood starch-stiff away from his skin. His cologne was a pleasant blend of spices and cedarwood.

So different from the stink of my first kill, that my mind wandered for a split second. *Focus.*

"You have many talents." His voice turned breathy. "Perhaps you can show me instead."

My left hand continued to knead his flesh while my right hand retrieved my Baby Browning pistol from my pocket. The little gun tucked discreetly in my palm, ready to work. In a split second, I had the muzzle pressed against the upper left side of his sternum, angled downward. I fired one shot.

His body barely jerked at the impact. His heart merely stopped beating, interrupted by the tiny lead bullet passing through.

I balanced his body to remain upright as I crawled backward and off the bed. I rounded the footboard and stepped back into my shoes while rebuttoning my shirtdress. I left him in his bedroom, staring into nothingness, and quickly searched his home. The schu-up, schu-up of the exhausted shellac recording ticked away the minutes from the gramophone.

Ten minutes later, with his agenda and a file of names, dates, and places secured against my bosom, I turned off the music player and descended his front steps, with the schu-up, schu-up still looping in my mind, keeping pace with the pounding of my heart. The neighbors wouldn't notice another afternoon visitor leaving his home. This was his routine—or rather, it had been.

14
SATURDAY, MAY 5, 1945, LATE EVENING

The dining car quieted after the couple left. Kohler summoned the porter with a snap of his fingers.

Van Dyke shot me a worried glance as he approached. "Yes, sir?"

"Two more of these." Kohler waggled his finger at his empty glass. "And dinner for the young woman." He indicated to me. "You are hungry, eh?"

"Yes, thank you." I directed my answer to Van Dyke. Once he'd made a quick bow and left, I offered my hand across the table. "I hope I'm not too presumptuous. My name is Penelope Tompkins."

He took my hand and held it gently for several seconds. My fingertips rested on his wrist—his heartbeat quickened. I gazed into his hazel-gold stare, and his pupils widened. Not fully dilated, but enough to tell me what I needed to know. And he studied me as intently as I assessed him.

Kohler was one of those men who, by his sheer presence, turned any suit into a uniform, the epitome of the Hitler Youth

Program. Though he was a few years older than I, his jaw still curved with the fullness of a younger man. His light brown hair curled around the crown, and I suspected that if he waited too long for a haircut, he'd also develop unruly wisps at the nape of his neck.

If I had known nothing about his life—his beliefs, his cruelty—I would find him quite attractive. I contemplated his past for a second.

What fills a man with so much hate they delight in the whole-sale murder of strangers? This man not only enjoyed the slaughter but played an active role whenever he could. He had not simply called the Jews despicable names and humiliated them but herded them like cattle to extermination camps. To gas chambers. To firing squads. He often requested to be the one to throw the switch for the poisonous gas or pull the trigger.

Who was he trying to please? Or was it revenge? A tyrant father? An unaffectionate mother? Both? I had read the psychological studies; they'd intrigued me. I needed him to tell me why he was this way. I was going to kill him, whatever his motivation, but I needed to be sure his journey to London was an escape from justice and not part of a more sinister plan.

"Good evening, Fräulein. I suppose you already know my name?"

"Yes, sir." I curled my lips and blinked through a slow breath. "Your reputation precedes you."

"And yet you still joined me." He paused for a moment as our drinks arrived. "I wonder why."

"Perhaps I'm intrigued by men of power. Your orders send people scurrying." I picked my words as one might select flowers for a bouquet. And in return, he smiled, enjoying the sweet aroma of adoration.

"You like power?" His brows rose, bringing his chin up, too. Even at the higher angle, I noticed his gaze lowering to my lips, dropping to my collarbones, and settling on my bosom. I drew a deep breath to emphasize my neckline.

"What else in the world matters but power?" I didn't let him answer. "A man such as yourself can have whatever he wants with a snap of his fingers."

He flexed his left hand into a fist and picked up his glass with his right. He swirled the last of his drink a few times before replacing it precisely where it had been. This was working. I parted my lips enough to release a whispered moan, which caused a flutter of a blink in Kohler.

"Being close to you," I started, but let my voice trail off into a sigh. "So many things I want to ask you."

"Such as?" His tone was confident. His hands smoothed a wrinkle in the white linen tablecloth, but his eyes still roamed over my body.

"Such as why a true believer like yourself takes a train to London instead of one bound for Germany at this point in the war." I had to be careful. While the war was almost over for the rest of us, for Kohler, this might be the launch point he needed for something else. I pushed my lips into a thoughtful pout and arched one brow.

Kohler smirked at the gesture. "You think my work can only be accomplished in Germany?"

"Certainly not." I paused as Van Dyke centered a plate of herring and potatoes in front of me. The savory scent of herbs wafted to my nose, and I almost forgot what I was saying.

"May I be of further assistance to you, miss?" Van Dyke asked with pleading eyes. He still grasped the edge of the plate as if I might change my mind.

"No, thank you, porter. I'll let you know if I require you again." I wanted to reassure him of my intentions, but I dared not, and he released the plate, leaving with a disturbed expression etched on the deep creases of his forehead.

His concern refocused my mission. Without missing a beat, I resumed. "I simply doubt London will be of much benefit to your cause."

"Are you trying to discover my plans, Fräulein? And why would you want to do that?" His golden eyes met mine again.

"I only thought that if you intend to spend a few months in London, perhaps we might see each other again. Perhaps even share another dinner." From behind me, I could hear Jack clearing his throat. It was for me, and I knew it. I ignored his efforts to curtail my plans.

Kohler raised his chin and blinked. "Perhaps this and perhaps that. Why do you not speak plainly?" Kohler's voice softened against the rigidity of his words.

This was the test. I had to remain calm. Even a hint of fear or nerves could give me away. He again smoothed his hands over the tablecloth while his chilling stare bore hard against my façade.

I swallowed a bite of fish, savoring the seasoning. I let my thoughts wander to a specific memory from a year ago, purposely causing a blush to rise on my cheeks. "Sir, I am still enough of a lady not to speak too plainly about certain things."

Another cough from Jack, followed by Alice chirping, "Darling, drink some water."

But I kept my gaze steady and ran my tongue over my upper lip for a split second.

Kohler's eye twitched in the corner. "However, not enough of a lady not to think about… certain things."

My lashes worked again. "Some men can't help but cause such thoughts."

"And what do you think about me? It is not proper dinner conversation, maybe?" He leaned forward a few inches.

I mirrored the shift, leaning over my plate, my voice a mere whisper. "Let me assure you, what I'd like to do with you is not at all appropriate dinner conversation." It wasn't.

The German leaned back in his seat, self-pleased. "Finish your dinner. We can talk further over another drink." He snapped his fingers in a request for two more drinks from the steward.

A genuine laugh rippled over my lips, and Kohler's grin broadened.

"It's late," Jack said louder than necessary. "Let me escort you back to your cabin, Miss Fairchild." Behind me, I heard the scrape of chair legs on the floor.

"Thank you," was her more subdued response.

The couple said goodnight to Mr. Graves and the soldier. Jack and Alice strode past us to the steward's counter behind Kohler's chair. Jack thanked the man, palming him a gilder for his trouble. Alice followed behind him, her nose in the air and her arms crossed impatiently.

The task done, Jack turned to face us. "Good night to you both."

I reached for his sleeve without touching it. "Oh, Mr. Vogel. May I trouble you for a favor?" Alice glared, her mouth agape.

Kohler watched me without acknowledging Jack or Alice at all.

"Of course; how may I be of service, Miss Thompson?"

"It's Miss Tompkins, actually."

"Of course. My apologies."

His request, I stand down, and my refusal.

"Would you mind terribly checking on Mrs. Lundt after you

see Miss Fairchild to her compartment? I may be a little while, and I'd hate for her to wait up for me."

He bowed his neck slightly. "I'd be happy to stop in on the dear woman." He exchanged a glance with Alice almost apologetically. She shook her head and leaned an elbow against the bar impatiently. "And shall I retrieve you if she needs assistance?"

Another request.

"I'm sure it won't be necessary. She's quite well and self-sufficient. Simply a bit tired."

Another refusal.

Jack grimaced. "Then I shall bid you both a good evening."

He'd turned to leave when Alice looped her arm around the crook of his elbow. She shot a fiery smirk at me, which I ignored.

Within a few more minutes, Graves and the soldier left, and Kohler and I were alone in the dining car with the single steward to chaperone.

I met Kohler's icy stare with the most wicked gaze I could feign. "And now we're all alone." I kept my voice low and sultry.

"Except for our friend here." Kohler raised his finger again, and the man snapped to attention beside our table. "Clear this table and bring another round of drinks."

The steward shuffled away the remains of my dinner, shooting a withering grin at me and a brusque nod to the German. "Yes, Herr Kohler."

Dismissing him with a flip of his hand, Kohler made a quick move to conceal the burn on his wrist. Why? He hadn't made a secret of the identifying scar before. Did he suspect me of something? I needed to shift his attention.

"The city is so lovely this time of year," I said, hoping to keep his mind on lighter things.

"I prefer the city to the country. The air is not as fresh, but there is always something to do in the city." Kohler's eyes again focused on my body. I was safe for the moment.

We talked a bit about London rain and the summer weather, and soon the fresh drinks were set before us. Kohler picked up his glass and pitched the cocktail back with a single gulp. "Let's go to my compartment and let the man clean up." He flicked a finger toward my drink. "You can tell me all about London."

The train car bumped, and I reached for my drink on instinct. The cool glass soothed my warm hand, already aching in anticipation of the task.

I could use poison; I had a vial in the lining of my clutch purse, but no syringe. I'd need a way to get it into him without a fight.

No, perhaps strangulation was better for Kohler. I would use his necktie, the cord from the window shades, or, as a last resort, my hands. I didn't like to use my bare hands; it took too long and too much energy. But it was bloodless, and I was always sure when the job was done.

However I did it, I knew how to make it look like a suicide when I was finished. It would be best for everyone on board.

I picked up my glass and gulped the whisky. The fiery liquid blazed from the tip of my tongue to my gut. Kohler twirled his finger as if to hurry me. As we stood, the train rumbled harder than before, causing us both to sway. I let the swaying rock me into his body, and he cinched his arm around my waist.

"Will your old woman mind too much if you are with me for a little longer?" Kohler kept his arm around me, but loosened his grip.

"She is probably already asleep," I whispered. I followed him through the transition and into our car. "I doubt if she'll know the dissonance." I paused, hearing the wrong word. It was as though someone else was speaking. "I mean, the diff-er-ence." My tongue moved slower than my brain.

Kohler loosened his arm from my side as we reached his compartment and swayed a little more. He raised the latch to slide open the door on the third try. "It's a little sticking."

He stepped in and took my hand, pulling me inside as he closed the door behind me. I heard the latch click as I watched Kohler dive head-first into his bench seat.

Reaching out to catch hold of his arm, my fingers wouldn't close on his sleeve. Something was wrong. The tiny room bumped and turned and knocked me to the rug before the lights dimmed. I tried to cry out, but a heavy shroud of the blackest night dropped over my head.

15

SUNDAY, MAY 6, 1945, MORNING

Sunlight screamed through my eyelids as the train whistle split the quiet of the early morning. My head pounded, and my stomach lurched. I was sprawled on the floor of Kohler's cabin, and he sat on his seat, looking down at me with a cold, unblinking stare. His lips turned up at the corners in a bizarre smirk. I'd seen the expression before, but my mind couldn't quite place when.

"What happened?" I asked, knowing full well I'd been drugged. I struggled to string together a coherent memory of the night before, praying I hadn't allowed any of my secrets to slip.

Kohler didn't answer.

The feeling started to return to my hands and feet, and I worked myself up to an unsteady sitting position. My heart slammed against my ribcage with an unnatural crash that echoed in my ears. Still, the Nazi didn't move.

A memory—not from last night—filled my brain, and I instantly recognized the man's grin. Panic washed over me, and I scanned the floor. There it was at the man's feet. A small pistol. A Baby Browning. My Baby Browning.

This was not the plan. Something had gone wrong. Had I done this? My mouth went dry. My body tremored with every slamming beat of my heart. I scrambled to my feet, shaking with a mix of confusion and fatigue. The din of the rails softened as the train slowed. We were coming into a station, and Kohler would be discovered.

I reached for my weapon.

"Stop!" Jack barked from the cabin's open doorway.

My hands went up, and I shook my head. "I didn't do this."

But I looked at Kohler, who still sat frozen, his eyes staring down at the rug. Jack stepped inside and closed the door behind him. The shades on the door and windows to the hallway were lowered, concealing us for a few minutes more.

We moved closer to see exactly where the German had been shot, but I already knew. Looking down his unbuttoned collar, I saw the short drip of blood on his chest. One shot through the heart at very close range. By the smile on his face, I knew he hadn't even felt it.

"This *is* you." Jack pointed to the wound.

"No."

Jack scowled. "You as good as told me last night you were going to kill him. Against orders. And now, after this? This is the method that you described to me from a past mission; I took notes. Now you deny it?"

"I did say that. And I did do it this way before. But I do deny it now." My mind sputtered. I drew a deep breath and began again. "I did intend to kill him. I planned to strangle him." I gestured to the pistol, still on the floor. "I didn't even have my gun with me last night. It was still in my cabin. I didn't kill him."

"This is your signature. Nobody else could have made a shot like that. Nobody."

"Well, someone did, and it wasn't me." I couldn't stop shaking my head. "I didn't kill him."

"Just tell me what happened." His face flushed with anger as he scanned the room.

What had happened? My mind raced to remember. "I had my dinner, and we talked and drank. Before long, he brought me back here—and I don't know what happened next."

"How much did you drink?" Jack sounded like my father.

"You know me well enough to know drinking wasn't a factor. I was drugged, and I don't think it was Kohler." I pointed to the dead man sitting at our side. "Considering his current situation."

The door slid open, and Dahlia and Alice stood in the hallway, their mouths hanging open.

"Oh my," Dahlia gasped. She looked up at me in pity. "Penny, dear, are you all right?"

Before I could answer, Alice shrieked, "Mr. Kohler is dead!"

Jack pulled both women inside the compartment and closed the door again. Dahlia hurried to my side and patted my hand. "I couldn't find you this morning. I was afraid something had happened to you. Oh, my dear, such a tragedy." Her voice dripped with calming compassion.

In stark contrast, Alice's breath heaved in and out of her quivering lips until her complexion was a dull green.

"Calm down, darling," Jack muttered. "You should go back to your cabin before you're ill."

"But he's—what happened to him?" She raised trembling fingers to her lips. Her eyes were pale green saucers.

"It appears to be something with his heart." Jack's simplified answer calmed her slightly. "Now, take Mrs. Lundt back to *your* cabin—put as many compartments between us as you can. You both need to sit and calm down. We don't want to upset the woman."

I regarded Dahlia, who was the least upset of us all. As if on cue, she raised the back of her hand to her forehead. "Oh, heavens! How dreadful for the poor man. Miss Fairchild, do you mind?" Her voice developed a shudder as she reached out for the younger woman. "I must sit down. My heart, you know. Such a shock."

Alice regained a measure of composure and offered her arm to Dahlia. "Of course."

The two stepped into the corridor, only to be met by Van Dyke.

"What's all this?" He leveled his gaze on Alice. "Mr. and Mrs. Hadsell said you were yelling about a dead man." He peered into the compartment at Jack, at me, and next at Kohler. "Oh, *God in de Hemel*," he said, crossing himself.

Jack stepped forward, gesturing to Van Dyke to come inside. "I told the ladies to return to Miss Fairchild's room before I came to get you. Mr. Kohler is dead, plainly."

Van Dyke shooed away Dahlia and Alice, sending them down the hall. He shot me a panicked glance. "Miss Tompkins?"

"I didn't do it." I reached for his arm, but he shrank away from me.

"But last night?" the porter asked.

"I know what I said last night." I took a deep breath and allowed my eyes to glisten, hoping for his sympathy. "But I assure you, I didn't kill him."

Van Dyke stepped in and looked at Kohler's face. "Natural causes?"

"I'm afraid not," Jack replied, tugging the dead man's collar enough to reveal the congealed drip of blood.

Van Dyke saw the pistol and looked back into my eyes. "Miss Tompkins, you were with him." His voice begged me to contradict his accusation.

"I was." I sniffed appropriately. "I woke up on the floor a few minutes ago, and he was like this. But I didn't do it."

As if punctuating my sentence, the train stopped completely, and we all swayed with the halting. Van Dyke removed his porter's cap and raked his fingers through his short hair.

I lowered my shoulders to become as diminutive as possible. "Please believe me."

"We've already crossed the border into France. I'll have to tell the conductor. You should both go to your own rooms and stay there until I come back for you. I'll have to lock this compartment, and… I'll help as I'm able, but this is quite a position I'm in now." He frowned at Jack and softened his expression to me. "Don't touch anything. Leave the gun here, please."

We followed his instructions as we shuffled out of the compartment. We watched Van Dyke lock the door and release a long low sigh. I half-expected him to spit on the door.

"Mr. Van Dyke," I asked. "Would you mind if Mr. Vogel stayed with me until you return? I'm not sure my nerves will stand being alone."

"I shouldn't allow it, but I think I can make an exception in this case." He sighed again. "But you must stay put. Nobody is to come out of the room until I say. Do you understand?"

"Yes, sir," Jack and I said together.

We agreed and backed into my compartment, closing the door after us. Jack placed a tender hand over mine, but dropped it as soon as he saw Alice and Dahlia sitting on the seat in my cabin, staring at us.

16

SUNDAY, MAY 6, 1945, MORNING

*A*lice leaped from her seat next to Dahlia and threw her arms around Jack's neck. "Darling, I was so frightened!"

"Everything's fine now. Don't worry about anything." Jack's voice was calm but unconvincing, and Alice spun off into whimpers and sniffs.

Dahlia reached out for my chilled fingers and directed me to sit next to her. "What a dreadful experience for you, dear. My, your hands are like ice. Let's get a blanket for you. You're in shock, don't you think?"

"I'm quite all right," I lied. My pulse pounded in my ears, and the taste of bile lingered on my tongue. My thoughts spun in a hundred different directions.

Kohler was dead—and I hadn't done it. That meant someone else had followed him. Followed us. And framed me. I couldn't imagine who had drugged us, or who might be mimicking my method of assassination. Why would anybody do it if it wasn't to place the guilt squarely on me? I racked my brain to remember even the slightest memory from after dinner. Nothing. I turned my attention back to Dahlia. "But you must be shaken at such a sight."

The older woman bobbled her head. "It was a wretched thing to see, of course, but all I could think of was you and what you must have gone through."

Dragging Jack to stand closer to Dahlia, Alice whined, "Darling, I think, under these terrible circumstances, you and I should be the ones to chaperone Mrs. Lundt for the rest of the trip to London. Don't you agree?"

"What?" Jack's brow arched as he squinted.

Alice continued without taking a breath. "I mean, Miss Tompkins is obviously not the kind of person who should be a lady's companion."

"What's wrong with Miss Tompkins?" Jack's brow reversed into a furrow.

"Well, she's not," she began and paused when she realized both Dahlia and I were staring. Alice swallowed hard and straightened her spine before continuing. "She's… she should have known better than to have dinner with a man like Mr. Kohler. He is a German… after all… well, he was. And to go back to his room with him, well, it doesn't show good judgment." She looked down her nose at me. "I don't say these things to be mean; I'm stating facts."

"Alice, that's not a very charitable thing to say." Jack clicked his tongue.

"Facts are facts," Alice replied. Her green eyes shot daggers into mine. "I think Mrs. Lundt deserves to have a traveling companion who'll look after her interests first. Not act like some sort of good-time girl."

"Alice, stop," Jack demanded.

I tried to decide how to proceed. I couldn't explain to Alice why I had gone into Kohler's room. *I wasn't looking for a cheap thrill, Miss Fairchild; I went to Kohler's room to kill him.* No, that wouldn't do.

Dahlia spoke up. "I'm afraid this was all my fault. I'm the one who pushed Penny—Miss Tompkins—into having dinner with the man."

My jaw dropped open, and I had to snap my mouth shut before Alice noticed.

"Of course, it's not your fault, Dahlia." I shook my head. "He said that he wanted to show me a photo of the house he intended to rent in London. I shouldn't have been so stupid. I should have insisted he wait until morning to show me."

If I hadn't been drugged, my mind would have been sharper. I could have dealt with this nonsense in mere seconds. But the tiny cabin was closing in, making everything louder and more ridiculous. If I hadn't been drugged, I could have thought through everything. But then again, if I hadn't been drugged, none of this would be happening now. Who could have done it? How did they do it? And why?

Alice pulled on Jack's sleeve as her protesting continued. "See? Even Miss Tompkins agrees about her lack of judgment. Mrs. Lundt won't be a problem. I'll take good care of her."

"I am not a stray dog who needs someone to clean up after." Dahlia held her head high. "Miss Tompkins has been a perfect lady in every respect, and I shall not dismiss her now when she needs me." Dahlia reached her thin arm around my back to rest her shaking hand on my shoulder. "Thank you, Miss Fairchild, but no, thank you."

The blonde blinked at Dahlia's refusal as if it had been a slap in the face. "I was only trying to help the situation. Some people have no sense of appreciation."

"I do not need your assistance right now." Dahlia turned to face me. "Now tell me, Penny, what can I do to help?"

I released a long sigh. "I truly don't know. I'm a bit tired. Maybe we should let Miss Fairchild and Mr. Vogel go back to their cabins."

"Good idea," Dahlia said.

"Remember what the porter said." Jack shoved his hands into his trouser pockets. "He wants us all to stay in this room until he sends for us."

I narrowed my eyes. "Yes, but that was when he expected Dahlia and Alice to be in Miss Fairchild's cabin." I decided to be a tiny bit uncharitable toward Alice. "He sent us both to my cabin so I wouldn't have to be alone." I regarded Dahlia with a placid smile. "But now I have Mrs. Lundt, and you have Alice. I suggest you go to her cabin and find a way to occupy yourselves until the porter returns."

Alice's face flushed red, and Jack cut his eyes to meet mine. "Maybe it is a good idea."

A knock at the door interrupted him.

"Come in," Dahlia called in her sing-song way, though now it carried a tremor.

Mr. Van Dyke stepped in and heaved a quick sigh of relief. "Good, you're all in here, safe and sound. I looked in Miss Fairchild's cabin, and it was empty. Scared me for a moment."

"Yes," Alice said. She took a step away from Jack and toward the porter. "I thought Mrs. Lundt would be more comfortable in her own cabin."

"Gave me quite a start." Van Dyke wrung his hands together.

"I'm a bit on edge, as you might imagine. This kind of thing doesn't happen every day."

"Yes, well, what can you tell us, Porter—what was your name again?" Jack slouched against the door frame.

"I'm Mr. Van Dyke." He shot me a worried glance. "I've spoken to the conductor, who called the French police. I've been instructed to keep everyone in this car in their rooms until a team of investigators arrives. They should be here soon. Once that happens, we'll all be escorted to an inn until the authorities get this incident sorted out."

"They won't be holding anyone in jail?" Alice asked, tossing an accusing look my way.

"Not until the investigation calls for it." Van Dyke grimaced at Alice. "For the moment, I'll have to ask you all to stay in here. But it won't be a long wait. Mrs. Lundt, Miss Tompkins, you may want to get your bags ready. And I'm afraid the police will have to inspect all of your belongings."

"Will we have the opportunity to gather our things as well?" Jack asked before Alice had the chance to protest.

"Yes, sir. I expect the police will give you plenty of time to pack before you leave the train."

Jack's nod was confident. "I hate that the whole train will be delayed on our account."

He was a master at getting people to talk. Almost as good as me.

"The train will merely be delayed an hour or so while the police inspect the crime scene and remove the victim. When it's done, and we're all secured at the inn, the train will resume the trip."

"What about us?" Alice continued her whining. "When will we

be allowed to go? I have a wedding to plan. My mother and father are waiting for me. I can't be delayed."

I watched the porter inch back against the door as Alice spoke. The room was too small for this many people with this much emotion.

It was my turn to take over; there was no more time for too-close quarters or a muddled mind. I had to put my emotions on hold and act, as Mother had trained me. "Thank you, Mr. Van Dyke." I shook his hand with a gentle squeeze. "We all appreciate you for keeping us informed. We'll be ready when the police arrive."

"Yes, miss." Van Dyke tipped his chin and backed out into the hall, sliding the door closed between us.

I spun around and faced the others in the room. "Dahlia, why don't I pack us up while you visit with Mr. Vogel and Miss Fairchild?"

"Of course, dear," Dahlia motioned to the space beside her on the seat. "Come along, Alice. May I call you Alice? You should have a seat. You look pale as a ghost."

Alice dropped into the seat with Dahlia, who comforted the poor girl.

I glanced up at the luggage on the shelf above the water closet. "Mr. Vogel, would you be a dear and help me with this?"

"I'd be happy to." As he reached for the case, I sidled up next to him as we'd practiced many times before. He pretended the suitcase was stuck for a moment. "We need to have a conversation," he whispered.

"Shall we have it here?" I muttered sarcastically. "Or in the police station?"

He rolled his eyes. Lowering the valise, he said, "Here it comes.

It must have been hooked on something. Let me look the bag over and ensure you don't have a loose strap."

He and I opened the suitcase and hunched over the bag as Dahlia and Alice chatted behind us.

"Hmm, look at this," he said and dropped his volume. "I need to know what happened to Kohler." He inched his body closer to mine, and I could smell his cologne.

"Oh, you're right. It does look loose." I huffed and matched his whisper. "I'd like to know, too." I stepped back, refusing to be influenced by his smell or touch, no matter how much I longed for them.

"I wonder how this happened without you noticing it." Jack's tone was back up, and as I understood it, Kohler's dead body was now the suitcase in question.

"Well, I don't know. It must have been damaged by someone else on the train." I shrugged. "You know, we're not the only travelers here."

Jack smirked. "I understand, but it looks like something someone like you would have done."

An accusation? He didn't trust me? "Something I'd have done?"

"Considering the damage, I'd think it was done by someone of your height, roughly." Jack held out the case as though he were pointing at the bullet hole in Kohler's chest.

"There are plenty of other people on this train—in this very car—about the same height as me, roughly."

"But I question their ability to do this kind of damage."

I kept my ire from escaping and pulled the suitcase from his hand. If he didn't believe me, I could handle this problem myself—couldn't I? "Well, I'm more careful with my things than you think. And if you ask my opinion, the damage isn't too bad, anyway."

"What's wrong, dear?" Dahlia asked, interrupting her conversation with Alice.

I directed my sweetest smile toward the woman. "It's nothing. Mr. Vogel found a scratch on one of our suitcases. But it's hardly noticeable." I held out the case for Dahlia to see, and she agreed.

"I can't see anything amiss," the old woman said. "I suppose Mr. Vogel's eyesight is sharper than mine."

"You should both call me Jack," he said.

"Jack?" Alice complained, offended by his informality with me. "Considering the circumstances… and the kind of woman she is."

He took a step toward Alice, ignoring her last remark. "Look, dearest, we're all in this little pickle. So let's not worry about etiquette right now. Call me Jack. Call her Alice." He pointed back at me. "We'll call you Penny."

Alice harumphed and pressed her lips into a tight line. She turned back to face Dahlia. "You, of course, should call me Alice."

The older woman bowed her chin and patted Alice's hand. "And I'm Dahlia, dear. I do think we'll all become fast friends, despite the situation. Don't you think so, Penny?"

"Of course. We shouldn't let the death of a stranger keep us from making friends." I glared at Jack and next set a wicked curl to my lip as I glanced at Alice. "I enjoy new friends."

17

SUNDAY, MAY 6, 1945, LATE MORNING

*W*ithin the hour, Van Dyke and the steward from the dining car were leading all the first-class passengers to the corner of the train platform, where we signed documents attesting to the ownership of our luggage. We watched as each piece was loaded onto a truck and driven out of sight.

Another man, tall with wavy dark hair combed back from a squared forehead, directed us into three black automobiles that headed down the road toward a grove of trees amidst a broad expanse of farmland. Dahlia and I rode with Graves and the soldier. By this time, I was positive it was the same soldier I'd seen before in Amsterdam.

The young man tipped his head toward me. "You're Miss Tompkins, eh? I'm Hans Rutgers." He positioned his wrapped arm forward and across his waist.

Graves spoke up. "Pardon my manners; I should have introduced you."

I greeted him with a bob and gestured to Dahlia. "Mr. Rutgers, Mr. Graves, may I present my friend, Mrs. Lundt."

The gaunt, young Rutgers bowed and settled his focus back on me. "I wanted to thank you, Miss Tompkins."

I blinked and offered a placid smile. "For what do I deserve your gratitude?"

He leaned toward me and softened his voice. "Mr. Hadsall says you killed the Nazi. My hat's off to you."

A flush of heat radiated from my cheeks. "I'm sorry, but I'm afraid Mr. Hadsall is mistaken. I assure you, I didn't kill anyone on the train."

Rutgers flinched and cocked his head. "I must have misunderstood him. My apologies." He shrugged. "Hadsall said the blonde screamed after finding you in the dead man's compartment."

"That much is true, but I didn't kill him." I'd barely gotten the phrase out when he raised a brow and slipped an index finger alongside his nose.

"Of course, you didn't." He winked. "But if you did, I wouldn't think less of you, miss."

"See here, man," Graves interrupted. "This is highly inappropriate. This young lady has been through a traumatic experience. How could you accuse her of such a crime?"

"I wouldn't consider it a crime if the man deserved it." Rutgers held his free hand palm up. "As I said, I'd thank her."

Dahlia shook her head. "Now, now. Miss Tompkins didn't do any such thing. Mr. Vogel said it was the poor man's heart." She patted my knee. "I suggest we don't speak anymore on the matter."

Graves straightened himself in the seat. "I agree with Mrs. Lundt."

But Rutgers couldn't let it go. "They don't bundle us all off the train and search our things because someone suffered a heart attack. So, no, this was murder, most certainly."

Dahlia gasped and clutched her hand over her bosom.

I glared at Rutgers and turned toward Dahlia. "Are you all right? Should I lower the window for some air?"

"Thank you, my dear. Yes, please."

"Now you've upset Mrs. Lundt," Graves said.

And yet, Rutgers persisted. "It's a shame even to call it murder, you know. If this had happened last week on the street, the man would have been merely another casualty of war."

"Please, Mr. Rutgers. Please, let's change the subject." I pleaded as I cranked open the window beside Dahlia.

The man relented as the car pulled up to a small inn at the end of the road. The building was once a grand estate home. It was a formidable grey-brown cut stone with a century of ivy climbing up to the blue slate roof. The heavily leaded glass windows blinked in the sunlight popping over the hills beyond.

A tall, thin youth hurried out to open our car door and help Dahlia and me inside the small lobby. The men followed.

The lobby shone with dark paneled wood walls and marble-tiled floors. There was a broad front desk with polished brass cherub lamps at each end. Beyond that, the end of a staircase curved out with an ornately carved balustrade and a newel post shaped into a miniature statue of a Greek muse. The figure carried a long, narrow trumpet and a scroll clutched to her semi-nude body. The post was topped with a globe etched with stars.

Though the house was tired with war, the innate opulence glowed all around us. The boy directed us into a smaller, less grand sitting room.

"The inspector requests you have a seat here in the parlor until he can sort you all out." The boy repeated this as the passengers from the other cars arrived.

We all took seats in the shabby little room appointed with mismatched chairs and drab grey wallpaper. Brighter blue rectangles punctuated the walls where paintings had once hung. The old home had undoubtedly been a grand inn before the war, but, like everything else, had been starved into a gaunt shell.

A quiet little woman seemed to appear from the shadow in the corner. "May I bring tea or coffee for you? We have both, though not much milk or sugar."

"Thank you, please," Graves said, still standing until all the women had settled in the chairs.

The woman hurried away, leaving us all to stare at each other with wide eyes and unspoken questions. Alice, Dahlia, and Mrs. Hadsall jumped at the rattling sound the tea cart made bumping over the threshold. "Here we are now," the hostess chirped.

"Allow me to help serve," Graves said. He deferred to Dahlia. "Mrs. Lundt, may I bring you some tea?"

"Thank you, yes. A tiny splash of milk, please. And no sugar for me." Dahlia smoothed her skirt and shifted forward in her seat.

In a few minutes, Graves and our hostess had served everyone a warm cup, with still a bit of milk to spare.

"I'll leave the cart here if anyone would like more." She bowed herself out of the room.

China cups clinked into and out of saucers as we sipped over the pregnant silence that filled the room.

Finally, Rutgers leaned from his chair toward the husband and wife, the Hadsalls. "Miss Tompkins said she didn't kill the Nazi." His whisper might have been a full-lunged shout in the quiet parlor.

As if he'd tossed a grenade into the room, everyone erupted

with a gasp followed by an exasperated statement of disbelief. Everyone except Dahlia and me. We watched as the men hopped to their feet and the women let their jaws slacken.

"Please, let's calm ourselves." Jack's voice rose over the cacophony of the others. "The police will manage without our speculation."

"That we will, *s'il vous plaît*." The tall man from the train station stepped into the room and commanded a hush by slapping his black leather gloves into his palm. His blue-black uniform fit his broad shoulders perfectly, giving the impression of an imposing figure. Everything about him was polished, from his tight gold buttons to his glowing black boots. "I am Inspector Toussaint. I expect your full cooperation in my investigation of the death of Monsieur Kohler. Yes, I'm afraid it was murder."

"Not his heart?" Alice asked.

"*Mais oui*, mademoiselle, it was his heart. It stopped pumping when the bullet passed through it." He raised his full brow until it created a third crease across his forehead. His tone became almost playful. "But I believe someone else put it there for him."

At this declaration, all eyes turned to me. Shaking my head seemed as ineffective as denying the accusation, so I remained still.

"*Eh bien.*" Toussaint pulled a notepad and pencil from his breast pocket. "Mademoiselle Tompkins, is it?"

"Yes, sir." I drew a steady breath, keeping my fingers loose and my feet unmoved.

Toussaint waved his pencil around the room. "They all—obviously—believe you had something to do with Kohler's death."

"They do." Back straight, head high, and not too much breath in my voice.

"And why is it so, may I ask?" He poised his pencil to begin. His dark green gaze bore straight through me.

I cut my eyes to Jack, and he blinked twice. *Proceed with caution.* I'd been insubordinate enough already, and I decided to comply. "They have their reasons, but they are wrong. I would be most happy to explain my situation privately."

Mrs. Hadsall released a low gasp as though I was trying to seduce Toussaint in front of everyone. Maybe I should have, but it wasn't my intention.

Toussaint clapped his notebook closed. "This is satisfactory. I will speak with each of you one at a time. I will make myself an office here, and Madame DeSalle will provide you with rooms for the night. After luncheon, I will begin my interviews."

Graves put his teacup down and stood with a finger raised. "Sir, I appreciate you have a job to do, but under the circumstances, is it necessary for all of us to stay? Some of us are anxious to get to London. I have appointments."

Toussaint smeared a smile from one side of his mouth to the other. "*Oui,* monsieur, I understand. It is why I am sure you will all be forthcoming with whatever information you might have. So that," he paused, holding out his palms in a beseeching pose, "you may all continue your journey as soon as possible."

Mr. Hadsall stood alongside Graves. "But we have no information to give you." He rocked a thumb between Graves and himself. "We had nothing to do with the matter."

Rutgers rose and stepped in with them. "Same for me."

Toussaint's smug smirk widened. "Ah, I see. So the rest of you had no reason to want Kohler dead? He was a Nazi officer. He decimated your homes and starved you all nearly to death. Were you all so happy to forgive? In all my days, I have never seen such a merciful congregation."

The men retook their seats.

"Yes, I do see." Toussaint's expression grew more serious. "Mademoiselle Tompkins may have had the most obvious means and opportunity, but from what I have gleaned from the barest of details, you all had the motive to kill Kohler." He closed his eyes and placed his palm to his chest. "For that matter, I had motive as well. But, of course, I had no means or opportunity. I was not on your train."

As he finished, Madame DeSalle entered, wiping her hands on her apron. "I'm ready to check you into your rooms." She curtseyed to Toussaint. "Whenever you're ready."

"*Oui, madame.*"

We all rose, placing our cups and saucers on the cart before filing into a line toward the lobby. Toussaint bent his head toward me in a respectful bow. "I should like to speak with you first, if I may?"

Before I could answer, Dahlia reached her hand toward Toussaint's. "Inspector, Miss Tompkins is my traveling companion. I will need her assistance getting up to my room. Would you mind terribly delaying your meeting with her until I'm settled? It will be but a moment or two."

Toussaint studied Dahlia's frail frame before agreeing. His sharp edges seemed to soften and melt in the wrinkles around her eyes. "Yes, Madame Lundt. I will allow it." He glanced up at me. "But do not keep me waiting. I am anxious to hear your story."

"Yes, sir." I took Dahlia's hand in mine, and we left the inspector alone in the parlor.

The men were kind enough to insist Dahlia register first, so we moved to the front of the line. Once we signed in, Jack stepped out of the queue.

"Please allow me to see you both up to your room. The stairs look steep." He popped his elbow out toward Dahlia. "Mrs. Lundt?"

As she reached her fingers around his arm, Alice turned to face us. "Jack, I'm sure Mrs. Lundt can manage with Penny's help."

Jack glared. "Darling, I would hate for anything to happen to her. I'm sure you're concerned for her as well."

Guilted into submission, Alice simmered into a nod. "Of course, but hurry back down, dear." She bit the word off with a glare.

"Of course."

With Jack on one side of Dahlia and me on the other, we followed the youth up the wide staircase to the last room on the right.

Dahlia handed me her wristlet, and I drew out a coin and pressed it into the old woman's trembling hand. She turned to the boy. "What is your name?"

"I am Allard." He paused as Dahlia gave him the coin. "Whatever you need, please, ask for me." He opened the door to our room. "May I show you the room?"

"Please do," Dahlia said, smiling.

Jack pulled me back gently. "Tell Toussaint the truth about last night."

I interrupted. "I know. The truth, but not all the truth. I understand. I remember the training."

"In the meantime, I'll see what I can discover, too. Someone is setting you up." His face moved toward mine.

I edged a half-step back to keep a respectable distance. I didn't want to put Dahlia in the position of having to lie to the police. "You know what you're saying? The implications?"

He straightened his stance and tipped his head forward in the slightest nod. "It means someone knows who and what you are."

"Thank you, Mr. Vogel, for seeing us up." I held out my hand to shake his. "Be careful," I added under my breath. "If they know who I am, they may know about you, too."

His voice went back to a conversational volume. "My pleasure. I'd best get back to my fiancée. Cheers."

His term for Alice stabbed my heart. I wondered if it was intentional, aimed just at me, or for show, to keep up appearances in front of Dahlia. It hurt, either way.

Jack trotted back down the stairs with Allard a few paces behind. I turned and joined Dahlia in the small room.

"According to the boy, this is the finest room in the whole inn. We even have a private bath." Dahlia gestured to the door behind her. "Would you like to freshen up before your interview with Toussaint?"

"Interrogation, you know." I sighed. "And thank you for giving me this little respite." I patted her hand. "You're a good friend."

She placed her trembling fingers against my cheek. "My dear, I know you didn't murder the man. I *know* you. It's not who you are."

My heart lurched. Dahlia trusted me. She saw me as someone so much better than I was. I couldn't let her know the truth. "Yes, I think I would like to freshen up."

18

SUNDAY, MAY 6, 1945, LATE MORNING

"And what is your age, mademoiselle?" Toussaint licked the lead of his pencil as he paused for my answer. I assessed him as he studied me from head to toe.

I guessed he was in his early to mid-thirties, perhaps a year or two older than Jack. His tanned complexion indicated that he spent much of his day outside, and his overall build suggested that he had enjoyed a healthy measure of sports as a youth. I supposed he had spent time at the front—maybe even suffered a minor injury. Not enough to send him home, but enough to put him behind a desk. His manners were impeccable, so he must have come from a good family. Not necessarily wealthy, but that wouldn't surprise me. I wondered if a seduction tactic would be appropriate. Maybe.

"I am twenty-six years old." I shifted my crossed ankles in his direction and kept my expression placid.

The inspector wrote in his notebook much longer than it

should take to jot down a two and a six. I waited patiently for his pencil to stop as if I hadn't noticed.

"One thing to begin," he added, not looking up. "You are a British subject. Why were you in Amsterdam?"

Nodding, I spilled the answer I had ready for this question. "I'd always wanted to be an artist and had begun studying in London. But when the war was launched in earnest, I decided to finish my education in Amsterdam, where I could study Rembrandt and other masters. I had a good teacher for a while, but the bombs began falling there, too. I still like to draw and paint, but I fear I will never be able to sell my work."

"I understand. So, what did you do to keep food on the table? Is that when you went to work for Madame Lundt?" His gaze finally reached mine.

"Oh, no. Mrs. Lundt lived in the house next door to mine. It's how we became friends. But no, I worked at a nightclub." I paused to let his imagination work, noticing that he glanced at my ankles and back to my face, then added, "I worked in the cloakroom." I feigned a yawn to test his empathy for my situation, and he reacted with a brief yawn into his notebook.

"Pardon," he said, recovering. "Well, it must have been disappointing for you. Wishing to be an artist, only to work in a dark closet of a nightclub, eh?"

Pleased with his response, I lowered my chin and lifted a wide, sorrowful gaze to his. "Yes. I tried to sketch caricatures of the patrons, but the manager refused my suggestions. Said I was better with a lint brush than a paintbrush."

"Ah, the toll of war, I'm afraid." He saluted by tapping the end of his pencil to his forehead and poised to write again. "I know this may be difficult for you, Miss Tompkins, but of course, I must have your account of what happened last night, as best you remember, between you and Kohler."

"Of course." I straightened my back and glanced up to the right, ensuring he saw the gesture, just in case he'd studied the tells of body language. "I had accompanied Mrs. Lundt to the dining car for dinner, but before we could order, she grew tired and asked to return to our car. Traveling can be quite exhausting, especially for a woman of her age. I left with her and made sure she was comfortable in our compartment. When I returned to the dining car, there was an empty chair at the table with Mr. Kohler. I sat there with him, and he ordered me a drink and dinner."

"There was no other empty chair?" Toussaint raised his brow. His expression contained no trace of judgment, merely intense interest.

Again, I lowered my chin. "Well, there was the table Mrs. Lundt and I had left, but it was right inside the door—the farthest from the steward's counter and with more train noise and the draft from the door. The chair at Kohler's table was the closest to the counter."

"I see." He tapped his pencil against his full bottom lip. "And Kohler didn't mind?"

"No, sir. As I said, he ordered for me." I maintained a matter-of-fact composure and continued. "We talked about the weather and such. A little about my art. He said he also liked to draw. He wanted to show me some of his work. That's why I agreed to go back to his compartment after dinner." I studied his face as he took notes. His moustache curled neatly around his lips, drawing attention to the way they tilted down when he wrote.

As though he could sense my gaze on his lips, he looked up before continuing. "Of course. But you must know the others may not see this as the innocent encounter you present."

Sensing the need for sympathy here, I melted into a woeful air of distress. "I know now. But at the time, it simply seemed like a shared interest. I was naïve." I sniffed twice, and Toussaint handed me a linen handkerchief from his breast pocket. I allowed my fingertips to brush his as I took it. His hand was hard and firm, but not rough. "Thank you."

"My pleasure." He waited as I knotted the linen square around my knuckles and whimpered for a second.

The handkerchief carried a freshly laundered scent, with a hint of spice and leather. I couldn't focus on that now; I had work to do. I tugged at my dress collar, hoping to draw his attention to my throat.

"We each had another drink, and we got up to leave the dining car soon after. We were the last ones left, besides the steward. As we walked, though, we struggled not to stagger." I dabbed at my eyes. "I think we were drugged somehow."

"It was not simply the drink?" Toussaint asked. "You had two drinks? How many had Kohler?"

"Yes. I had two cocktails, but they didn't taste strong. No stronger than wine. I have no idea how many drinks Kohler had. He didn't act intoxicated before, though."

"But you think there was something more in the drinks? Why?" He leaned forward to the edge of his chair now. His dark green gaze bore into mine.

I rocked an inch forward in my chair and focused again upon his lips. They looked full and soft, and I wanted him to notice me looking at them.

Licking my own lips, I raised my eyes slowly to meet his and nodded. "I do. The feeling I had—it isn't easy to explain." I paused and drew a deep breath. "By the time we got to his cabin, we could hardly stand upright. It all happened so fast. In fact, almost before he got the door closed behind us, Kohler fell dead away." I let my voice tremble with tears. "That's all I remembered. Afterward, everything went black."

Toussaint's face contorted with sympathy. "*Oh, ma cherie.* What a terrible thing." He paused for a second. "And this morning? What is the next thing you remember?"

"I awoke on the floor, exactly as I had fallen, I suppose. And Kohler was sitting on the seat. At first, I thought he was looking at me, but then I realized he was dead." I sniffed again, playing on his compassion for everything I could get. "I was about to scream when Mr. Vogel opened the door. He made sure I was all right, checked on Kohler, and afterward, Alice, Miss Fairchild, summoned the porter."

"Yes, I see." Toussaint wrote furiously in his notebook, nodding and humming as he scratched away. He glanced up after a few moments. "You did not know Kohler before yesterday?"

"I knew his name… and his reputation, of course." It would benefit me nothing to deny that fact.

"And yet you sat with him? He is known, even here in France, mademoiselle, for his cruelty."

"Perhaps part of me wanted to see if it was true." I shook off the whine in my voice. "I have met many people these last few years who didn't live up to their reputation."

Toussaint suppressed a laugh and eased back into his chair. "Perhaps you are naïve, perhaps no." He flipped his notebook closed and tossed it and the pencil onto the table at his elbow. He cocked his head and raised a brow toward me. "Did you find Kohler," he inserted a strategic grimace into his sentence, "attractive looking?"

The question caught me off guard enough that I blinked. "Really," I tried to sound insulted, "I hadn't thought about it." I took a breath, trying to decide what answer would serve me best. "I suppose I did. Yes, maybe it's why I wanted to know if he could really be such a horrible man. He didn't look horrible."

"Yes, *oui*. It is as I suspected." He shrugged his shoulders and let them drop. "Innocence is hard to overcome, except in war. It is refreshing to see."

Yes, innocent. See me as innocent. "It comes with its own trouble; I'm learning."

"My dear, there is always trouble." He gripped the arms of his chair and appeared as though he would stand, but waited. "About the drinks, who do you think may have drugged you?"

Toussaint wasn't going to be quite as easy as I had hoped. "I'm sure I don't know," I said. If I thought someone drugged my cocktail, I certainly wouldn't have drunk it."

"Of course. But what I mean is… since you did drink it, and since Kohler was murdered immediately afterward, can you guess who might have done the deed? To me, it seems reasonable that whoever slipped the drugs into the drinks was the same person who murdered Monsieur Kohler. Don't you think?"

I coughed a slight laugh. We weren't underestimating each other. "It does make sense."

"Still, you cannot guess? Who had the opportunity? Surely it was someone in the dining car; the number is limited. Think. Try to remember." Toussaint finally stood and gestured for me to do the same.

I sighed into the handkerchief as I rose beside him. Standing within reach, I noted that my eyes were even with his shoulders. Taller than I had estimated. Taller than Jack. I tilted my face toward his. "I don't know who knew Kohler. As you suggested, perhaps everyone had a reason to hate him. I'm grateful whoever it was didn't hate me, too." I held out the linen square to redirect his attention.

"No, mademoiselle, it is for you to keep." The inspector walked me to the door and put his hand on the knob, though he didn't turn it.

"Thank you, monsieur. You have been most kind." I fluttered my lashes.

"Just one more thing I forgot to ask you," he said over a raised finger.

"Yes?"

His gaze met mine as he opened the door, and his tone turned surgical. "The pistol on the floor of Kohler's cabin—the one which killed the man—that pistol belonged to you?"

19

SUNDAY, MAY 6, 1945, NOON

From the lobby doors facing the back garden, I watched the Hadsalls enjoy another serving of tea on the terrace. The sun danced above the stand of oak trees on the horizon, casting a brilliant green over the stretch of meadowed expanse that reached out from the inn.

Behind me, I heard Toussaint and Rutgers arguing, and I adjusted my stance for a view of the exchange. Toussaint insisted he needed to see Jack immediately, while Rutgers pleaded to be the inspector's next interview.

"Monsieur, I understand, but I should speak to the ones who found the body first. Were you in the group that found the dead man?" Toussaint crossed his muscular arms over his chest as if in a challenge to the man whose arm still languished in a bandage.

"No, not at first." Rutgers shifted his sling to square his shoulders. "But the Hadsalls told me what they heard, and I want to be sure to tell you before I forget."

Toussaint rolled his eyes to the heavens. "It is not the way."

He tried to step around Rutgers and gesture to Jack, but the man pressed him again. "Please, Inspector, it's important."

Pointing to Jack, Toussaint gave in. "All right, but Monsieur Vogel, I will see you directly."

Jack saluted the man and gestured between Alice and the gardens. "Look, darling, why don't you enjoy some fresh air. The inspector will call me in a few minutes. See if there are any roses on the hedge."

Alice shot a sharp glance in my direction before looking past me toward the Hadsalls. "Maybe I'll join them for tea. Oh, won't it be grand to be back in London? I'll be glad to be away from this sordid situation. Can you imagine what people might think if they heard?"

"Yes, dear." He held the door open wide for her. "When I'm finished, I'll come to find you."

Alice patted Jack's cheek as she passed him on the way outside. "Soon, it will be my turn, I suppose?"

"I expect so." Jack closed the door and waved as Alice glanced back over her shoulder.

Trying not to react to their exchange, I turned to look at the one painting hanging behind the lobby counter. Jack snickered as he stepped beside me.

"Admiring the art?"

"It's what we artists do; you know?" I motioned to the woman in the portrait. "Not a Rembrandt, but not bad, either."

"The basics?" Jack asked, knowing there was nobody close enough to overhear our conversation.

"Yes. But Toussaint is not a pushover. He asked about my pistol." I kept my voice low, still on guard.

"What did you tell him?"

"That I didn't know how it got there. I told him I traveled with a pistol for protection, but didn't have it with me at dinner or afterward. I suggested perhaps someone realized I had a weapon in my compartment and took it." I shrugged. "After all, it's what I believe *did* happen. You said I should tell the truth." I cut my eyes to the floor and back up, level with the bridge of Jack's nose. "He's quite tall, isn't he?"

Jack's brown eyes took on a jealous glint. "I hadn't noticed."

I shifted to stare at the painting. "Then you're not really doing your job, are you?"

"Look," he said, stuffing his hands into his trouser pockets. He shook off my insinuation. "I know I ordered you not to touch Kohler, and the order came from above, but if you did it, we could work something out."

"I didn't do it." I kept my eyes focused on the portrait, not wanting to give Jack the satisfaction of eye contact.

"But Penny, I can't figure out who else could have." Jack's voice tightened. "The way he was—the wound, the loosened necktie, the stupid grin on his face. Come on, who else could it be?"

"I know it looks like me." From the corner of my eye, I could see him staring at the side of my head, willing me to face him. "You want it to be me, don't you?"

Jack reached for my elbows and gently turned me toward him. "Honestly? Yes, I do." He dropped his tenuous grip and looked into my eyes. "If you did it because you were drunk or running on instinct, or even if you just wanted to kill him to spite me, I can deal with that. It's an easy fix, Penny. A little trouble, but not much, you know."

"But if I didn't do it?"

"Then we have a lot more on our hands. You've been compromised. And me, too. You know how Mother deals with agents who have been compromised. I don't want to be sent out on a mission with a parachute that won't open. And I don't want it for you, either." His eyes pleaded with me, but I couldn't give him the answer he wanted.

Glancing beyond him to the garden where Alice sat with the Hadsalls, I spoke softly through gritted teeth. "Jack, I didn't kill Kohler." I swallowed hard, knowing we were both in danger. "I wanted to." I had to come clean with him. If I lied to everyone else, I couldn't lie to Jack. I took a deep breath and prayed he'd understand, shifting my gaze back to his. "I was going to. I'd planned to strangle him and then make it look like suicide. Like in training. But someone got to him first."

Jack shook his head and drew a breath for a lecture.

Interrupting, I said, "Trust me, I wondered if I *had* done it. Lost my memory or something. But you know me better. I wouldn't have defied you and then left the body like that for everyone to find. And I certainly wouldn't have done it that way—the one way that would uniquely point to me. You trained me better than that, and I'm not stupid."

He rubbed his jaw, and the tension in his eyes eased. His gaze searched my face and roamed over my hair and shoulders. I could almost feel his hands cupping my jaw, holding his lips to mine. The expression I'd seen a hundred times. The scratch of his whiskers against my cheek. Now I watched it from an arm's length away. I wanted to linger in the look, but it wasn't safe. One of us had to think rationally. Anyone walking in on us now would see… much more than acquaintances eyeing a painting.

I looked away. If he were lost in a memory, it would be solely his. Not mine. Not right now.

He sighed, took a step closer to the portrait, and looked as though he might say something. We both turned at the sound of swishing skirts and footsteps, and a housekeeper flitted into the room, dusting shelves.

"Oh, pardon." Her face was pale in stark contrast to her raven hair knotted at the nape of her neck. "May I help you?"

As she spoke, Jack and I inched away from each other.

Jack pointed up. "Just admiring the painting. Do you know the artist or the subject?" He affixed his most charming grin as he turned to the slim young woman.

"No, monsieur. I am new to the inn." Her naturally pink lips pursed as she paused. "But I can find out, I'm sure."

"Don't go to any trouble," Jack said.

The young woman curtsied and went back to dusting. A moment later, the parlor door opened, and Toussaint and Rutgers emerged. Rutgers saluted the inspector and hurried up the stairs without a word to us.

Toussaint raised a brow at us lingering in the lobby together. He gestured to Jack, and the two men retreated for the interview.

I drew a deep breath and shifted toward the stairs when I heard the housekeeper hum a tune that stopped me in my tracks. It was the first bar of *Beethoven's Fifth Symphony*. Did I really hear it?

Again. "Hm-hm-hm *hummm.*"

My brain whirred into action. Short-short-short-long. Morse code for the letter V. V for victory. I stood at the newel post anchored to the first step. Did I dare? I had to. I rapped out the same message with my knuckle on the wood and waited.

Her tune changed to *Frère Jacques*. The right response. She was definitely with the French Resistance. I turned to face her. She couldn't have been older than twenty or twenty-one. So young for such a dangerous game.

"Miss, can you bring up my messages in a few minutes. I'm in the room...."

"I know your room, miss." She bobbed. "I'll be up right away."

20

SUNDAY, MAY 6, 1945, LATE AFTERNOON

Ifound Dahlia back in our room, resting in a chair by the window. Her head tilted down, like she were surveying the garden below, but her eyes were closed as if in a peaceful dream. However, she wore a smile that said she was very much awake.

"How was the interview?" she asked, not opening her eyes.

"Fairly routine. Inspector Toussaint is a clever man. I expect he'll sort everything out soon." I hoped I would sort it out before he did.

"I suppose he'll want to speak with me, as well, though I don't know what I could add." Her eyes popped open suddenly, and she beamed at me. "But I should be happy to speak to your character. I dare say Miss Fairchild would like to soil your reputation. I won't have it, you know."

"I know, dear friend." I took the chair beside her and reached for her hand. It trembled in mine, cold to the touch. "Are you all right?"

When she beamed, the loose wrinkles around her eyes tightened into two deep creases, and her lips thinned to almost nothing. "My dear, these chilled old bones never warm. I'm used to it." Her eyes softened. "I never thought of London as warm, but after spending these last winters in Amsterdam, London should be like the Côte d'Azur."

"Perhaps when France is all cleaned up, we can take a trip to the Riviera—just the two of us."

Dahlia rocked her head and turned back to the window. "Penny, this was your first war, but it wasn't mine. Things will be very different for us all for a long time to come. War changes everything."

I watched the old woman's expression alter as she closed her eyes again. She drew her hand from mine and lowered it to her lap.

"Of course, we'll all have a lot of work to do to get things back to normal." I smoothed my hands over my pleated brown tweed skirt.

Her head tilted back a fraction of an inch. "There is no normal now. Not for a long time. War is a monster, leaving nothing untouched. It floods through nations, from the smallest villages to the greatest cities. It leaves everything broken. Buildings, roads, families, and bodies. There are no survivors. Even if the blood still pumps, if the arms and legs still move, the brain—the heart—is damaged. Whatever innocence remained, war scrapes it away."

Her hands balled into fists as she continued. "And good riddance. Innocence after a war becomes a handicap. It keeps us from seeing the ugly truth. From recognizing what we must do to keep the evil from ravaging again. Innocence pretends, and we haven't got time for such things. Pretending we haven't seen, haven't heard, haven't felt—haven't known." Her head bobbed with emotion. "Moving forward takes honesty. We all must be brave enough to say it."

I leaned forward in my chair until it creaked. "What must we say?"

Dahlia didn't move. She barely breathed. "That no one is innocent anymore." The words came out in a whisper and raced down my spine.

"But we must hope," I began.

The old woman snapped back to life and turned her warm blue eyes to face mine. "Oh yes, you're right. Hope is the one thing that will see us through." She spread her hands over her skirt and afterward raised them to pat her hair. "I suppose we should get dressed for dinner. Do you think we'll all be dining together tonight?"

Her demeanor changed so abruptly from morose to cheerful that I had to blink away a dizzy blur from my eyes. "I can find out if you like."

"That would be lovely, dear." She turned back to face the window, and the last rays of afternoon sunlight played on her cheeks before tucking behind the growing clouds.

I rose from my seat. A knock at the door startled me, and I spun in place. "I'll see who it is."

In the hall stood the young woman from the foyer. She held a basin of water in her hands and two towels draped over her elbow. "Good evening, miss. I brought these in case you wished to freshen up before dinner."

"Very good." I directed her to the table in front of the mirror. "And did you have any messages for either Mrs. Lundt or me?"

She dipped a curtsey as she handed me the folded towels.

"Only that the early dinner seating will be in forty-five minutes, and the late seating is at eight-thirty. Do you have a preference?"

"Yes." I paused when my fingers touched a paper folded between the towels. "We would like the earlier seating if there is room for us."

"*Oui,* I will reserve your places. Tonight we will have rabbit stew and fresh-baked bread. It is not extravagant, but we are only now getting more staples for the kitchen."

"It sounds delicious." I smiled and placed the towels on the foot of my bed.

"Girl," Dahlia called before the young woman could leave.

She stopped over the threshold. "*Oui,* madame?"

"Come here for a moment, please." Dahlia's hand shook as she reached for the woman. "What is your name?"

Again, dipping into a slight curtsey. "My name is Madeline Cazeaux, madame. What may I do for you?"

"What time do the letters post?" Dahlia tapped on the arm of her chair. "I want to write to my family in London—to let them know of our delay."

Madeline twitched her lips to one side. "The boy takes the letters into town after lunch each day, though often the spring rains delay him."

I thought it was an odd comment at first, but out the window, the clouds were growing like a tower over the horizon.

"That's fine. I'll write my letter tonight and leave it at the front desk in the morning." Dahlia sighed and dismissed the young woman with a quick, "Thank you, Madeline."

The woman curtsied again and swept out of the room with a quiet, "Madame."

I glanced between Dahlia and the towels. "Would you like me to refresh your dress while you wash for dinner?"

"Thank you, Penny." Dahlia shook as she stood. "You know, I can manage by myself. You're not a servant."

I chuffed, placed one of the towels next to the basin, and slipped the note into my skirt pocket. "But I am your traveling companion, and I'm happy to help." I picked Dahlia's extra dress from the wardrobe and retrieved the garment sponge from my vanity case. "I'll have this done in a few minutes, and we'll have plenty of time to go downstairs before dinner."

Dahlia sat back in the chair and began fussing out of her brown brogue shoes. "Before you start on my dress, would you mind terribly taking my shoes down to see if someone might give them a quick shine? They're coated with so much train soot they almost look black."

"Of course," I said, happy to have a moment out of the room.

"Mind you don't get your hands too dirty."

"I'll be careful." I scooped up the shoes and backed out into the hall with a smile. "I'll be back before you can say *Jack Robinson*."

I closed the door and hurried down to the lobby with the shoes. The young Allard at the desk waved me over when he saw me.

"Need a shine?" He reached for the shoes and gave me a cheeky wink. "If you don't mind waiting, I will be done in minutes."

"Thank you. *Merci*." I gestured to a chair under the window. "I'll be over there."

He lowered his chin and scurried behind a door as I strode to the chair. I made sure I was alone in the room before retrieving the note.

The iron mask has served its purpose, and the king is still on the throne.

The ladies in waiting must do their job before the crow has flown.

. . .

WHAT WAS this supposed to mean? Who was the king? Was I supposed to be a lady-in-waiting? And what other job was I to do? Oh, the French were so tiresome. Always in rhyme and riddles. Jack had always hated the Mother Goose codes and refused to send messages that way.

I studied the note again. At the bottom, there looked like a drawing of a bird flying, but it had only one wing. I looked more closely, turned the page on an angle, and the bird became a musical note. Humming to myself, I tried to set the verse to a tune. But which tune? Nothing fit.

The one tune I could conjure was *Frère Jacques*, which Madeline had hummed earlier. But unfortunately, it didn't fit the verse, no matter how I metered it.

"All ready for you, Miss," the young man interrupted my humming.

I jumped to my feet and slipped the note into my pocket, bringing out a coin for a tip.

He spread a broad smile and handed me the shoes. "Wait," he said, still gripping the freshly polished leather. "If you like, I can take them up for you."

"That won't be necessary; I'm going right up now. But thank you." I took them and turned toward the stairs. "You've done a fine job, too."

"*Merci*, mademoiselle."

As I climbed back to our room, I thought about the verse. The Iron Mask must refer to the book by Dumas. The novel ventured that Louis XIV had his twin brother, the rightful king of France, imprisoned, wearing an iron mask to hide his true identity. I couldn't see how this applied to the murder of Yann Kohler. I needed to think.

Before I knew it, I was standing at our door. As I entered, I heard Dahlia singing.

"Frère Jacques,
Frère Jacques,
Dormez-vous,
Dormez-vous?"

HER LITTLE VOICE quivered the same way her hands did.

I was back in my first year. On instinct, I joined her, singing in English.

"Are you sleeping,
Are you sleeping,
Brother John,
Brother John?"

WE FINISHED the children's song and laughed for several seconds. Dahlia beamed at me. "I don't suppose they'll ask us to sing for our supper."

"We're certainly not the Andrews Sisters, are we?" I placed her shoes on the floor in front of her chair.

Dahlia shook her head. "It was still fun to sing. For a moment, I was transported back to my childhood. I haven't thought of the song in ages. What made you think of it?" she asked. She fanned at her face as though the exertion of singing had worn her out.

I blinked at her question. "I sang it because you were singing it." I picked up the sponge and dabbed a dusty spot over the shoulder of her dress. "Why were *you* singing it?"

Dahlia turned a confused expression to match mine. "Now,

Penny, please don't tease. I already question my sanity most days. I heard you singing out in the hall."

My stomach lurched. Madeline must have been in the hall humming—probably as a summons—and I hadn't been there to hear it.

"Oh, when I was in the hall. Yes, I forgot about that." I hurried to finish the dress and tossed the sponge into my case. "Dahlia, I remembered something I was going to ask about dinner. Do you think you can dress without me? I'll be back soon. I promise."

"Of course, dear. After all, I've been dressing myself since I was a child." She reached out her hand and cocked her head. Her eyes took on a veil of concern. "Is something wrong?"

"No, nothing at all. I had a question about who else will be at the early seating."

Dahlia displayed a knowing grin. "Checking to see if your young man will be at the table? I understand. I was young once, too."

I raised my hand to my cheek as though I was hiding a blush. "You're so clever."

She shooed me out the door with a flick of her wrist, and I turned to see Jack coming out of his room. I steeled myself for the conversation I knew had to come soon. I'd allowed myself to be compromised, which meant his cover was tenuous as well. He'd trained me to be better than this, and I'd let him down. But he'd also trained me to fight, and I wasn't about to roll over and give up.

He waited for me at the head of the staircase. "Toussaint is the real thing, isn't he? No pushover there."

I agreed. "What did he say?"

"Everything you'd expect—maybe a little more." He offered his elbow to me for the trip down the steps.

"Does he still think I killed Kohler?" We took a slow pace and kept our voices low.

"I'm not sure he ever did think it." Jack's lips barely moved. "Kept asking who else was watching you and Kohler in the dining car. And he wanted to know why I might have been the one to find you this morning."

This morning? Yes, it was still the same day. This morning seemed like a week ago. "Did he give you any hints?"

"No, he's a cool one." He looked me over. "Why are we going downstairs?"

"I had a question for the maid we met this afternoon."

Jack's eyes sparkled as we hit the lobby again. "The maid, eh?"

"The maid." I glanced around us for Madeline, but she was nowhere to be found. "She'd reserved our places for the early dinner, and I wanted to be sure of the time."

"For someone who spends half her life lying, you're not very good at it with me." He tugged me gently to the corner and moved close enough that I could feel his breath on my cheek.

So he wasn't angry with me. Perhaps disappointed? His warm body so close to mine didn't feel like disappointment. But he could be offering me a false sense of security to push me to confess my failures. As with everything else, this could be a test.

He slipped his hand to rest on my hip. "You know as well as I do, she's French Resistance. Did she give you a message?"

"Did she give one to you?" I countered.

His gaze lowered to my lips. "You weren't going to share with me? That hurts." He took my hand and placed it over his heart. "Right here."

If we weren't careful, everyone in the inn would know all our secrets. I pulled my hand away and took a half step back. "I thought we'd have a chance to share later. After dinner, maybe."

"What if Alice and I are having a late dinner?" His brown eyes gleamed as he again closed the gap between us.

My hands flexed, ready to push if I had to. I didn't want to. I wanted to wrap my arms around his neck and sink into his embrace. But that wasn't possible now. Maybe not ever again. "Then perhaps I'll have to share with someone else."

Jealousy flashed over his face again. "Inspector tall, dark, and official, I suppose?"

I sighed and pursed my lips. "You're the one with the fiancée, not me. You've no right to be jealous." I jabbed a finger into the middle of his chest.

He jerked his head a fraction of an inch, and his lip curled on one side. "Hmm. If that's how you feel, I'll see you across the table."

Jack turned and headed away from me toward the desk. He rapped his knuckle on the wooden top—three shorts and one long —and Madeline appeared a few seconds later. He shot me a two-can-play-at-this-game glance over his shoulder. When he turned back to the girl, he affected his most charming grin. "Is it too late to change our dinner reservation?"

"No, monsieur. I will go and set your place right now. For you alone, or for your lady-friend as well?" Madeline gestured toward me as Jack laughed.

"For two." He watched the maid leave and turned back to face me. "It looks like we're all set."

I scowled as he sauntered to my side. I planted my hands on my hips and scolded. "You know, I'm not your little doe-eyed secretary you can control with a bit of lovemaking in the hallway. I saw what you did there."

"And what did I do?" He shrugged and held out his palms in

surrender. "I simply changed my dinner reservations to accommodate you. You should be grateful."

"Grateful?" I seethed, peering at Jack through a wicked squint. "You knew I wanted to speak to her, and you sent her away."

"Oh, you wanted to see her *now*?" He pasted on his most naïve expression. "I didn't realize."

"*And* you didn't tell me what was in your message from Madeline."

"Why would you think I got a message at all? I didn't even know her name was Madeline." He clicked his tongue. "You know you really shouldn't go around making assumptions."

I growled under my breath. "Never mind. But understand, I will not share unless you do."

"Share what?" Alice's voice called from halfway up the stairs. "There you are, darling," she said to Jack, immediately ignoring my existence. She stopped on the third step up.

He spun to face her. "Right here."

"Jack, dear, I've been waiting for five minutes. I thought perhaps you'd take me for a walk in the garden."

Jack took another step away from me. "Change of plans. I was down here talking to the hotel maid, and she suggested the early dinner would be more enjoyable. Fresher and with plenty of seasoning. They may run out of ingredients for the second seating, and I thought you'd prefer the better meal."

"And after dinner? You'll take me for a walk in the moonlight?" Alice slipped a fingertip between her teeth and batted her lashes.

Jack responded the way most men did to such a childish expression. "Of course, darling. The moonlight will be more romantic, anyway."

Alice reached out for Jack, who hopped to her side and escorted her down the last three steps. "Perfect," she purred.

"Now, let's allow Miss Tompkins to scurry back to her room. She obviously hasn't had a chance to dress for dinner."

I raised a brow at the woman, ignoring Jack's embarrassed throat-clearing. "Is that what you're wearing?" I pretended to ask. "Good. It won't take me any time at all to get ready."

"Jack!?" Alice whined.

I marched up past them both without looking back.

21

SUNDAY, MAY 6, 1945, EVENING

Madeline seated Dahlia and me at the far end of the dining room. The other guests from the train sat close enough that every conversation could be overheard. Graves and Rutgers sat at a table on one side of us while the Hadsalls' table was on the other. Jack and Alice were on opposite side of the room. Toussaint sat alone at his table by the fireplace, where he could observe us all.

"I suppose we're all under suspicion," Dahlia whispered. She cut her eyes to Toussaint. "I think I'm the only one the inspector hasn't interviewed."

I glanced up at Toussaint, and he nodded, indicating he could hear everything from across the room. Turning back to Dahlia, I surveyed the once-grand room. The dark paneled walls looked dull, leaving me to imagine the luster they must have had in years past. At eye level, the room showed the same darker, more vibrant rectangles where paintings had hung. I wondered if the artwork had been hidden by the owners or stolen by the Nazis.

"This is ridiculous." Mrs. Hadsall gasped, drawing everyone's attention. "We should be almost to London already. Why we're sitting here, I cannot say. The inspector knows who killed the man. He should either arrest her or give her a medal—I don't care which. But the rest of us should be allowed to go."

"Evelyn, please." Mr. Hadsall leaned close to his wife, waving his hand in a warning gesture. "I'm sure Inspector Toussaint must make sure he has all the conspirators identified." His chin jerked toward Van Dyke and the steward from the train, sitting at the inspector's side.

"Don't shush me." Evelyn flourished her napkin as she slipped it onto her lap. "I have as much right to speculate as anyone else." Whatever timidity the woman had earlier had vanished with the train.

At her outburst, Van Dyke clicked his tongue. Without a hint of discretion, he said, "There's a significant difference between speculation and accusation."

"Here, here," the steward responded. "And we all had motive to kill the Nazi. Isn't that what you said, Inspector?"

Evelyn gasped again as if the man had slapped her. "Well!" Her chin quivered. "Edward," she whined.

Edward waved his spoon at his wife. "What would you have me do? Kill them for you?"

Toussaint focused on the bowl of soup set before him. I suspected he, like the rest of us, was trying not to react. I saw his moustache twitch with a repressed grin.

Dahlia's lips curled at the corner, obviously relishing the discord she'd instigated.

I shot a glance at Jack. He gazed submissively at Alice, and I suppressed a laugh.

"I say," Edward Hadsall continued. "He's right. Either of us had plenty of motive to kill the man. What he did to us… to our business. If the war had gone much longer, we'd have starved." He slurped at his soup and pointed his spoon at the other tables. "I suppose everyone here feels the same. Whoever killed Kohler did the world a service."

Rutgers, no longer wearing the sling on his arm, held up his glass of sherry. "Agreed. Cheers to whoever did it."

Before anyone could join the toast, Toussaint stood, shaking his head. "I beg of you all. Do not make a hero of a murderer. There is law. There is justice."

Graves rapped his knuckles on the table. "Absolutely. We must let justice run its course."

Rutgers pushed himself out from the table, and everyone fixed their gaze on him. This was quickly becoming a spectacle, which was fine with me. People often said things in anger or passion that they'd never say with their emotions in check.

"What are you? Some kind of pacifist?" Rutgers directed his remark back to Graves.

Graves squared his shoulders. "Actually, I am." He held his chin high.

The rest of us raised a collective brow.

Graves fixed a smug expression on his face. "So you see, I couldn't have killed Kohler. Whatever *he* was—*I* am a man of peace."

"Bah!" Rutgers spat out. "Pacifists think if everyone thought like them, there would be world peace." He scowled. "But pacifism doesn't produce peace. Instead, it paves the way for tyrants to roll through a country and enslave those who can't fight for themselves. All because those who can fight aren't willing." He drew a deep breath. "If I had killed Kohler, I'd admit it proudly." He angled his glance in my direction. "And to whoever did the blessed deed, I'm grateful."

I grimaced.

Dahlia patted my hand. "He's quite excited, dear."

Rutgers acknowledged her statement. "That I am. Any of you would be if you knew what I'd been through. I watched my whole regiment be decimated by Nazis. They outnumbered us seven to one." He held up seven fingers, then switched to his thumb.

Graves sniffed at the display.

"Why? Because the Dutch army had been pared back by politicians and pacifists. Neutral? Hah! Our guns were old. Our soldiers—the ones we still had—were either untrained or exhausted. I spent the last two years hiding, hoping to find other troops to join. But there weren't any. All I could do was ambush the soldiers ignorant enough to wander around alone. The difference between Kohler's killer and me? A few days. Think whatever you like; I'm glad Kohler is dead."

"Amen," Van Dyke added and was answered with a few more amens from around the room.

Rutgers turned his chair slightly out from the table, a not-so-subtle expression of his disdain for Graves.

Unruffled by the whole conversation, Graves shrugged and went back to his soup.

Toussaint resumed his seat and jotted something in his notebook. I almost felt pity for him. His investigation was most certainly an uphill battle. I wondered what I'd have to do to manage a peek at his notes later.

Dahlia silently pointed toward Jack and Alice's table. I looked up to see Alice cringing at the stew in front of her.

"When will they bring out the main course?" she asked, sotto voce.

Jack shook his head. "Darling, this is the main course. It's stew." His tone was low. "It's quite good."

"Ugh, I ate better than this in Amsterdam. I thought the war was over." Her nose wrinkled, and she pushed the bowl away.

"What can you expect in a week?" Jack's whisper hovered over their table like a fog.

Dahlia shot me a smirk. "Isn't this stew lovely? My, I haven't tasted anything so delicious in years." She kept her tone conversational but made sure that Alice could hear her.

"It's quite delightful," I agreed. The two of us behaved as though no one else was in the room. I nibbled the bread crust on the side plate. "And the bread… It's so nice to have bread made with wheat flour and not crushed tulip bulbs."

Toussaint chuffed with a gracious nod toward me. "We French are particular about our bread." He raised his glass. "And our wine."

Dahlia tipped her glass toward the inspector. "My second husband was French. And a fantastic cook. It was my favorite thing about him."

I matched their unspoken toast, and the three of us took a quick sip of our wine. "Perhaps I should look to marry a chef." I giggled.

"Just be sure he's French and not English." Toussaint cast a bemused smile toward me.

I was charming him one word, one glance at a time.

"I wouldn't know the difference between bread dough and cake batter," Jack said in a beleaguered attempt to join the conversation.

Alice's scowl grew sourer. "I don't think she was talking about you. And you won't need to know about such things. We'll have a full kitchen staff. Daddy will see that we won't live like refugees," she said.

Jack choked on his mouthful and swallowed hard. "And how will we afford a full staff?"

"I'm sure Daddy will continue my allowance until you get set up in his business."

Within minutes, the room filled with overlapping conversations, and I had to focus to hear anything specific. One glance at Toussaint told me he was doing the same, though he had the advantage of his notepad. I would have to rely on my memory.

We finished our supper, and Madeline and Allard brought out small currant tarts for dessert. Dahlia and I spoke of how nice it was to have something made with real sugar *and* real butter. And though not everyone may have appreciated the rabbit stew, the tarts were a great success.

By the time supper was over, I had gleaned motives for murder from almost everyone. The Nazis, perhaps Kohler specifically, had destroyed the Hadsalls' bookshop. Making an example of them by burning the "unsanctioned" books in a grand pyre in the street and setting the storefront ablaze a few months later when it was discovered that the Hadsalls were smuggling the forbidden books into town anyway. They were lucky they hadn't been sent to a concentration camp.

Van Dyke and the steward, whose name, I learned, was Johannes Dieter, had roughly the same motive as each other. Both worked for the railroad for a dozen years or so. Both learned that instead of helping their Jewish friends out of a Nazi-infested city, they were escorting them to death camps. Both wanted revenge.

Rutgers had explained his motive most eloquently. And Graves had given his protest, though I still believed there was more to his story.

The truth was that any one of them might have drugged our drinks. Deiter especially had the means to do so without being noticed, though with a little work, it wouldn't have been impossible for any of the others.

My problem was the way Kohler was killed and the fact that *both* he and I had been drugged before it happened. Nobody seemed to have a reason or foreknowledge to implicate me specifically.

Why not just poison him? Why shoot him, and why with my pistol and with my method? This was definitely a plot to point to me. But not only would the murderer have to know who I was and how I killed, but they would have to believe the authorities would also discover this information. Setting me up for a murder charge would be easy enough by the simple fact that I was in the room with the dead man. Drugging me accomplished that.

But they could have used any pistol and placed it in my hand. Instead, they searched my things and found mine. They could have shot him through the temple or through his shirt, at least. But they didn't. They shot him at close range right through his heart—nice and quiet—at an angle that avoided blood spatter and all the other indications of violence. They knew the angle to hold the pistol to keep the bullet from bouncing off a rib. They murdered him precisely as I might have done.

But Toussaint couldn't know this. No ordinary French inspector could. So, this message was for me. Me alone.

I ran every scenario I could imagine. Were the Hadsalls, or anyone else for that matter, agents of another government? If so, why would they kill such a prominent Nazi and pin the murder on me? Had I offended or been an obstacle for them? I just couldn't see it.

Was it Jack? After all, he was the only one who knew my

secret. Had he been playing with me from the start? Running a long game and using me? Playing with me? My heart said our relationship had been genuine. He'd saved my life a dozen times before. But what if I was wrong?

How could I be?

If I was wrong about him, everything had been a lie from the very beginning. I pushed the idea out of my head.

But in its place screamed a complete lack of any other plausible explanation. Were my instincts wrong? Had Mother changed the plan and kept me in the dark on purpose? Had I made mistakes I was unaware of? After all, I was suddenly called back with my assignment unfinished.

Perhaps Jack was told to cut me loose. Maybe Mother had nothing to do with it. Jack might have decided that if I were going to defy orders and kill Kohler, it would jeopardize his career with Mother. Was I now nothing more than a fun pastime on the tedious journey home?

Dahlia's quiet voice seeped into my mental arguments. "Penny, dear, I'm tired. Would you mind seeing me to bed, please?"

I startled from my thoughts and peered across the table. Dahlia sighed, holding her hand to her cheek.

"Of course." I had no idea how long I'd been lost in my thoughts. As we stood, Inspector Toussaint rose from his chair and offered a bow toward us. It was not a grand gesture, but it served to calm my nerves. He was a gentleman, no matter how he might feel about the situation.

He took a step toward us. "Madame Lundt, I hope you will feel better tomorrow. I do still need to interview you about the incident on the train, but I will allow you to rest tonight if you will give me your word that you did not murder the man. And that you will not abscond into the darkness." He gave her the slightest wink.

Dahlia fixed an amused smile to her lips. "Oh, Inspector Toussaint, you have such a sense of humor. I can assure you it's been a few decades since I've absconded anywhere."

He nodded into another bow, this time more directly to me, and I suspected that if he indeed believed me guilty of the murder, he didn't hold it against me as any great sin.

I watched the old woman closely as I walked her up to our room. Her steps seemed slower than usual. Each movement was more apprehensive. She was like a China doll being held together with brittle string. One misstep, one little jolt, and she'd come undone.

In the room, I drew back her bedcovers while she donned her nightgown.

"Thank you for the company," she said, settling into the once-lush bedding. "You should go back out and have a nice evening. Find your young man and have a drink with him. Steal him away from that dreadful girl."

I laughed. "She is dreadful, isn't she?"

"In my day, we had a word for young women like her. But I'm too much of a lady to use it." Dahlia chuckled to herself, but the laugh turned into a cough.

"Are you ill?" I patted her hand. "Would you like me to stay?"

"No, child. No need. Just an old woman whose body isn't used to traveling."

I started to protest, but she held up her hand, and that was that.

"What ails me is years, not disease. Don't trouble yourself. I'll be fine. I'm returning to London, and I assure you—I won't die before I see my home again. Now go on and find your man." She waved her hand toward the door. "I only need a little rest."

I left her in bed, closing the door quietly behind me. I had to think. My mind raced back to this morning. Yes, it was merely this morning.

My thoughts went right back to second-guessing. Who else would know how I killed? Unless Jack had become a double, he wouldn't do this. But he was the only one who knew. Had he betrayed me? He knew all my methods, but I couldn't believe he'd do this.

Had he let our secret slip? To whom? The one other person close to him was Alice. She didn't seem the type, but then again, neither did I. Had Jack made the mistake of trusting her? Maybe even trying to turn and train her as an asset? Surely not. But what other explanation made sense?

Nothing made sense.

I was back in the lobby, staring at the painting behind the desk again. Madeline was nowhere to be found. I pondered the idea of Alice.

If she knew who and what I was, she would know I had a pistol. She might have gotten access to Jack's notes, with or without his knowledge, and read about my assignments. She might have even slipped something into our drinks at the steward's counter last night as Jack was saying goodnight. It wasn't beyond the realm of possibility. But why? Why kill Kohler? Convenience? Not likely. Why make it look like I had done it? To have Jack all to herself?

In the grand scheme of it all—the war, the Nazis, all of it— having Jack wrapped around her little finger seemed a bit trivial. He was a catch, but worth killing for? I had a difficult time believing it. After all, if she wanted him so badly, why not simply kill me?

Still, unless Jack had set me up himself, Alice was the only other option.

A flash of light shot through the glass doors to the garden as the leading edge of a rainstorm tapped against the slate roof. Thunder rolled in from the stand of trees across the meadow, sending a cool shiver down my spine.

"Oh! We're too late. The rain has already begun," Alice whined from the doorway.

"Don't fret, darling; tomorrow morning, you can show me the gardens." Jack stepped into the lobby with Alice on his arm.

"But what shall we do tonight? It's too early to go to bed." The blonde frowned as she peered out the doors.

"We could have a nightcap or find a deck of cards somewhere. You know how to play Gin Rummy."

I turned my back to the couple and thrummed my fingernails on the desktop. It was our signal that we needed to speak. I had to hope Jack could hear the sound above the thunder and Alice's complaints.

"I hate Gin Rummy." She put on a baby's voice. "Can't you come up and tuck me into my beddy-bye?"

"Alice, please," Jack said in hushed tones. "Consider how people are talking about Miss Tompkins. You don't want them saying the same things about you. About us."

Though I wasn't looking, I could hear Alice's voice change again, and I knew she was talking with her lower lip out in a pout. "No, I don't want anyone to think such things about us."

Though I was fuming, I didn't dare turn toward them. I knew this was his best play to get rid of her.

Jack responded in his low gravel, which always melted me.

"Darling, go on up. You have your book. I'm going to get a quick drink, if I can find one, and I'll be off to bed myself. I have a little paperwork to catch up on, especially being delayed a day."

"And no card games?" Alice had moved to the bottom step, at the edge of my peripheral vision. Her tone shifted from flirtatious to cautioning. "Promise?"

"No games at all."

"Then kiss me goodnight," she demanded.

From the corner of my eye, I saw her leaning forward from a step or two up. Her bosom poised just below his eyes, and her lips puckered like a duck's bill.

Jack stepped to meet her, and Alice maneuvered him to be in my line of sight. "On the cheek," he said, stepping to her side. But as he leaned in to kiss Alice's cheek, she turned her face and kissed him full on the mouth. Much more than a goodnight kiss. And she wanted me to see it.

Jack took a step back from her as she ascended the stairs. Jack watched her go—perhaps a little too long for good taste, but it was his cover.

When Alice was out of sight, Jack drew a deep breath and sighed. "Where do they keep the liquor in this place?"

"When you find out, let me know. I need a stiff one after your little show," I whispered.

"There's a little covered area in the corner of the portico, behind the dining room. It should be protected from the storm. Give me five minutes." Jack stood at the doors without a glance in my direction.

"Five minutes." I regarded the woman in the painting. Her smile hadn't changed. But I had.

22

JANUARY 4, 1945, AMSTERDAM, LATE EVENING

Five months earlier...

My head pounded in time with my steps as I mentally choreographed the plan.

Changing techniques would be a challenge, but I could do it. All the preliminaries were arranged. I would meet the Nazi after the club closed and accompany him to his flat.

But from there, I was to diverge sharply from the arrangements I had made.

I'd planned a quiet evening for the two of us. A bottle of wine, a bedtime snack, and a lethal dose of poison. Simple.

But when I read Jack's note last night, *simple* went out the window.

Before the club opened, Vera dolled me up with her lipstick. I flashed my most knowing smile at Hermann Walter when he handed me his hat and scarf. He bent his neck in a secret bow, acknowledging our upcoming liaison without speaking. Perfect.

Walter was to become a message. An example of the worst

kind. A poisoning that mimics a heart attack would not do. Tonight would need to be a spectacle.

"You're quite lovely, fraulein." Walter helped me into his car.

I hadn't been in a car in months. The heat blowing from the dashboard reminded me of how cold everything was in Amsterdam. The streets. The buildings. The people.

"I've never been in a car so nice as this one." I pressed my fingers into the leather seat next to his thigh.

His gaze turned hungry, as I hoped it would. "What is your given name?" he asked.

"Penelope." What would it hurt to share that information with him? He'd never repeat it.

We ascended the stairs to his flat, and I marveled that this city still had such luxury. His foyer was almost as big as my whole place. The dark paneled room smelled of lemon oil and floor wax.

"It's beautiful." I handed him my coat, and he hung it on a peg.

"And what did you bring for our special night?" He led me into his parlor and gestured to the bag I carried.

"I traded this week's pay for a bottle of wine from Maddock." Of course, it wasn't entirely true, but I didn't want Walter to know I was anything but virtuous.

"We'll start with yours, then. And I have a few of my own bottles you may enjoy."

Walter excused himself to remove his uniform, returning moments later dressed in silk pajamas and a smoking jacket. He stoked the fire on his hearth and directed me to his couch.

As I sat, I wondered about the family that once resided here. I suspected they might be Jewish—probably in a camp a hundred miles away. Perhaps already dead. And now this piece of human filth infested their place like the rat he was.

I disguised the hate inside me as lust. It was a sort of lust, after all.

He poured out two glasses of wine and offered a German toast. I tapped my glass to his and sipped. His expression telegraphed his expectations.

I stalled for a second, studying his face and his body. He was handsome enough. Well-built and fit. Tonight would be a challenge.

His grey-green eyes didn't blink as they roamed my body. He tossed his wine back and poured himself another glass. "Drink up, my dear, Penelope. The night is just beginning."

I took another sip, then set my glass on the side table. I unbuttoned my neckline and smiled without a word.

"Why don't you stand in front of the fire? You don't want to be cold."

I rose and took a step toward the fire. "And better for you to watch?"

He leaned back onto the sofa cushions and untied the belt on his jacket, letting it fall open. "Just so."

I shifted at an angle, ensuring the dagger in my garter faced the fire—away from Walter. I unfastened the rest of my buttons and let the dress fall to a puddle at my feet.

"Take one more step back." He pulled open his pajama shirt. "Too much of you is in shadow."

I stepped free of my dress and, as I bent down to remove my shoes, I retrieved my knife at the same time. I faced him more squarely, hiding the now-hot blade behind my back. "Is this better?"

His gaze swallowed me whole. He gulped his second glass down and reached out his arms. "Better still if you're within reach."

"My thoughts exactly."

My hands itched, anticipating their work. It was time. I slithered toward Walter, allowing the straps from my bra to drop off my shoulders.

His smile broadened.

My brain settled into the calm before the storm. I had to be precise. I needed blood, and lots of it, which meant his heart had to pump for as long as possible. I didn't want this to be interpreted as anything but rage. But I also had to incapacitate him quickly. He was strong enough to overpower me if I didn't.

My heart slammed against my ribs as I tugged one strap down, drawing his full attention away from the weapon in my other hand.

One last step forward, and I planted my dagger into his upper thigh. A stream of crimson covered me when I withdrew the blade, assuring me I'd hit the artery.

His eyes went wide, and he screamed. His body convulsed as I stabbed his abdomen a dozen times. His arms flailed wildly, trying to push me away, but his slick hands slid over my body. Blood sprayed everywhere. Spatter on the ceiling, the furniture, the rug, and the mantle.

He bolted upright to chase me, but slipped in his own blood, spreading the pool in every direction as he only scrambled a dozen more steps. He tried to speak, and perhaps he did. What sounded like gibberish to me might have been the worst German curses he could manage. But soon, he was quiet. And that's when the real work began.

I found a cleaver in his kitchen, wrapped the handle with a tea towel, and covered it with Walter's blood, careful not to leave my prints. I hacked into his arms and legs enough to make the weapon appear appropriate to the wounds.

I took my blade to his face, removing his tongue and an ear. Rolling him onto a velvet blanket from the back of the couch, I dragged his body over the slick wood floor into his bedroom and, using a leverage technique I learned in training, rolled him onto and around on his bed. I pulled his blood-soaked pajamas off and draped them over the bedpost.

While the mattress absorbed more blood, I ran the faucet in his bathtub. I used the cold water to clean myself as much as possible. When the tub was half full, I wrapped Walter's nude body back into the blanket and hefted him over the side, dumping him into the pink water.

The adrenaline I felt at the beginning was waning. The effort spent dragging him from one room to another had exhausted me.

I walked into the parlor and stepped back into my dress. I had a few more tasks before my work was done. I washed the wine glasses and poured two half-servings of bourbon into the crystal cups next to his sink. I placed the drinks, along with a few of his severed body parts, strategically around the flat.

Back in the parlor, I tossed the tea towel into the fire along with a few blank papers from his desk. I scooped up a diary and a few other official documents from his office. They went into my bag.

I stood in the foyer, surveying my work, and bile crept up my throat. It wasn't the blood or the violence that sickened me, but the knowledge that I could render such a scene without hesitation. I swallowed hard; I'd be sick later.

Walter's home was over a mile from mine, and as I walked, an icy rain began to fall. I ran, anxious to be in the warmth of my blankets and out of the weather. Lightning struck a few miles away, and I felt a rush of God's wrath. A hot wave of guilt flooded my mind, and bile shot from my lips. I couldn't breathe. I was drowning in the burning shame and the freezing sleet.

As I came around the last corner before my block, a man stepped from a shadow and into the meager streetlight. I recognized the silhouette immediately and ran into Jack's open arms.

"Are you all right?" His voice barely rose above a whisper.

I pushed the bag of papers into his hands. "It's done." His arms held my trembling body tight against him.

"But you?"

"I did what you asked." I stepped out of his embrace and stared into his dark eyes. "Don't ask me to do that again."

"I'm not the one who wanted it like that." He put a warm palm to my cheek. "It was just orders."

I turned away from him. "We can't be seen together. You've put us both at risk."

"I had to be sure you were all right." He raised my chin to face him. "I can't imagine what you've been through."

Lightning flashed on the horizon, and thunder rolled in from the sea.

Turning toward home, I didn't look back. After another fifty steps, I was inside, stripping off my clothes and sobbing over my washbasin. I grabbed my nightdress and wrestled it on.

I still felt the knife in my empty hand as I crawled into bed and pulled the covers to my chin. "I'm all right now. I'm all right now." I mumbled my mantra a thousand times and stared at my itching, trembling hands.

23

SUNDAY, MAY 6, 1945, LATE EVENING

I stood in the shadow on the garden-side porch, watching the cold spring rain fall in sheets off the inn's slate-tiled roof. Goose flesh prickled over my arms and down my back as I waited for Jack to join me. I lingered for a few seconds in a memory of a stormy evening five months ago. His arms were warm that night, but not enough to thaw me from the icy shock that had taken over my body.

I'd killed a man. That fact wasn't unusual. It was the very reason I'd been sent to Amsterdam. But that night was different than the others. My other assignments had been quick and, from all outward appearances, clean. A bullet or injection, placed with unemotional precision, and the target simply ceased to be. That night was different. My assignment was different.

My orders on that particular occasion were to make a mess. Not merely of the man's place and things but of him. I'd done it perfectly. There wasn't one inch of his home that didn't reflect the violence I'd wrought upon him. Blood spattered the papers on his desk, the blankets on his bed, the floors, walls, and ceiling. I'd taken the man apart and left him in several places around his home. Sickening.

Sickening to know that I could do that to another human being. Sickening that someone wanted that done to another person. I didn't question it. I had my orders.

By the time I'd gotten back home that January night, the sleet had felt warm against my frigid skin. Jack had been waiting for me, for my delivery.

The body had been discovered the next morning, and the man's suspected murderer, another German officer and rival, was in custody. I was good.

Good. I laughed to myself. There was nothing good about me.

"Something to warm you up," Jack said, startling me out of my trance. He slipped a whiskyglass into my shivering hand.

"Thanks." I took a sip and let the liquid burn down my throat. "If I drink enough of it, I'll be able to feel my feet again."

Jack sipped at his glass, releasing a cough afterward. "It's not very good."

Shaking my head, I said, "You've been spoiled. This stuff is better than I've had in a long time."

We clinked our glasses together and rocked our heads back into a full swallow. When our eyes met again, we were ready to talk.

I pulled the message from my pocket. "Something to show you."

He produced a matching scrap of paper from his jacket, and we exchanged notes.

I held the paper to the dim light filtering through the window. It contained the exact wording as mine. I flipped the page over to study the back. Jack held his up to look through the paper for hints of more than the simple verse.

"Bloody French." Jack folded the note and handed it back. "Always the nursery rhymes."

I took my note back from him and slipped it into my pocket. We faced each other for several long moments, letting the storm fill the silence. I didn't know how to bring up my ideas with him, but the whisky had lit a bold fire in my gut. I gazed up into his brown-gold eyes.

"I think I know who killed Kohler," Jack said.

At the same moment, I said, "I know who killed Kolher.

Jack laughed as thunder pealed from somewhere beyond the black horizon. "Of course, you do. It was merely a matter of time and simple deduction." He took the empty glass from my hand and set it on a rock ledge by the door. He slipped his jacket off and wrapped it around my shoulders. "I should have done this first."

His whisky-breath puffed hot on my cheek as he snugged me into his embrace. I leaned into his chest.

"What do we do with her?" I pulled his jacket closed between our bodies. "On one hand, she did the world a favor."

"But on the other hand, she set you up for murder." He rested his chin on the top of my head. "I don't think Mother will approve of her methods, do you?"

"No. But how do we handle it? Do we turn her over to Toussaint? Or Mother?" Pressed against his shoulder, I could hear his heart pounding. "I'm not sure we can do both, but without handing someone over to Toussaint, we won't be free to return to Mother. And I'm not sure Mother can dole out her justice remotely, unless you or I do it."

"It's tricky." Another roll of thunder after a distant flash in the sky. "I'm afraid—even with Madeline to help—getting word to

Mother won't be easy. Toussaint is itching to have it all wrapped up before any message gets through. Meaning, he'll have you wrapped up." Jack paused for a moment. "No, I don't think we can wait for orders from Mother."

"You think we should let Toussaint have her?"

"The only other option is to take care of her ourselves." Jack's shoulder rose and fell with a shrug. "But it would have to look like an accident. Or perhaps a suicide with a confession in the note?"

"And if Mother objects to our decision?" Of course, these last few days revealed I wasn't above disobeying orders, but I didn't want to make it a habit. Mother's discipline could be brutal. I feared that even telling Mother of our situation might bring repercussions for us as it was.

"Better sometimes to ask for forgiveness than permission, eh?" Jack quipped.

"And you're willing to take responsibility for the decision?" I was a little surprised Jack would so willingly offer Alice into Toussaint's hands… or mine.

"I am. And we can even make it look like natural causes. Expected, you know." Jack's arms loosened from around my body, and his fingers inched up to my shoulders. "But we should talk to her first. See why she did it. Make sure there wasn't someone else involved."

"I agree. She might have a perfectly good explanation." I knew she didn't, but if Jack was going to play nice, I could as well.

"Brilliant," Jack's dark eyes gleamed in the shadows. "Will you talk to her tonight?"

"Me?" My voice scratched. I wasn't sure if it was because of the rain or the drink. "Why would I talk to her? Don't you think you should be the one to question her?"

His forehead creased, and he took a step back. "You're closer to her."

The cold air rushed into the space between us. "In age, perhaps."

Jack's face tilted forward with a confused frown. "What are you talking about?" He blinked as the raindrops blew onto his face. "Just ask Dahlia if she was under orders from someone."

"How would Dahlia know if Alice was under orders to kill Kohler?" I paused as his words sank in. "Wait. What are you talking about? Do you think *Dahlia* killed Kohler?"

"Who else?" Jack's realization came slowly. "You thought I was talking about Alice?"

"Of course, it was Alice." I shook my head. "Why would Dahlia have anything to do with it? She's a sweet old woman."

"Not nearly as sweet as she plays up to be," Jack said. "The killer used *your* pistol. The pistol was in your bag in the compartment that you two shared. She had the easiest access to it."

"She's not a killer," I insisted.

"Well, *you* are."

His words stung more than they should have done. "I am." I shook free of Jack's coat and pushed it back to him. "And I tell you, Alice is the only one who could have done it. She's the only one who had reason to set me up."

He pushed his arms into his jacket sleeves and jerked it into place. "What reason would she have to set you up?"

"You—you jackass."

He didn't react to my suggestion, but simply continued his explanation. "And how would Alice know precisely how to kill him to make it look like you did it? How would she know to use *your* pistol? How did she know you *had a pistol*?"

"Hmm," I said, my voice dripping with sarcasm. "Those are all excellent questions. Maybe you talk in your sleep?"

That finally got a reaction. Jack stepped forward and huffed. "I do not talk… It's not…." His face reddened as he became more flustered. "Alice couldn't have learned any of the information from me." He turned to face the storm. "Dahlia could have known all of it."

"How could she?"

"She's your friend." He balled a fist and gaveled it against the side of the porch post. "You have tea with her every day. Who knows what you might have mentioned to her without thinking?" He yanked his jacket back over his arms and shoulders. His voice took on a mocking tone. "She's a poor old woman who can barely walk."

I wanted to slap him. I marched into the rain to face him. "You're accusing me of letting secrets slip out over tea, but *you're* far and away *above* mentioning anything after your second or third bottle of wine? And how many drinks have you had tonight? Don't try to convince me this one was your first." I tossed an accusing finger toward the empty glasses.

Jack's face became stone. His voice turned low and steady. "I am your superior. Do not accuse me."

"I'm not accusing you. I'm accusing her!" I pointed to the window overhead.

He stared until another bolt of lightning flashed behind me. "You're wrong," he said, and the thunder rolled over his words. He took a step back and turned away from me. Picking up the empty glasses, he went inside alone.

With all my heart, I wanted to believe that Jack was on my side. I wanted to trust him. But he'd just called me a common *murderer*. And now he was accusing Dahlia of the same. How could I protect her?

24

SUNDAY, MAY 6, 1945, MIDNIGHT

The door of our room latched with a single click. I crept quietly to the lavatory, where I peeled my rain-soaked clothes off and hung them to dry. As I tugged my brush through my hair, I thought of using it on Jack.

I looked across the darkened room at the silver shimmer of Dahlia's hair. She was no killer. And she'd never do anything to incriminate me. I'd bet my life on it.

I slid into bed, and my mind was as clouded as the sky. Twenty-four hours ago, I was alone in the train compartment with Yann Kohler, drugged into oblivion. My thoughts raced as I tried to remember one glimmer more.

Edward and Evelyn Hadsall? I hadn't seen them after they left the dining car. Carl Van Dyke? I might have seen him without noticing, such is the way with porters and stewards. But Johannes Deiter was the one who made our drugged drinks. I struggled to remember if I had seen him make them. I couldn't be sure.

Hans Rutgers and Collin Graves were seated in the dining car near us. Had they left before or after us? Before. Everyone had gone before us.

Jack and Alice, too. And they'd said good night when they left.

I replayed the morning. Waking up to Kohler's dead stare. The pistol by my hand. I was floating around the room, seeing myself on the floor. I could see the top of Kohler's head. His hair was still perfectly in place. Looking down the collar of his shirt—two buttons undone, his tie loosened—a short drip of congealed blood on his chest over his heart and a stupefied grin on his mouth.

My eyes drooped even as my brain whirred.

The cabin door slid open, and Jack stepped in, wearing an iron helmet over his head. Van Dyke followed, and Jack handed the heavy mask to him. He put it on for a minute before Hadsall, Graves, Rutgers, and Dieter crowded into the cabin. Each took a turn wearing the mask. Finally, Toussaint entered and announced, "I need to speak to John."

Hadsall, Graves, and Van Dyke left the room, joining Evelyn, Alice, and Dahlia in the corridor. They stared into the tiny compartment with their faces pressed against the windows. I watched my body slowly rise to a sitting position. "Who is John?" I asked.

"I am," answered Rutgers, Deiter, Jack, and now-alive Kohler, in unison.

My thoughts raced. Hans, Johannes, Jack, and Yann were all forms of the name John.

"And you are, too," a voice—my voice—whispered, and all the men stood, pointing accusing fingers in my face.

The whispers grew louder, layering on top of each other.

"You are Penelope *Ann*."

"Ann is the feminine of John."

"Penelope Ann."

Jack took a step toward me and, with the help of all the other men in the room, lowered the iron mask over my head.

The men all began to sing.

Frère Jacques,

Frère Jacques,

THE SONG LOOPED IN A ROUND; over and over, they sang.

I couldn't see or even breathe. I fought to lift the mask off, but it wouldn't budge. I was suffocating. My body flailed under the weight of the thing. I tried to scream, but no sound came. I pushed, kicked, and scratched.

"Penny, dear," Dahlia's voice shattered the mask, and a bright light flashed in my eyes. "Wake up."

She sat on the edge of my bed, clinging to my hand. She was already dressed in her grey tweed day suit, and her hair was perfectly coiffed into a silver knot at the top of her head. Her round cheeks flushed pink with life. Staring into her shimmering blue eyes calmed me. I could breathe. I gulped at the air until my throat ached.

"That must have been a frightful dream." Dahlia's honied voice rattled. "But after all you've been through, of course, it was."

Sunlight flooded through the window, and I struggled to sit upright. Though I'd slept, I hadn't rested, and my body ached from exhaustion more than it had last night. "What time is it?"

Dahlia worked on a pleasant expression. "It's almost eight o'clock. The girl came by a few moments ago to see if we'd be down for breakfast." She patted my hand. "You should stay here. I'll see if I can get one of the men to walk me down. The inspector asked to see me directly after."

Her words rallied my body, if not my mind. "No. I'll simply be a moment." I hurried into the lavatory to find my dress still damp. I shook my head as if that would shake the vague terrors of my dreams away. I freshened up and slipped into my brown tweed skirt and white blouse.

"I'm ready," I lied, offering my arm to my friend. "Let's go down and face the day."

25

MONDAY, MAY 7, 1945, MORNING

In the dining room, a long buffet table glistened with what I guessed was every piece of silver and crystal the inn still owned. Breakfast consisted of toast and marmalade, scones, and tea. My tongue still reveled in the delicacy of wheat flour. The milk and the butter were luxuries to us, and we savored them slowly.

"Perhaps when I'm back home, I'll look for a place in the country where I can have a cow," Dahlia said. Her hands shook as she lifted her scone to her pursed lips. "Or maybe I'll find a generous neighbor with a cow."

"Or perhaps a rich husband?" I teased.

She raised a narrow brow and grinned. "I haven't had a husband in over a year. It might be nice." She shot me a quick wink. "What about a husband for you? It shouldn't take you long to find one. Maybe your young man will propose?"

I pointed my butter knife toward the lobby, from where I

heard Jack's voice. "Remember? He has already proposed, but not to me."

She scoffed and shooed away such nonsense with a flick of her wrist. "Don't worry about Miss Fairchild, dear. She may have him wrapped 'round her finger now, but once they get to London, I suspect she'll find someone with a bigger purse than Mr. Vogel."

"You may be right." I picked up my teacup for the first time and then set it down without a sip. I tipped my chin toward the door, where Jack and Alice were entering. "It appears there is a little trouble brewing."

Alice had her arms crossed and wore a prominent scowl over a cornflower blue day dress. Jack reached out for her elbow, and Alice responded by flinching away from him.

"Of course, I'm right, dear." Dahlia leveled her chin toward the not-so-happy couple. She lowered her voice to a whisper. "If there's one thing I know about, it's husbands, and Jack is definitely not going to be hers."

I suppressed a laugh as Jack glared in my direction. Over his shoulder, I saw Toussaint poke his head into the dining room. His eyes met mine, and he jerked his head slightly to one side in a discreet summons.

"Excuse me for a moment, won't you, Dahlia? I need to have a word with the inspector. I won't be long." I gave the old woman's hand a gentle squeeze.

"Don't let your tea get cold," Dahlia chirped, tapping on the edge of my saucer.

I hopped from my chair and regarded Toussaint at the same time. Without a word, he gestured to the interview room. Madeline appeared behind the buffet and began working on the tea service.

I addressed Dahlia and motioned toward the buffet. "Look, the woman is already making more. But if mine starts to cool, you go right ahead and drink it, and I'll get fresh."

I dipped my chin to Madeline as I hurried across the hall to Toussaint's court.

"Bonjour," he said, indicating the chairs in front of the large French window. His midnight blue uniform mirrored the crispness of his expression.

"Good morning." I sat, nudging my chair closer to the table between us. I hoped to catch a glimpse of his notes as we talked.

The inspector studied me for a second and let a faint smirk peek from beneath his moustache. "You did not sleep well?"

I wanted to be offended, but I was sure my appearance betrayed the night of shadows. "Understandable, don't you agree?"

"Of course." He dropped his hand atop his notebook and rapped his fingertips on the cover.

If Jack had done that, it would have been a signal to me that we needed to meet privately. But Toussaint? I wondered how much he knew.

He stopped tapping and stretched his fingers over his notepad. "I shall do my best to make this simple for you." He paused and blinked. "I did hope to speak with your employer first."

"First?" I straightened my spine. "Did I misread your summons? Were you requesting Mrs. Lundt instead?"

"Not at all." He chuffed and tilted his head. His moustache twitched, and I suspected it hid a hint of a smile. "I'm not worried so much about her. I only meant I hoped to speak with her before you confess." He held out his hands as if to accept a gift. When I didn't move, he tapped a single finger in the center of his notebook. "You wish to know what I have concluded, to see what I have noted about you. About all the others."

"You're a clever man." I crossed my legs and relaxed in the

narrow armchair. "But I want more than to know your thoughts on this tragedy."

Toussaint chuckled and suddenly returned to a severe expression. "Tragedy? I doubt anyone would consider Herr Kohler's death a tragedy." He said *Herr Kohler* as though the words tasted like castor oil on his tongue.

My expression remained as placid as I could manage. "The man was a monster, I understand."

He agreed, rocking his whole body in a slow nod. "So, if you confess to killing him, I should shake your hand. Or give you a medal?" He pulled his pencil from his breast pocket. "This is what Monsieur Rutgers says."

"You think I could kill a man in cold blood?" I fluttered my lashes and leaned toward him. I wasn't sure he would respond to seduction, but I hoped to distract him, if only for a second.

"Mademoiselle, I think anyone can kill, given the right circumstances." Toussaint picked up his notebook and licked the pencil lead. He seemed oblivious to my suggestive pose. "And if the man was abusive to you, one can certainly sympathize. Self-defense, you know?"

I bobbed my head, and my mind flashed with an image of Harriet's battered body. "One can imagine the man did terrible things. Especially to a helpless woman." I played the hypothetical victim to see what he might offer, what he might reveal.

If I did confess—portray the evening as though I was a victim of a monster, would he let me go? Would it be worth doing if it allowed us to deliver Alice to Mother?

"But, of course, you claimed to have been drugged. And, according to your statement yesterday, Kohler was drugged, too. So, self-defense may not apply to this situation." He tucked his chin down to his chest, and his stare came through his heavy brows. "And the shot which killed him—the single shot with your pistol—was quite precise. Someone who had been drugged to near unconsciousness couldn't make a shot like that."

"And yet you believe I *could* make the shot?" I fingered my neckline and rested my fingertips over my heart as if shocked by such an idea.

"If you were fully conscious, I do believe you could." The man now opened his book and poised his pencil. "Shall we get to it, mademoiselle?"

"How closely have you worked with the French military during the war?" I thought I'd learn a little more about him since I had no intention of confessing.

"See here, I appreciate your attempts to… gain my trust. Under different circumstances, we could perhaps enjoy each other's company. In fact, I do enjoy your… but now is not the time. We should put these games aside for now. I am—" Before he could finish, a shrill scream ripped through the quiet of the morning.

We both jumped to our feet as we heard Jack's voice. "Call for a doctor now."

Toussaint reached the door before me, but he had no intention of leaving me alone. "Come quickly."

We hurried to the dining room, where I saw Madeline hunched over Dahlia, who was sprawled on the floor, half under our breakfast table. My heart pounded in my ears as panic gripped my stomach.

I dropped to the other side of her body and saw Jack stretched over Alice. She was prone on the floor as well. Evelyn Hadsall stood beside the buffet table, sobbing into her husband's shoulder.

I peered down at Dahlia's face. Her skin was grey-white, and her lips were blue. A froth of foam traced over her cheek, and a faint smell tickled my nostrils. No—no. That smell. Bitter almonds. I knew it too well. Cyanide. A teacup lay on the floor beside her, split into three pieces.

Madeline's ear was pressed to Dahlia's chest, but I knew she was gone. Her liquid blue eyes were already dull.

My vision blurred with tears as my mind searched for answers.

"She is gone," Madeline whispered. "*Dieu au paradis*, she is gone." The woman rocked back on her knees and looked me in the eyes. "I am so sorry."

"It was in the tea," I said. "You put it in her tea?"

Madeline shook her head. "No. You cannot think I would ever harm an old woman."

Our voices were low and calm, though both of us wiped tears off our cheeks. All around us, the room was in chaos. Jack continued to yell—but I couldn't tell to whom he directed his ire.

Toussaint ordered the hotel boy not to touch the teacups on any of the tables. He was already in charge of the situation.

I raised my bleary gaze toward Jack. He rose and staggered back a few steps, leaving me a clear view of Alice. Like Dahlia, she was ghostly pale, with foam around purple-blue lips.

"Toussaint, this was poison." His body swayed.

"I know," the inspector said with a nod. He commanded the others in the room with a wave of his hand. "I want everyone to go to the parlor and take a seat. Do not touch anything in this room. Do not eat or drink anything else. Do not speak to each other." He pointed at me. "Mademoiselle Tompkins, you must step away from Madame Lundt and go with the others. Monsieur Vogel, you as well."

I rose to my feet, more shaken than I expected. Jack took a step toward me.

"No, monsieur, do not speak to her. Not to anyone," Toussaint warned. His hand flexed between a fist and an axe.

"She's in shock." Jack moved closer and took my elbow. "I want to get her to a seat."

"Very well." Toussaint's face burned red with anger. "And keep everyone in the parlor. Nobody leaves." He snapped his fingers at Madeline. "You." He snapped until she responded. "You stand watch in here until I return. At the door. Not alongside the victims. At the door where you can be seen. Understand?"

"*Oui*, monsieur." She rose and staggered toward the archway.

Jack and I followed everyone else into the formal room and took seats. Evelyn continued to sob, and her husband consoled her with quiet shushing.

Van Dyke and the others frowned without making any conversation, but everyone's eyes shot accusations all around the room, most landing upon me.

Toussaint stepped inside and drew the door almost closed behind him with an exaggerated flourish. "I need everyone's attention."

Evelyn and I sniffed through the sudden quiet. I watched Toussaint pace a wide circle in front of each person, but with every step he took, I seemed to detach from my body a little more.

He spoke, but I could barely make out the words. I saw him pointing from one side to the other but heard little morc than a hum—like a bee in a garden, hopping from one flower to another.

My fingers trembled, icy cold. All I could see was Dahlia's grey face. Her eyes stared through me. How could this happen? Was it in her tea? A thought gripped my heart. Was it in my tea? Oh, no. Please, God, no. Was this my fault?

The lovely old woman, my sweetest friend, was dead because of me.

26

MONDAY, MAY 7, 1945, MORNING

My senses rushed back to me when Toussaint said, "Mademoiselle Tompkins?"

An electric current sped down my spine, and I blinked away the tears that clouded my vision. Every inch of my skin prickled, and the smell of dust and nervous sweat battered my nose.

Jack's voice boomed. "I already told you, man. She's in shock." He stood at my side, and the heat from his body warmed me.

"I understand, monsieur, but we cannot bring everything to a halt while we wait for her to feel better. Three murders. Three." Toussaint wiped his palms down the sides of his coat as he clicked his tongue. "And she is the one closest to them all."

"So why are we even here?" Evelyn Hadsall whined through a sigh. "When you know it was her. You said so yourself. Why not allow the rest of us to go on to London?"

"Here, here," her husband agreed.

Others chimed in.

I pondered the puzzle of the Hadsalls. When they boarded the train—even later as they passed our compartment on the way to dinner—Evelyn seemed meek and scared. She cowered in her husband's shadow. But now, ever since Kohler's death, she spoke with a bolder demeanor. And now her husband was the mouse, the echo of her demands. What had changed for them, apart from Kohler's death?

"Because," the inspector said with a sweep of his hand, "I do not believe she is the only one involved."

"Well, we have nothing to do with any of this." Edward Hadsall wagged his hand between his wife and himself. "We don't even know the woman. We don't know any of them."

Colin Graves got to his feet and planted his fists on his hips. "Miss Fairchild was traveling with Mr. Vogel. Mrs. Lundt was with Miss Tompkins. Hold them both. And Mr. Kohler traveled alone. His murder happened on the train, so keeping the railroad employees makes sense. But for the rest of us—I do think we've all answered your questions."

Toussaint nodded once in his direction.

"And at this point, we should be allowed to continue on with our journeys." Graves gestured toward me, his clunky, wide watchband sliding down on his wrist. "As you stated, Toussaint, she is the one at the center of this."

As Rutgers and the Hadsalls joined Graves in protest, my stomach flipped.

I felt the blood drain from my face. Then, holding my icy fingers to my hot cheeks, I felt beads of sweat forming in my hairline.

Toussaint must have noticed. He opened the door wide, snapped his fingers, and called for Madeline, who hurried from the other doorway to his side.

"Take her outside for some fresh air, *s'il vous plaît.*"

She dropped a curtsey. "*Oui*, monsieur."

Madeline took my arm and walked me through the back doors to the garden. The cool morning air filled my lungs. Unfortunately, it was too late to prevent me from becoming sick. I raced to the edge of the lawn and retched.

Madeline held my hair back with one hand and patted my shoulders with the other. "You can breathe in a second. You'll be all right soon." Her words comforted me through another wave of bile.

I struggled for breath between heaves, but no air came. How long could I go without breathing? I was already dizzy and faint. I clutched my knees to keep steady, and I finally managed to stand and take a slow breath. I wiped my mouth with the back of my hand, and Madeline gave me a handkerchief from her apron pocket. When I'd finally reclaimed a modicum of dignity, she passed me a small silver flask.

"This will help," she said.

Unscrewing the tiny lid, I took a quick sniff at the neck of the bottle. Alcohol, and strong. I kissed the opening and tilted my head back and forward in one swift motion. Even the shortest sip of brandy burned my mouth and throat all the way to my freshly emptied stomach.

I pushed the flask back to her. "I'm not so sure."

"We should sit for a moment." Madeline gestured to a stone bench next to a rose hedge. "Clear your head."

The bench was in the sunniest portion of the garden, and the stone warmed me. Within a minute or two, the tremble in my legs had stilled.

"Thank you." I gestured to Madeline, and she bobbed back.

"I need you to do something for me," Madeline said.

My mind scrambled to make sense of her request. What could

I do for her? And why should I help her? She might have been the one who poisoned Dahlia and Alice. But, no. My gut knew she didn't. I hadn't even hesitated to take the flask from her. I trusted her. "If I can."

"You're the only one who can. Toussaint respects you."

I laughed, and my stomach muscles ached. "I think you mean he suspects me."

"I always say what I mean." Her expression pleaded through a tortured smile. "If he suspects anything about you, it is that you—unofficially—work for the government. And he is correct."

I returned a weak smile without answering.

"But you did not kill Kohler?"

I was surprised that she made it a question. No one else seemed to have any doubt. I shook my head. "I did not."

Madeline responded with an almost relieved sigh. "Who wanted him dead?"

"Everyone."

"You are not wrong." Madeline glanced around us. "But the question is, who benefits from his death?"

I pondered her query for a moment, but my mind sputtered. And then I remembered something she'd said before. "You need me to do something for you? What is it?"

She tilted her head. "Toussaint may have guessed your situation, but he doesn't know mine. I need it to stay that way. As I'm sure you understand, the people I work with would be in extreme danger if the wrong people discovered they were part of the resistance."

I shifted my shoulders a fraction of an inch. "The war is almost over."

"This end of the war is near, perhaps. But there is always

another to take its place." Madeline scoffed. "Do not be fooled. We are not heroes. Not yet. Not for a long time."

"What can I do? How can I prevent him—or anyone—from discovering your secret? Toussaint is clever." I turned toward the doors and saw the inspector staring out the glass panes. "He watches us even now."

Madeline patted my shoulder again and stood to face me. "All I ask is that you keep my secret. And ask Vogel to do the same."

I agreed. From the corner of my eye, I saw Toussaint step outside. "Thank you, yes," I said, louder than necessary. "A glass of water would help, I'm sure."

"Very good," Madeline said with a curtsey. "I will be back straight away."

Before she went through the door, Toussaint was at my side. He gestured to the empty stretch of bench at my side. "May I?"

"Of course." I inched to one end to leave more room. "I apologize for leaving so abruptly." I offered a weak grimace.

"Are you feeling better?" His eyes softened as they met mine.

My training told me never to trust anyone. And how many times had I vowed to myself that I never would? But something formed between this man and me, and I didn't know what else to call it, but trust. I understood that he'd lock me up in a heartbeat if he thought I'd murdered Kohler, and yet… somehow that made me trust him more.

"Much better, thank you." I took a deep breath. The cool morning air filled my aching lungs, and I relished it. "And will you be sending the others on to London as was suggested?"

"No." He bit the word off almost before it left his lips. His spine straightened like a spear. "I do not fold to the wishes of the majority. I will complete my investigation before anyone can leave."

Toussaint's shoulders squared as he continued. "And I am sorry for your loss. I know Madame Lundt was dear to you."

I blinked at his sincerity. "Thank you." I glanced back at the doors. "The others think I killed her. And Kohler *and* Miss Fairchild."

"They hope it was you." Toussaint sighed. "It would make everything simpler if you did." He glanced upward as if to heaven. "For me, too."

"But you don't believe I did it?"

"I cannot rule you out. They are correct when they say all the evidence points to you." He drew a thoughtful breath. "But I believe you *can* help me find the killer—or killers." His gaze held steady on mine as though waiting for a reaction.

I tried to maintain my composure upon hearing his revelation. "You don't think the same person killed all three?"

His lips curled, raising the ends of his moustache. "You see? You ask the right questions. You are the only one who does."

"And am I the only one who notices when you don't answer any questions?" I matched his grin.

"*Ah, ma oui.* I think perhaps you are." He slid his hands over his thighs, stopping them at his knees. He sighed heavily and looked out at the garden.

"And shall I be forced to assume things about you as you assume things about me?" I leaned back on the bench.

"It is part of my job—or maybe a consequence of my job— which keeps me from answering questions. It requires me to make assumptions. You know how it is, do you not?" He drummed his fingers on his knee.

I was sure he'd noticed the signal between Jack and me. But did he know what it meant? I dipped my chin and pivoted to face him. "If you want to know something, you can ask me directly.

Dangling these hints and suggestions before me wastes both your time and mine. I have told you the truth, and I will go on telling you the truth—as far as I can."

"The truth," he murmured as though I had made a joke.

In for a penny, in for a pound, I decided. "I did not kill Kohler. I wanted to. I fully intended to kill him. But before I could do it, I was drugged. I woke up, and he was dead."

Toussaint's brow hovered high above his eyes. "Murdered in a quite peculiar manner."

Maybe two pounds. "How he died was specific to a method I had employed in the past." I pressed my lips into a thin line. "Designed to implicate me. Much more than simply using my pistol. It was a clear message to me. They know who I am. And I have to assume they want you to know as well."

I watched the gears turn in Toussaint's mind. More than processing what I'd said, he was working out what to do with it. How to proceed. "The war made us all…."

"Into monsters."

He clicked his tongue, his habit quickly endearing me. "I was going to say it made us all do things we never thought we would."

I lowered my head a fraction of an inch. "It is the same thing."

27

MONDAY, MAY 7, 1945, LATE MORNING

Toussaint and I spent the next half hour discussing a mutually beneficial arrangement, while a doctor and other local officials attended to the crime scene in the dining room. By noon, the unusually bright morning had dulled to a grey more befitting London, and I yearned to return home.

"Are you absolutely sure you can trust Vogel?" Toussaint asked. "Because if he is the killer, you will most certainly be next."

"Isn't that our plan? I'll be the bait to draw out the murderer. Short of revealing my secret, Jack and I will appear to have given you the information necessary to solve the case." I shrugged through my words. "Don't you think it will work?"

He placed a warm palm over my hand, then removed it quickly, as though it were a tactical mistake. "Making yourself a lure will put you in extreme danger. If Vogel can't be trusted, he may put you in a position from which you cannot extricate yourself." His words were brief, but his message was deep and clear. "I would never forgive myself. You must be utterly sure."

I glanced toward the doors. Not to see if anyone watched us, but to hide whatever doubts my face might reveal. "I've put my life in his hands many times. And—if it comes to it, I can handle him. But I don't think it will. I trust him as much as I trust anyone."

The man rocked his head back for several seconds and then down to focus on my expression. "I suppose it is the answer I expected, if not the one for which I'd hoped."

A little scoff escaped my lips before I could stop it. "I wish I could be more assuring." I met his steady gaze. For a split second, I entertained the notion that Jack had set me up for a hard fall. My gut knotted. If he did, the result would be deadly for one of us, and I was determined it wouldn't be me. I chased the idea from my mind. "Have you ever been betrayed?"

"Not in a long time." He stood and offered his hand to me.

"How do you avoid it?" I took it and steadied myself at his side.

"I stopped trusting people." His curling lip peeked from beneath his moustache.

I held up my hands as if to surrender. "Then this is all for naught?"

He clicked his tongue and shook his head. "It is a good plan."

Madeline met us at the door, holding two glasses of water. "Pardon," she murmured. "I intended to bring this earlier, but the police needed me."

Toussaint took the glasses. "*Merci.*" He glanced at me with a question behind his eyes.

I furrowed my brow. I wanted to trust Madeline, but her motives were still unknown. And at the moment, I couldn't stomach water. "No, thank you."

He handed the glasses back to the woman. "*Ah, merci.* I think we will both wait until luncheon."

"*Comme tu veux.*" Madeline dropped into a curtsey and took the glasses away.

From the lobby, we could see into the dining room, where two police officers paced and took notes. Alice and Dahlia had been removed, and Allard and Mrs. De Salle waited patiently to set up the space for luncheon.

Toussaint walked me to the stairway and raised his chin upward. Without preface, he said, "We shall see."

I bobbed over my shoulder to him, and he bustled away toward the other officers.

Jack stood at the top of the stairs, waiting for me. His blood-shot eyes softened as I approached.

"I'm sorry," he whispered. He took my hand and pulled me down the hall toward my room. He pulled me into a tight embrace when we were out of sight of anyone else. "Are you all right?" My shoulder muffled his question.

"I will be fine," I whispered. "But we shouldn't be seen like this. People will talk. They're already talking."

Jack took a half step back. "Is that what the inspector said? Others think we're conspiring? For what? Why?"

His suspicions boiled over, and I did my best to calm him. "Not about you. But there is some talk I may have wanted Alice and Dahlia out of the way because they stood between us." The words almost caught in my throat as I said them. I knew Jack would want to know what Toussaint had said. But his sudden rush of questions unnerved me.

My expression must have given my thoughts away, and maybe Jack could read my face like no one else. He scoffed. "That's ridiculous."

"You know it, and I know it. But others…" My words trailed off. I adjusted my voice to be loud enough for anyone else who might be eavesdropping. "How could anyone else understand? Unless they knew our true situation."

Jack stiffened his lips the way he did when holding back something he wanted to say.

I stepped out of his arms and studied his face. "What is it?"

His eyes darkened. "Who could know? I thought—before—maybe you had told Dahlia. And perhaps she had used it against you. Like you suspected that I had told Alice. But we were both wrong."

"The fact that they are both dead now doesn't mean we were wrong. Though I didn't tell Dahlia, and I trust you didn't tell Alice." *Trust.* Since my talk with Toussaint, I didn't like the taste of the word in my mouth. A shadow crossed his face, and I knew he felt the same. I lowered my voice. "And even if we didn't tell them, it doesn't mean one or both of them didn't find out about us."

"I was careful." Jack raked his hand through his hair, and he paced in a small circle in front of me. He was almost too defensive. Why?

I took another step away from him and planted a fist on my hip. "So was I."

"I know. I didn't mean to imply you weren't." He stopped and leaned against the wall, reaching for my hand half-heartedly.

"I'm sorry about Alice." I tried to sound sincere as I hooked his hand with my index finger. "I know you liked her."

"I did. She was a good secretary."

I tilted my head. "Not more than that?"

"Perhaps a little more. A good asset." He swallowed hard, and the cleft in his chin thinned as he flexed his jaw. "She was smitten with me—that kind of thing is hard to ignore. She was fun. When everything around us was crumbling, she was a good time."

"Don't feel guilty. This is what we're trained to do. To be." I struggled to maintain a casual tone. I had lost a good friend, but part of me wondered if Jack had lost more. "Did you love her?" I paused to fortify myself for his answer. "I won't be angry if you say you did."

Jack's spine straightened. "How was Toussaint with you? Rough?"

He changed the subject, as he always did when he was uncomfortable, and I decided to let him. I pushed a hint of a smile onto my lips. "Have you ever known me to have trouble with a man?"

"I have not." He laughed under his breath. "I don't know why I worry about you at all." His gaze settled on my lips, and I curled them a little more.

"You worry about me? Why? Is it a little self-doubt you're feeling? After all, you're the one who taught me."

His fingers laced through mine. "It's not because I think you can't take care of yourself. Honestly, you were my best student."

I pulled my hand free and slid my palm to the side of his jaw. My thumb rested on his bottom lip. "I'm not angry. And I like it when you worry."

"You should come to my room. We can talk in private." He nodded toward his door.

"No," I whispered, moving my mouth close to his ear. "I don't think we'd get much talking done. And, given the suspicion already surrounding me, I need to stay virtuous right now." I stared at his lips. "The temptation would be too great."

"Temptation for whom?" His gaze roamed over me. "You're steady as a rock."

A bell clanged from the first floor, and we jumped apart.

"That would be luncheon." I drew a deep breath. "I should wash my face."

"I'll walk you down."

I shook my head and gestured toward the stairs. "Wait for me at the bottom of the steps. And make sure others see you there alone." I wanted to tell him about the plan Toussaint and I had devised, but I decided he was clever enough to see it without my explanation, and I didn't want anyone else to discover it.

Jack's sulk sat stiffly on his features, as if he wasn't quite sure how to wear it. "I suppose it's best."

"I'm always right, you know." I left him in the hall and slipped into my room.

The bedroom seemed smaller than it had that morning. Colder and darker, too. Dahlia was gone. Her absence was as palpable as a hole in the floor. I switched on the lamp, and from the nightstand, a small piece of paper, folded in thirds, caught my eye.

I scooped it up as I sat on the bed. Holding the page under the lamp, I squinted as my eyes adjusted to read the scrawled missive.

King Louis has no challenger for his throne. He must be toppled.

I didn't recognize the handwriting. Not Jack's, certainly. And it didn't look like the note from Madeline, either. My heart pounded. Should I show it to Jack? To Madeline? To my dear inspector?

King Louis? Another reference to *The Man in the Iron Mask*. And this time, not a poem. More urgent in tone than that, but still in code. If it was from Madeline, I didn't dare share it with Toussaint. He would ask questions, and I wouldn't have answers. Not an ideal way to garner trust.

That word again.

Perhaps Jack was the only one I would show the note to for now. He hadn't had much to say about the first nudge from Madeline; I couldn't guess what he'd think about this one. My genuine concern was who might have sent it and how it got into my room.

How long had it been there? I hadn't noticed it this morning, but I was a little distracted then. Had the killer put it there? Why would he? Or her? There was no reason to. An enemy? An ally? My mind reeled; I needed more time to think.

And what did the bloody code mean?

I pushed the paper into my pocket and went to the mirror. I looked terrible. Like I had lost my best friend.

I had.

My eyes were still puffy, and my throat raw from the bile. I took a swallow of water from the bedside decanter, swished it around in my mouth for a few seconds, and spat it into the washbasin.

A comb through my hair helped. And maybe looking sad wasn't a bad thing. I could use a little sympathy. I pinched the apples of my cheeks and sighed. Good enough. I started to walk out and realized I should take my handkerchief for any necessary tears or sniffles. I shifted the note to my left pocket for safety and tucked the tulip-embroidered linen square into my right. I didn't want it tumbling out with the hanky.

Jack waited, in position, with his foot propped casually on the bottom step. His head angled from his neck in a sulk. I wondered if it was authentic or for show.

"I don't look forward to breaking the news to her parents." He was speaking to Van Dyke. "They're planning a wedding. It will devastate them to plan her funeral."

"Perhaps the inspector could make the call?" Van Dyke shrugged.

"No." Jack rocked his head from side to side. "It's the coward's way out."

"Probably right." The porter glanced up and met my eye with a meek smile. He tipped his head forward. "Good afternoon, Miss Tompkins."

"And to you." My voice was appropriately hoarse.

Jack straightened his stance and offered his elbow as I reached the lobby floor. "Allow us to escort you to a table. They have everything set up in the parlor." He made sure to include Van Dyke in the *us,* conscripting him to lead the way through.

Van Dyke pulled out a chair for me and sat to my right as Jack sat to my left. Besides Toussaint, I felt they might be my last allies in the room.

Before luncheon was served, Toussaint stood and cleared his throat. "I'm afraid I have some news for you all, good and bad."

The entire room fell silent, and everyone turned to the inspector.

"This morning, there was a radio announcement that Allied forces had accepted Germany's unconditional surrender in Reims, France."

The room erupted in joyous gasps and whispers of "thank God" from everyone.

Toussaint held up his hand. "But there is more." He lowered his eyes for a second and crossed himself. "I just received word about a situation in Amsterdam." He swallowed hard. "This morning, there was a celebration in Dam Square. Thousands of residents were enjoying their liberation."

A low murmur jumped from table to table.

Toussaint's hand raised as he continued. "While the people celebrated, a few remaining German soldiers opened fire into the crowd. I've been told at least a dozen are dead and many more injured."

We all joined in a collective moan. I didn't expect that Hitler's suicide would tie up everything in a nice, neat bow, but to hear of sniper fire against civilians broke my heart.

"I'm afraid we are not the only ones still fighting the last battles of the war." Toussaint dropped his chin to his chest before taking his seat.

My heart pounded as my brain absorbed the news. I wished the inspector could provide more information, but I was sure there was no more to be had for now. This kind of thing could embolden the true believers, or it may have been nothing more than a distraction, something to keep the Allies busy while the top brass Nazis made quiet escapes. Whatever it was, the war certainly wasn't over. And we still had our own battles to win.

Madeline brought in a tray of cold sandwiches and set up the tea service. Toussaint watched every move she made as if she had poisoned the morning tea and might try again. Her hands fumbled with the milk pitcher, and she almost spilled.

The Hadsalls, Mr. Graves, Mr. Deiter, and Mr. Rutgers watched with equal interest. As Madeline picked up the tea tray, everyone else's gaze shot away from her. Not mine. I had to be the one to go first.

I beckoned to the young woman and fingered my teacup in an unspoken request. She hurried to our table and filled my cup with tea and milk. I stirred exactly enough and drank. The room held a collective breath as I swallowed and bobbed my head in approval.

"Very good. Just what I needed." As I took another sip, Jack and Van Dyke also held their cups for tea.

Madeline moved to where Toussaint sat with Rutgers and next shifted to the table with Graves and the Hadsalls. Evelyn Hadsall was the last to take a drink, and even at that moment, it was the most meager sip.

Trust was a rare commodity in this congregation.

We had all made our way through the sandwiches when Madeline brought in a cart with a soup tureen and bowls. She ladled out a brothy chicken stew and served us in reverse order as the tea. As she set my bowl in front of me, she mumbled, "I am so sorry about your grandmother. She was a kind woman."

Tears filled my eyes, real ones, and a lump heaved in my throat. "Thank you," I choked out. Dahlia had been the grandmother I'd never known. She was the only family I'd had in a long time. I grabbed my hankie and pressed it to my eyes. "Excuse me," I whispered and stood.

Both men at the table stood automatically.

Jack offered a hand. "May I assist?"

I shook him off. "I'll be fine. I need a moment."

Madeline took my elbow. "I'll make sure she's all right." And the two of us hurried to the lobby hall.

28

MONDAY, MAY 7, 1945, NOON

"We have but a minute before someone will come looking for you," Madeline said, leading me toward a bench in the lobby. "But I've been thinking about the message from earlier. About *The Man in the Iron Mask*."

"King Louis?" I was fishing. If she hadn't written the second note, did she know who did?

Madeline blinked without emotion. "I wondered—assuming it referred to Yann Kohler—perhaps Kohler has a brother. A twin, maybe, like in the book." She shot me a hopeful glance. "It is a guess, but maybe not a bad one, eh?"

I agreed with a nod. Over her shoulder, I saw Evelyn Hadsall poke her head out from the doorway. Her dark eyes flashed in our direction, so I dropped my head to my hands as though I were crying. She retreated back to the parlor.

Keeping my voice low, I continued. "I don't know if there is a brother, but it might be possible. You might want to check with your contacts and see if they can find out. It would make sense with the message." I pretended to wipe tears from my face. "Perhaps whoever sent you the message in the first place expected me to know. But it wasn't in his file. Not the file I saw."

Madeline dipped her chin. "I'll see what I can find out. We should meet again later. After supper, I can bring fresh towels to your room."

"Yes, that will be fine." I stood and coaxed my hair back into place.

"Merci," Madeline said with a curtsey and hurried toward the kitchen.

"You should have asked to have your luncheon served in your room." The deep voice startled me, and I turned to find Rutgers at my side. "It's difficult when you suffer such a loss. Especially for women. Trying to carry on as though nothing had happened."

I sniffed and pasted a smile onto my lips. Best to let the soldier assume I was fragile; it would buy me some time. "I think it's all catching up with me."

"Of course, it is." He poked his elbow in my direction. Though it was the injured one, the muscles in his arm felt quite healthy to me. "I'm happy to escort you back through, or if you prefer, upstairs."

I clutched the steely arm beneath his linen shirt sleeve. I certainly didn't intend to be alone with him for any stretch of time. "I think I'd like to join the others again."

"That's the spirit. Chin up, as they say." Rutgers led me to my seat next to Jack. He pulled the chair a few inches out and waited for me to sit before taking a step back. "If I may be of further service, don't hesitate to let me know." He bowed and stepped back to his chair at the next table.

"All better?" Jack asked.

"Yes. Much." I slid the napkin back across my lap. "And hungrier than I expected."

Van Dyke pulled the small silver tray from the center of the table toward me. "The boy brought another round of sandwiches. They're quite good. You should eat. Keep up your strength."

His long, narrow face grew even longer as he raised his brow and smiled.

"Thank you." I took a triangle-shaped crust smeared with an olive pâté of some kind. "It does look delicious."

After three or four of the tiny sandwiches, my stomach felt content. My mind, on the other hand, whirled with ideas. A brother? I didn't know anything about that. Could a man with such a reputation have a hidden brother? If I were related to Kohler, I would certainly not wish for anyone else to know the fact.

Van Dyke excused himself, leaving Jack and me. Within another ten minutes, the other guests had finished their lunches as well, and we were alone in the parlor.

"What are you thinking?" Jack asked.

"Did Kohler have a brother?" My voice was no more than a whisper.

"Not that I know of." He tapped his index finger on the table for a second. "You're thinking about the iron mask?"

I shrugged. "An idea."

"If he'd had a twin, you'd think it would be known. At least in the file." Jack sighed and looked around. "What exactly was the plot of the book, again?"

"It's been a while since I read it, but as I recall, Prince Louis imprisoned his twin brother, making him wear an iron mask to conceal his identity so he could be king. I think he was the younger of the twins." I shook my head. "But if Kohler didn't have a brother—let alone a twin—what does the book have to do with him at all?"

Jack's eyes lit up. "Maybe nothing." He jumped to his feet.

"Why bother with such a message?" I started to reach for the second note, but Jack pulled my chair out and took my hand.

"Maybe it has nothing to do with what it said." Jack's hand went to my lower back as though he was leading me in a dance. "Maybe it was telling us where to look."

My brain finally clicked. "You think there's another message for us in a book? That particular book?"

"There's a library upstairs. I'll bet there's a copy up there." Jack pointed to the ceiling.

"How do you know there's a library up there?" I copied his gesture, pointing upward.

"Alice and I went for a walk around the place yesterday." He stopped for a second to swallow, and I could see the cloud pass over his eyes. "Beyond this room," he said, motioning to the doors at the far end of the parlor, "is a ballroom. From there, you can look up and see a loft filled with books. It must be right above us."

"Above this room?" I raised my gaze to the ceiling. It had to be fourteen feet high. Maybe higher.

"The space is probably used as an orchestra loft—or was once. It has a railing and looks out over the ballroom. But the walls are lined with bookshelves. Floor-to-ceiling books." He waved his arms up and down and back up again. "We should look."

My heart pounded with excitement. "That has to be it." I stepped toward the doors in question. "How do we get to this library?"

Jack frowned. "There wasn't a stairway from the ballroom. I suppose we should go up the main stairs and look around in this direction."

We hurried up the stairs from the lobby, but when we reached the top, we turned back along the narrow mezzanine overlooking the front desk instead of toward the hall to the guest rooms. At the far end of the balcony was a door.

"Is it locked?" I asked when Jack paused with his hand on the latch.

"I don't know." He turned the brass lever slowly. "It's not locked."

"Well, go on through." I pushed at his back.

The room wasn't large, but it was big enough to sit a dozen people or so. The walls were precisely as Jack explained. Books lined all three walls from the baseboards up, another twelve feet, to the crown molding at the ceiling. There was a table and chairs in the middle area to our left and a quartet of armchairs to our right.

"Which side do you choose?" I asked.

"I'll go right." Jack closed the door behind us and gestured for me to begin at the bookcase to my left.

I'd started at the highest shelf I could reach, scanning every title and author. "It's Alexandre Dumas, correct?"

"Yes."

The books seemed to have almost no sense of organization. They weren't in alphabetical order—neither by author nor by title. If anything, they seemed to be organized by size and color. My eyes blurred as I moved from the first section to the second.

"Oh, hell!" Jack swore.

"What is it?" I turned to face him, keeping my finger pinched between two books so I didn't lose my place.

"I just remembered. You are correct about it being Dumas, but 'The Man in the Iron Mask' is a chapter name. The title of the book is something else."

He was right. But what was the name of the book? "Do you remember the title?"

Jack shrugged and scratched at his chin. "It's something French, I believe."

"I should think so!" I said through a laugh. I racked my brain. "It's the last of the D'Artagnan tales. *The Viscount of* something."

"It's not Viscount in French. It's… oh, what is it?"

I laughed again. "Why don't we pull every book by Dumas?"

"Good plan. We can figure out the title when we find the hidden message." Jack moved back to his first shelf and started his search over.

I stared at my finger sandwiched between the tomes of Kipling and Voltaire. I was sure I would have noticed if I'd already seen a book by Dumas. Wouldn't I? I thought hard. Probably. But probably wasn't good enough. So I started over, too.

After an hour of searching, I'd pulled out three books and placed them on the table. Jack had added another one. We plopped into the chairs and stared at the books.

"Did you look through these?" Jack asked. "I flipped through mine, but it didn't have anything tucked inside."

I picked up *The Three Musketeers* and held it by the cover, letting the pages hang from the binding. "None of these have anything in them."

"Well, what did you find?" Jack picked up the next book. "This one is *Le Comte de Monte-Christo*." He ruffled the pages. "And nothing."

"I told you there wasn't anything." I picked up the last one I found. "This is *The Vicomte de Bragelonne: Ten Years Later*. It's the right book, but there's nothing in it, either." I flipped through until I found the section, 'L'homme au masque de fer.' I snapped my fingers to get Jack's attention.

"What?"

"This is the chapter. Look." I read through a few paragraphs and realized how rusty my French had become. My fingers traced line after line. I flipped a few pages. Nothing. I went back and scanned every page in the chapter. No writing in the margins. No underlined words or letters. No dog-eared pages. Nothing to indicate the book had been touched in decades.

"Check the binding." Jack held out his hands, and I gave the book to him.

"I don't see anything in any of these books." I leaned back in my chair and closed my eyes. "I even looked on the shelf behind the books. There's nothing there."

Jack hummed as he held one page after another to the light, looking for hidden messages.

My thoughts clicked through the messages we had. *The man in the iron mask has served his purpose.* What could it mean? And the note about King Louis? I'd completely forgotten about it.

I reached into my pocket. All that was there was my handkerchief. No, I'd moved the message to my left pocket. I reached inside. But it was empty. I patted both pockets again. It had to be here.

I hopped to my feet and searched around the floor. Nothing. The note hadn't fallen out in here. I shook my head, panicked. I couldn't have lost it. I couldn't be so careless.

"What is it?" Jack asked. He was on his feet, too, searching without knowing what he was looking for. "Did you find something?"

"No. I lost something." I felt sick. "There was a note."

"You found a note?"

"Earlier. In my room—I was going to ask if you had sent it." My heart thumped in my ears until I couldn't hear my own voice.

"It's gone." I shuffled the books on the table and then searched between the chair cushions. I rocked the chairs back to look beneath them.

"Calm down," Jack said.

How could I calm down? I turned my pockets out, but it was no use. The paper was gone. "It was another message. 'King Louis has no challenger,' or maybe 'rival' or something like that. I was going to show you."

"You had it with you?"

"Yes. And I was with you and Van Dyke. And then Madeline, and afterward Rutgers. Unless it fell out in the parlor or between there and here. But how could I miss it? I'd have seen it, I'm sure. Or you would have." I plopped back into a chair. "And it was about King Louis. Again."

"Maybe the messages *are* about the story." He gestured to the books in front of us. "They're certainly not about these dusty old books."

My head pounded, and I rubbed my temples. "I suppose you're right. And the messages were too story-specific to point us to this room alone."

Jack took my hand. "Listen. Let me take you back to your room. You lie down and rest for a while. I'll search the parlor and everywhere else for the note. And don't worry—if it's here, I'll find it. If I don't, I'll ask Madeline what was in it. After all, she's the one who wrote it, right?"

"It…" I hesitated, but why? "It wasn't the same hand as the other note. Oh, I wish I could show you." I leaned against Jack's shoulder, angry at myself. I felt helpless and hopeless. I'd failed the one person I could trust. He was the one reason I was still standing. The only reason I was sane.

The smell of his aftershave mixed with the dust of the books and made me light-headed in the very best way. His hands pulled at my waist, and I tucked my arms under his.

"I'm so tired. Why can't we have this for a little while?" I asked.

He rested his chin against my forehead. "Soon, Penny. We will soon."

29

MONDAY, MAY 7, 1945, AFTERNOON

*J*ack left me at the door to my room, and I went inside to search for the note. I checked around both narrow beds and underneath. I pulled the pillows forward and back, mussing the blankets. I knew the message wasn't anywhere in the room, but I didn't know what else to do.

I went through both my suitcase and Dahlia's in a panic. I'd had it in my pocket. I was sure of it.

If it had fallen out in the hall, on the stairs, or in the dining room, I'd have noticed it. Surely. What if someone had taken it from me? I was trained to pick pockets, but I was also trained to be aware of such encroachments on my person.

Jack was, too. And he was at my side most of the morning. What had he said when I told him I was missing the note? I couldn't remember. He acted shocked that there was a second message, but he hadn't denied that it was from him. He specifically mentioned I should ask Madeline, as she was the author. Hmm.

If he took it, why wouldn't he tell me he had it? If he wrote it, why wouldn't he tell me what it said?

I plopped onto my bed and leaned back to rest my eyes. My head was pounding.

Take a deep breath. And another.

The sound of my breathing filled my ears. I rubbed my chilled fingers into my temples, and my headache dulled a little more with each exhale.

I thought about Rutgers and Madeline. I considered Van Dyke. Someone else at this hotel knew I was an operative for the British government, besides Toussaint, Jack, and Madeline. Someone from the train. They knew how to kill Kohler to make me look guilty. They knew everything.

"Don't think so hard," a voice whispered.

I should have been startled, but I think part of me knew I was asleep. I didn't recognize the whisper. Seconds ticked by, and all I heard was my breath again. Perhaps the voice was merely my mind repeating the protocols I'd studied for so long.

Give yourself a chance to relax and remember.

It sounded like Dahlia's sweet chirp. I imagined her sitting by the bed and patting my hand. I wished she *were* with me.

My brain revisited every movement I'd made throughout the day. I saw myself walking down the stairs toward Jack. I saw his face, with its sad smile, when our eyes met. I took his arm, which had held me a hundred times. We floated into the parlor. We glided to our seats. A dance. Like we'd danced a thousand times.

I whirled around the long narrow room with Van Dyke, he in his light grey flannel porter's uniform. Then with Madeline, swaying into curtseys in her black dress and white linen apron. Next, I waltzed with the green uniformed Rutgers; he no longer held his arm in a sling. And lastly, I danced with Jack, leaning against his shoulder, my chin resting against his coal-black flannel suit.

I hovered on the ceiling and watched us searching through the bookshelves in the loft. Searching but not finding. And finally, I was in Jack's arms again. I could feel his breath on my neck. His fingers in my hair. His lips on mine. I knew I was sleeping, but I didn't want to wake up. Not yet.

"Soon, Penny," Jack whispered. But this time, he added, "It will happen again. And soon."

"What will happen?"

Before he could answer, his face vanished into a scream.

I launched upright in my bed. The room was silent, except for the pounding of my heart. No screaming. It was part of the dream.

But as I brushed through my hair with my fingers, a long, blood-curdling howl echoed through the inn. I hopped to my feet and ran to the door.

In the hall stood Van Dyke and Edward Hadsall.

"What was that?" I asked.

Hadsall rushed away from us toward the library.

"He said it was his wife's scream." Van Dyke gestured after Hadsall. "It came from that direction."

I hurried toward the open doorway to the library loft, and as I was about to enter, Edward and Evelyn Hadsall ran out. He sheltered her under his arm. "You shouldn't go in there," he warned as he passed.

Van Dyke caught my arm. "Wait. He said we shouldn't go in."

I pulled loose from his grip. "You don't have to, but I do. You can't stop me."

"Right," he said, and followed me inside.

The loft was empty. I took one cautious step and another

before hearing a commotion in the ballroom below. Toussaint's voice. And Jack's.

I went to the railing and peered down. Both men knelt on either side of Madeline, who lay sprawled out on the parquet floor, covered in blood.

"What happened?" I called down to Jack. There was a commotion behind Van Dyke and me as another person entered the library.

Toussaint gestured for Jack to step away from the woman's body. Jack raised his face toward me with cold fear in his eyes. "We cannot be sure." Jack nodded toward the inspector. "But it looks like she's been stabbed."

"The woman is dead." Toussaint's statement was definitive. He faced Jack. "Did you see anyone around her?"

"No, sir. I was in the lobby, and I heard two screams." Jack glanced up at me again. "Penny, get to your room right now. It isn't safe for you."

Toussaint concurred. "Do it, mademoiselle. Do it now."

"I'm not going to hide. I'm not—" As the words left my mouth, I felt a sharp, sudden push on my back, below my shoulder blades. My feet came out from under me, and my body flipped over the railing.

I was in free fall for a split second, and suddenly I felt a hand grasp my ankle. My body slammed back against the wall below the railing, knocking the breath from my lungs.

"Help!" Van Dyke yelled. "I don't have a good grip."

I dangled over Toussaint and Jack while Van Dyke held my leg with both his hands.

"Don't let go." Jack started to run out, but Toussaint grabbed his arm and stopped him.

"You must stay here to catch her if she slips. I will go upstairs and help lift her."

Jack's gaze met mine. "Hang on, Penny." He glanced above me. "Van Dyke, please don't let her go."

"I'll hold as long as I can. I don't know how it happened. She was right beside me one moment, and the next, she went right over."

"Pushed." That was all I could manage to say. My body ached already. I tried to pull myself up, but Van Dyke protested.

"Please stay still. My hands are slipping."

I couldn't see Van Dyke, as my pleated wool skirt had become a bell over my head. My legs and underpants were utterly exposed. If I weren't so terrified, I'd have been mortified. This was no position for a cold-blooded assassin. Jack didn't seem to notice. He just stared steadily into my eyes.

I reached my hands toward him, and he reached up to me. Our fingertips were still at least a yard apart.

"Do you trust me, Penny?"

My heart was in my throat. I didn't trust anyone. But at the moment, it was all I had. I could feel my ankle slipping in Van Dyke's grasp. And Jack was the one who had saved my life on so many occasions over the last few years. "Yes."

Without breaking eye contact, Jack said, "Van Dyke, let her go. I'll catch her."

The cold, damp hands around my ankle slipped away. Jack's arms caught mine and pulled me to him. My body slammed against him, dropping us to the floor a few feet away from Madeline.

"What's happening?" Jack's voice was low. He rolled me away from her and helped me sit up beside him. "Are you all right?"

"Yes. A little out of breath, but nothing broken." I smoothed my skirt back over my legs.

"Is Miss Tompkins hurt?" Toussaint's voice huffed from the loft.

Both Toussaint and Van Dyke clutched the railing and gasped for air.

"I will be fine. Thanks to Mr. Van Dyke."

Van Dyke waved to me and dropped his hand to his chest.

I glanced at Madeline's body and shifted my gaze to Jack. "I was pushed."

"By Van Dyke?" His eyes went wide.

"No. We were both looking down at you. He was at my side. His hands were on the railing next to mine. He didn't do it. Besides, he probably hurt himself trying to save me."

"He did save you."

"Yes, he did. It was a long way down." I dropped my head to Jack's shoulder. My whole body shook as the realization took hold.

His arms cinched me against his side. "Who pushed you?"

"I don't know. The Hadsalls had left the library. He wouldn't have had time to get her to their room and come back to push me. But someone else was there. I heard them behind us, but I didn't see who was there."

Jack stared into my eyes. "And you're sure?"

"Absolutely. Van Dyke didn't do it." I drew a deep, pained breath. "And who killed Madeline?"

"I suspect it was someone who knew she was working with the Resistance." Toussaint entered the room and gestured for Allard to attend to him. They exchanged a few phrases in French, and the boy ran out. "This has to stop. Someone is playing with us all, and I do not care for their game."

Jack rose to a knee and took my hand in his. "Very soon, there'll be no one left to play."

I steadied myself, and Jack and I stood, leaning on each other for support. "Four murders so far, and almost five." I shook my head and looked down at the darkening pool of blood. My heart couldn't stand anything else. "Poor Madeline."

"It appears the killer took our bait but was too quick for us. He distracted us, and now we must catch up." Toussaint shook his head in disgust. "This ends tonight." He scowled at the dead woman. "I'll gather everyone to the parlor, and we will have this out." He snapped his fingers at Jack. "Do not let her out of your sight."

30

MONDAY, MAY 7, 1945, EVENING

The whole inn grumbled as Toussaint directed everyone back into the parlor. The Hadsalls glared and shuffled inside, Evelyn still sniffling. Rutgers and Deiter followed Graves, and Van Dyke came along a few minutes later. His blanched face bobbed automatically as he passed.

Jack pulled me aside at the door to the room. "We should talk."

Before I could answer, Toussaint interrupted. "Mademoiselle Tompkins, I would like a word with you, too." He stroked his moustache, tilting his chin toward Jack. "And I must ask a favor of you, monsieur."

"Yes?" Jack edged between the inspector and me.

"Do you mind keeping an eye on the others while I ask the lady a few questions, *s'il vous plaît?*"

Jack shot a worried glance my way but conceded. "Of course." And he disappeared behind the carved wooden door.

Toussaint reached out and grasped my elbow, holding on firmly. "This has gone too far, and it is my fault. I have allowed you to keep your secrets. You *and* Vogel. I understand you need to keep some for your country. I made allowances for Mademoiselle Madeline as well. And now she is dead, and you, too—almost."

"You knew about Madeline?" I asked.

"Of course, I suspected she was with the Resistance. I have worked with them many times through this war."

My shoulders drooped as a wave rushed through me. Fear? Relief? Exhaustion? I wasn't sure. I drew a deep breath and pushed back my hair with trembling hands. "Please don't tell the others that Jack and I work for the British government."

He grimaced. "You need to tell me, honestly, what the dead girl was doing for you. Passing messages? Feeding you information?"

I would have to give him something if I wanted to keep my cover intact. "She was contacting her sources, trying to see what they knew about Kohler." I saw the blood rising in his cheeks. This wasn't helping. "We didn't receive anything from them. A few cryptic messages, nothing more."

A huff escaped Toussaint's twitching lips. "We had a plan, mademoiselle."

"I was going to talk to you about it." I held my hands up in surrender. "I was. But something happened. I found a note in my room earlier. One of her messages, I assumed. I had it in my pocket when I came down for luncheon, and I was going to ask her about it. But when I reached for it—to show Jack—it was gone."

Toussaint's face went from a rolling boil to a simmer. "And what did the note say?"

"It was in code."

My explanation was not enough for him. "I did not ask that. I asked what it said."

"It said that King Louis had no challenger. Something like

that." I stared into the inspector's brooding eyes. I needed him to believe me.

"You lie," he spat at me, squaring his broad shoulders with mine. His expression softened slightly, but his voice retained a razor-sharp edge. "Who is this King Louis? Ridiculous! I do not have time for this, and neither do you. I cannot keep your secret if you are not honest with me. You are a professional. I give you no pass because you are a woman." He stepped closer, our bodies only inches apart. I wondered if he was angry because I was keeping secrets from him or because I'd almost died.

My heart pounded as his face hovered only inches above mine. I couldn't think of a single response.

"Women remember everything. Word. For. Word. A woman such as yourself can tell me how many folds there were in the paper. If one corner was torn. If the loop of one L is fatter than the other." He seemed to regain his composure. He took a step away and scratched at his whiskers. When he continued, his voice was dark, barely above a whisper. "I ask you again. What did the note say?"

I managed a deep breath. "It said, 'King Louis has no challenger for his throne. He must be toppled.'"

Toussaint's eyes narrowed. "That is all?"

"Yes. I told you it was in code." I gulped another breath. "And the second L-loop in challenger was fatter than the first."

"What does it mean?" he asked.

I looked to heaven but found no answer. He asked the same questions I'd asked myself for the last two days. "I don't know for sure. I think it refers to—well, an earlier note referred to the man in the iron mask. Madeline and I wondered if Kohler had a twin brother." I shrugged at our musings. "It's probably silly."

"And yet she's dead now. I would say that idea is not so silly."

His frustration pushed through his calm exterior. "Two notes—and even after we agreed to be forthcoming, I knew about neither of them." Toussaint gestured to the room as the grumbling from within grew louder. "We should go in."

I reached for his arm. "Please. Are you going to expose Jack and me?"

"No, mademoiselle, I shall do my best not to. But from now on, no secrets with me. All of this subterfuge has certainly cost your friend her life." He took my wrist in a firm grip. "And nearly yours. I cannot help you if you lie to me." He held the door open and waved me inside.

His words cautioned, but his eyes expressed only concern. At that moment, I had no doubt he cared for me.

"I understand," I said, *sotto voce,* as I passed him and took my seat next to Jack.

Toussaint took his place in the center of the room, facing the semi-circle of suspects. His shoulders rose and squared. This was it. "The killing stops now." His voice boomed.

Evelyn Hadsall jumped, and after a heavy gasp, she sobbed into her husband's shoulder. Edward Hadsall held up a fist. "See here, man. There's no need to yell. The wife has already had a terrible fright today. No need to scare her further."

"But you should be afraid. You should all be afraid. One of you has been on a killing spree. First, Herr Kohler, on the train. Next, the two women this morning and another this afternoon. And if not for the quick reaction of Monsieur Van Dyke," Toussaint said, flipping his palm toward the Hadsalls. "Your wife would be the lone woman left alive right now."

With those words, Evelyn moaned.

Edward patted her shoulder and raised his chin to Toussaint. "You talk about all of this as though we had something to do with it. I thought you'd deduced Miss Tompkins killed Kohler. We all assume it to be true. So, it stands to reason she killed the others, too."

The inspector's stern scowl softened for a moment. His moustache quivered as though a hint of a smile pushed at the corner. "You are right, you know."

I wondered what he meant. Surely, he hadn't suddenly believed me to be the murderer.

Toussaint continued. "It does stand to reason that whoever killed Kohler killed the others. But why? Madame Lundt and Alice Fairchild and the girl Madeline—were they Nazis like Kohler? Why would we lump them all together as the victims of one killer?"

My thoughts reeled with his suggestion. When had I become so lazy? I was trained better than this. Was it because Dahlia was one of the dead? Was I too close to be objective? Was the real murderer counting on my lapse of objectivity? I had to pay attention. I had to focus.

"And how could Mademoiselle Tompkins push herself over the library railing? A sudden bout of remorse, that she should throw herself twenty feet to her death? I think not." Toussaint turned to face the Hadsalls. "You lost everything in the war—your shop, your books, and nearly each other. The Nazis destroyed your business, forcing you into hiding. Almost starving you both to death. Who would blame either of you for wanting Kohler dead? But the three women? I cannot see it."

He took a step toward Graves. "And you? You lost your wife and son to the war while you were stuck hundreds of miles away, useless to save them. So again, you have every reason to kill Kohler but no vendetta against the women."

Graves crossed his arms over his chest. "And I shall reiterate I am a pacifist. Whatever my feelings might be, I will not kill another person."

Rutgers released a sigh of disdain. "I, for one, am proud of my service in the war. I killed as many Germans as I could. I wish I *had* killed Kohler, too. I'd proudly tell you if it were so. But the women? Only a coward would harm women."

The inspector turned accusing eyes at Deiter and Van Dyke. "And both of you worked for the railroad. Holland has always been known for the excellence of its railroad. But when the Germans invaded, they forced you to carry the Jews and anyone who opposed the Third Reich to the work camps. You saw where they went."

Before he could say more, Deiter shouted. "Work camps? They were death camps. Thousands went in. Thousands. Far more than the camps could hold. And each time we stopped at them, we could see the truth. No more people than the last time. Where had they gone? Disappeared."

Van Dyke interrupted. "You say one of us killed Kohler. But he was the monster. He was the murderer. He and all of his kind." His voice faltered. Exhaustion hung on him like an old suit.

Deiter went on. "We went on strike. Maybe it was too late, but it was all we could do. We spent a year in hiding. What difference did it make? The Germans sent their own to take over the rails. Yes, I'm glad Kohler's dead. But I wouldn't have hurt a woman. It's not who I am. And it's not Van Dyke, either." Deiter swiveled in his seat to face Jack. "You should be looking into this man right here." He aimed his finger at Jack's face. "He's the one rubbing elbows with the Kraut soldiers, getting rich from their backroom deals."

Toussaint's brows rose high as he studied Jack's expression.

Jack preempted his accusation. "I didn't make deals with them.

On the contrary, I took advantage of them. I did what I could to survive, like the rest of you."

The room erupted into another din of arguments as I struggled to sort out the facts. If the same person killed all four victims, why? What did they have in common? Kohler was a Nazi, and Madeline worked for the Resistance. Dahlia had been married to a German officer, but Alice worked for Jack, who was sent by the British government. Was this some sort of tit-for-tat? Either way, someone else in this room had to know everything about Jack and me.

Toussaint held up his hands. "Stop! Be silent. You all believe Miss Tompkins to be Kohler's killer." He gestured to me without much flourish. "According to her, someone staged it all to appear as such. So, I ask myself, who knew that she would be on that particular train? The train that carried Yann Kohler."

Silence filled the room as all eyes turned on me.

"And I will ask her," he continued. "Mademoiselle Tompkins, who else knew you'd be on that train?"

My mind whirred through the last week. "Mrs. Lundt was the one who purchased our tickets. This was on Thursday. I had tried to buy passage that morning, but there were no tickets left."

"And nobody else knew?" Toussaint asked.

I glanced at Jack, who lifted his shoulders a fraction of an inch. Why had we not asked each other this question before?

"Until she told me, I didn't even know." My memory clicked. "Wait. That morning, when I'd tried to buy passage, I saw Mr. Rutgers at the station."

The room buzzed, and eyes shifted.

"And Friday morning, when I was checking on details at the train station, I saw the Hadsalls in line ahead of me. And Mr. Graves as well."

Edward Hadsall jumped to his feet. "See here! We were at the station because we were buying tickets for ourselves. You might have seen us, but that doesn't mean we saw you. *All* of us were at the station at some point for our tickets. That means nothing."

Rutgers and Graves made affirming *hmphs*.

Hadsall pointed toward Deiter and Van Dyke. "They could have easily learned she'd be on the train. More so than the rest of us, I'd say."

Rutgers shook his head. "And why her? If she's not the killer, if this is a frame-up, why choose her for the thing? Why not me or Van Dyke or anyone else?"

Another round of murmurs and protests. Toussaint growled and motioned for everyone to retake their seats. "Your points are heard, and they are valid," he said. His expression told me that his attempt had led the room in an unexpected direction, and he didn't want to have to explain why someone would target me specifically.

The room settled in stages until Evelyn's sniffs were the last sounds left.

"Thank you. *Merci.*" Toussaint bowed to me and raised a brow. "I happen to know someone stole a note from Mademoiselle Tompkins' pocket this afternoon. I will now ask everyone here to turn out *your* pockets. I want to see if anyone has it on their person."

I bobbed my head, pleased. This was good. Of course, any of them could have already secreted it to their room or even claimed they found it on the floor in the hall. It wasn't addressed to me, or anyone, after all. But let them say what they want; if someone had it with them, Toussaint would see. I would see, and I would know.

Toussaint again circled the room, starting with the Hadsalls. Edward emptied his pockets, and Evelyn handed her reticule to the inspector for examination. Nothing that should be in their possession.

Graves, Rutgers, Deiter, and Van Dyke turned out their pockets, revealing nothing more than a few coins and small pocketknives.

But when he turned to face us, I noticed the lines around Jack's eyes tighten, and I saw his jaw flex. He emptied his trouser pockets, the same as the other men, and before long reached inside his jacket. He placed a folded slip of paper into Toussaint's hand.

My heart sank. I raised my gaze to his, hoping for an explanation, but Jack only shook his head.

"Is this the note you lost?" Toussaint asked, handing the paper to me.

"What does it say?" Graves and Rutgers asked in one voice.

I met Jack's eyes, searching for a flicker of explanation, a signal that this was some plan we'd never spoken aloud. But Jack only looked away, and the silence between us was louder than any accusation. My heart pounded as I read the note silently.

King Louis has no challenger for his throne. He must be toppled.

31

MONDAY, MAY 7, 1945, EVENING

"How could you take it from me and help me search for it?" I wasn't sure if I yelled the accusation or whispered it. My throat ached and clutched, but the others in the room leaned forward in their seats to hear.

Jack gulped and finally made eye contact. "I didn't take it from you. I found it." He reached for my hand, but I inched it away from him.

I wanted to believe him, but how could I? He was the one who knew everything. He was the only one who could set me up for murder like this. My thoughts whirred. Why would he do it? On orders from Mother? No. If Mother wanted me gone, he'd have done it more discreetly, wouldn't he?

And Kohler's murder didn't merely threaten *my* cover, but Jack's, too. That thought resounded in my mind. It was the only way the other murders made any sense. *Jack's being set up, too.*

I'd believed he was the only one with the skills to frame me.

But was he? If the set-up were for both of us, someone else in this room had skillfully arranged everything. Who could do that?

My gaze drifted around the parlor. I didn't know these people. I took everything they told me at face value, and my training had taught me better. I had to learn more. I had to focus. Any of them could be… anyone. Jack was the only one I'd known before this trip besides Dahlia and Alice.

I stared at Jack again. "Where did you find it?" This time, I was sure to whisper.

"What does it matter where he found it? What does it say?" Graves asked again. He checked his watch as though he were late for something.

Toussaint shot a severe glance toward the man and clicked his tongue. "Where he found it is more important than what it says, in this case."

Jack leaned in and murmured, "I found it in Madeline's pocket. That's what I wanted to talk about with you."

Toussaint's brows arched high. He kept his voice low to match Jack's. "And was this before or after she died?"

Jack's expression told both of us he'd found the note on Madeline's dead body, though he remained silent.

"Inspector, I believe you can sort this out between the two of them without the rest of us." Hadsall stood and raised a fist. "I demand you allow us to be on our way."

"Here, here," Graves added. "We're all due back in London."

As the others stood to walk out, Toussaint motioned for them to stay seated. "We are not done here, I'm afraid." Nobody left the room, though no one reclaimed their seats, either.

Deiter shrugged. "And what else is there?"

The inspector shook his head. "There is everything. It is not as easy as you all may think."

Before he could continue, I flashed a threatening glance. He returned a softer one.

"As you say, perhaps I could sort out Kohler's murder with simply these two." Toussaint's finger waggled in Jack's and my direction. "But with three others dead, it cannot be so simple."

Deiter released a sigh of exasperation. "Listen, it's plain enough to us—why can't you see it?"

Toussaint frowned as if forming a question.

Deiter gestured to Jack and me with a nod and might as well have winked at Toussaint. "Graves and I were talking about it at luncheon. The two of them have something going on." He crossed his arms with a confident air. "And the women they were with got in the way, you know. I'd wager they're good for those killings, too."

"It makes sense to me," Hadsall said. Evelyn sniffed in agreement.

"And what about the other woman?" Toussaint challenged. "What about the housemaid?"

"One more pretty young thing, I suspect." Graves offered his hands up. "Or maybe she'd discovered their collusion and tried to get money from them—blackmail, you know. It would explain the note, too."

This was getting worse. Short of telling the others everything, I wasn't sure how Toussaint would explain why he didn't arrest us.

"Perhaps you are correct. Perhaps I am making this too complicated. Your suggestion is not—how do you say? Far-fetching?" Toussaint's self-effacing manner put the others at ease. "But I will tell you, in my many years as an inspector, the easy solutions are not always the correct ones. Often, they are the ones the guilty parties want me to see."

"Or perhaps it's the one logical answer," Hadsall added, shifting his weight from one foot to another.

Toussaint's defenses rose as he spun on the Hadsalls. "Madame?" He squinted at Evelyn, who lifted her chin in response. "What exactly did you see from your loft view?"

Hadsall stepped in front of his wife. "She's in no condition to answer questions. She witnessed a horrible sight."

"Did she? This is what I'm asking. What did she see?" Toussaint crossed one arm over his chest and, resting the opposite elbow upon it, laid a finger across his chin.

Evelyn sniffed and held her handkerchief in a knot. "I was sitting in a chair, reading the back of a book. I heard a scuffle below, which got me to my feet. The young woman said something in French; I speak a little of the language."

"What did she say?" Toussaint asked.

"Something like *'assassiné,'* and after maybe the word *'double,'* but I'm not absolutely sure." Evelyn dabbed the side of her nose with the hankie. "I couldn't see her at first. Not while she was talking. I supposed she was in the room beneath me—the parlor. But she made a choking scream and staggered backward into the ballroom. That's when I saw she had been stabbed." She gulped the air and pressed her eyes closed. "That's when I screamed."

Toussaint raised a finger. "You saw that she'd been stabbed, you say?" He took a step closer to the woman. "How did you know she was stabbed? Was there a knife visible? How do you know she was not shot?"

Evelyn Hadsall huffed, clutching her hands together against her heaving bosom. "I didn't hear a gunshot. But I saw the blood. So much… I assumed the maid was stabbed."

"And you didn't see anyone else with her?" Hadsall asked his wife. He dropped a hand on her shoulder to comfort her.

"No. Nobody. And I didn't hear anyone else speaking. I stood there, clutching the railing." She lifted her trembling hands, fingers curled like claws. "For what seemed like an eternity—and then you," she motioned to Toussaint, "came into the ballroom, and Mr. Vogel a few seconds later."

"I ran from our room to my wife's side," Hadsall said, glancing at Van Dyke for confirmation. "But Vogel could have been the one who killed the girl and waited for Toussaint to show up before coming to pretend to help."

Deiter pointed at Jack. "That's right. Mrs. Hadsall's scream led us to the library upstairs. Why did you go to the ballroom?"

Toussaint shook his head and shooed away the accusation with a flick of his hand. "Monsieur Vogel and I were downstairs, and we both heard the young woman scream a few moments before Madame Hadsall. So it was natural for us to investigate the first alarm." He turned to the others and pivoted back to Deiter. "And who was in the library? I saw Van Dyke and I know Mademoiselle Tompkins was there, too, but I did not see you."

The steward furrowed his brow. "I think we all were for a second." He exchanged a glance with Van Dyke. "Of course, the Hadsalls had already gone when I went in. I passed them in the hall. She was quite upset." He flashed Evelyn a weak grimace.

Graves concurred with a head bob. "Quite. I went in for a moment, looked over the edge, saw the girl's body, and hurried back out and down to see if I could help."

Rutgers cleared his throat. "I did the same. Deiter and I descended the stairs together when we heard the third scream." He gestured to me. "We stopped for a second, wondering which way to go." He paused to swallow. "And when we got to the ball-room, Toussaint turned us away. Said he was going upstairs to help Van Dyke."

My mind whirled as everyone spoke. I tried to sort the information chronologically with my flashes of memory. Assassin? Double? Not a brother, not a twin—but a double? I reeled with questions. Did Kohler have a decoy? If so, who was it? No one here could pass as Kohler.

I crossed my arms, stepped toward Toussaint, and faced the other men. "But who was it who pushed me over the rail? I was with Van Dyke, and I heard noises, but I didn't see anyone else with us."

Van Dyke reached out toward me. "You must believe me; I didn't push you. I never would do such a thing."

Deiter, Rutgers, Graves, and Hadsall shook their heads and shrugged. "It wasn't me," they said in staggered objections.

"I was with my wife—never left her side," Hadsall spat out and wrapped his arm around Evelyn's shoulders in a display of solidarity.

"What is that there?" Toussaint asked. I spun to see where he was pointing, but he stopped me mid-turn. "There, Mademoiselle, on your back."

Jack, from behind me, put a hand on my right shoulder as Toussaint placed a hand on my left.

"Hold still," Jack whispered. "Let us see."

"It appears to be a tiny smudge of blood on the back of your blouse," Toussaint said. He clicked his tongue. "Whoever pushed you, it seems, still had the blood of their last victim on his hands."

Whoever murdered Madeline was the one who tried to murder me. My mouth went dry.

At the revelation, Evelyn moaned and rocked on her heels. Her husband caught her mid-swoon and settled her safely into her chair.

"Miss Tompkins, I will need your blouse as evidence." Toussaint squeezed my shoulder. "Monsieur Vogel, please escort her to her room and guard the door as she changes clothes."

Jack nodded.

The inspector flipped his palm toward the Hadsalls. "You two may go to your room and have Madame DeSalle or her boy bring up some tea for your wife." He turned a stern eye on the others. "The rest of you?" He harrumphed. "I will speak to you individually."

"And we may go to our rooms until you call us?" Rutgers asked.

"No. You may wait in the lobby area." He turned to Deiter. "You, in the dining room." To Van Dyke, "You may wait at the foot of the stairs. I want all of you to be able to see each other." And to Graves, "I will speak with you first. Take a seat."

"Of course." Graves tipped his chin and returned to his chair.

Jack and I started out of the room, but the inspector took us aside and let the Hadsalls leave first. "I will want you after I speak to the others." He patted Jack's lapel and turned to me. "A double?"

I shrugged and whispered, "I think we'll soon meet our King Louis."

32

MONDAY, MAY 7, 1945, EVENING

Jack and I waited for the Hadsalls to go up before we ascended the stairs. We whispered our suspicions as we climbed out of earshot of the others, who were now taking the stations Toussaint had assigned them.

I watched the Hadsalls enter their room and close the door before I made a sound. "After hearing Evelyn's statement, I'm sure it's not a brother but a double. A decoy," I murmured. "It's the only thing that really makes sense."

Jack pressed his ear against the Hadsalls' door and listened for a moment before we continued to my room. "Who, out of this motley crew, do you think Kohler's double could be?" Jack strummed his fingers on the door casing as I fumbled with the key.

The latch clicked, and he followed me in. "Aren't you supposed to guard my room from the outside?"

He rolled his eyes. "Somebody should ensure you don't

smudge the bloodstain as you remove your blouse. Don't you think?"

Once he closed the door, I started unbuttoning. "I think the dead man on the train was the double. Kohler is King Louis. Doesn't that seem more likely to you?"

"It is logical." A hint of a smile formed in the corner of Jack's lips as the last button released. "But if that's the case…" He trailed off, waiting for me to slip out of the cotton top.

Turning my back to him, I whispered, "Now we have two big problems."

"Just two?" His fingers held lightly to the blouse as he led it down my back, low enough for me to free my arms from the sleeves. "I can think of at least five."

I pulled another blouse from my valise and finger-pressed a few wrinkles away. My mind hopped through ideas, trying to work out a hundred solutions at once. "Since we discovered the code wasn't leading us to a particular book, it has to be about the story."

Jack nodded, only half paying attention to my words.

I continued without giving him the attention he wanted. "If I'm right—if the man on the train was Kohler's double—he was murdered to make everyone believe Kohler was dead. 'The man in the iron mask has served his purpose.' If that's true, our first problem is that the real Kohler is still alive."

Jack folded the stained blouse carefully and set it aside. His gaze focused on my half-naked body as I pulled the fresh top over my bra. "The man on the train had the lightning bolt burn mark on his wrist. It was our positive identification for him. There aren't a lot of men willing to be branded like that to be someone else's decoy," he said.

"Burns are not difficult to replicate, especially if the original is available as a pattern." I tucked my top into my skirt, and Jack's gaze drifted back to mine. "He'd *had to have known* he was a decoy and been willing to sacrifice himself."

"Committed enough to be branded." Jack winced and then glanced at my bed. "A true believer."

I cocked my chin to admonish his subtle suggestion. "However, we were drugged—so perhaps he didn't know how great his sacrifice would be. *He* certainly didn't drug me and kill himself. Not with that method."

"You're right about that." Jack ignored my silent reprimand and let one hand rest on the coverlet.

"Once the word was out that Kohler was dead, the real Kohler could go anywhere he wanted. With the war drawing to an end, he could flee with the rest of the refugees. And with an incident like this morning's shooting, authorities won't be focused on refugees." I thought back to all the others on the train. The others still with us in the hotel.

"Where do you think Kohler is now?" Jack's hand gripped the bedpost, and his lips curled again.

"That's our second problem. He's here. Don't you see? He had to be sure his decoy was dead. He's the one who killed him. Or he had another accomplice." My mind raced. "Yes, he must have another accomplice. Or had."

"Who?"

I held up a finger. "Jack, don't be angry with me, but I still think it was Alice."

His expression balanced exasperation and sorrow as he gasped. "Alice is dead, Penny."

"That's why I think it was her. It's why I think Kohler is still here. He's making sure he doesn't leave any loose ends." I propped my knee on the mattress, hoping to distract him enough to manage his anger. It worked, but only momentarily. He glanced down at my thigh, lingering for a moment, and back up.

"By that logic, it could just as well have been Dahlia. She was married to a German officer. She could have been positioned next door to you to discover your secrets." Jack's face flushed with irritation.

"You know it wasn't Dahlia. The most logical explanation is that Alice was Kohler's accomplice, and so he had to kill her. With the way she was with you, a little of your charm could have made her talk."

"But he killed Dahlia, too," Jack argued.

"Maybe he meant to poison me. Dahlia may have drunk from my teacup." I took a quick breath to adjust my tone, refusing to let my emotions take over. "It doesn't matter who it was. What matters is who Kohler is. We cannot let him out of our reach. He must answer for the crimes he committed. All of them must be punished for what they did."

"Our identifying mark was the burn. That's not something you can erase. So, if Kohler is one of the guests here, he still has the scar." Jack tucked my soiled shirt into a towel to preserve the stain. "I shook hands with Hadsall a few times. He has no scar. And though his wife is no looker, she certainly isn't a man in disguise."

I recalled the last night on the train, remembering the man I had dinner with. I listed his features. "The man we all knew as Kohler was fit, an average height, with light brown hair over a high forehead. Hazel-gold eyes. Angular jaw and chin. Rather attractive. That's what we should be looking for."

Jack blinked. "That doesn't match anyone else here."

"It must. We simply don't see it. Kohler wouldn't have a decoy who wasn't a suitable double." Would he? In the book, King Louis made his twin wear the iron mask because he looked *too much* like him. My thoughts scrabbled to make sense of it. "The iron mask."

Jack sighed, and in the quiet of the bedroom, the slight sound jarred me.

"We have to identify the iron mask. What's the thing keeping us from seeing Kohler?" I paced to the window and looked over the garden. "Our dead man on the train looked like what we all expected Kohler to look like. But Kohler—the real one—*doesn't* look like what we expect right now. Forget about the scar; he's hiding it somehow." I spun to face Jack. "Who is wearing the iron mask?"

"As I said, nobody else looks like the man." Jack held up his hand and began ticking off on his fingers. "Van Dyke is too tall and thin. And I saw his wrists while you dangled from his hands— no scar."

My thoughts rolled through the other men. "What about Rutgers? He had his arm in that sling. And he's been very vocal about wanting to kill Kohler. Maybe it's a ruse to divert suspicion? *He doth protest too much, methinks?*"

Jack thought about my suggestion, then released a sigh. "I don't think so. Both Deiter and Rutgers are too short, six inches shorter than the dead man. Something like that would be hard to fake."

"Graves," I spat out the name like poison.

"Graves is bald and thick around the middle." Jack shook his head. "What little hair he has is grey."

"His hair can be done with peroxide and bluing." My heart raced. "And he can shave the top of his head. *And* wear padding. It's perfect, really." I recalled one more thing. "He wears a big, clunky watch on a wide band. It might be wide enough to cover the scar."

Jack's expression seemed to crumble. "If he made promises to

Alice or threatened her somehow—he could have even made threats against me, she might have done whatever he asked."

I considered that for a moment. What if I'd been in her shoes? Threats against me wouldn't have been a challenge, but against Jack? Training instructed us to disregard everything except the mission. But my heart might not be so strong. And Alice? If she was in love with Jack? And with no training... I refocused. "Jack, what did she know about me?"

He stared without responding.

I flew to his side, clutching his arm to plead. "We don't have time for pride or doubts. Tell me everything she knew. Everything she might have known."

His mouth twitched. "I... I don't know. She never seemed to know anything about you, or me, for that matter." He cut his eyes away. "But a few months ago, she was acting oddly; she lied to me about why she wasn't home one evening. I knew she was lying, but I convinced myself it was nothing. That it didn't matter. People lie about the most insignificant matters. But the next morning, things in the office seemed a little out of place."

"And you didn't question her?" Fire rose in my cheeks and my attitude. "Jack, we were trained better."

He pressed his fingers to his temples. "I'd had a few drinks the night before. I wasn't sure."

"You were sure, but you didn't want to believe it." I drew a deep breath, letting the accusations go. "I understand. I do. You didn't want to let yourself believe it. It was easier to imagine you remembered things wrong." I took his hand in mine. "But you're better than that."

"What if I'm not?" His eyes darkened, and he turned away from me. "What if I'm not better than that?"

"You were using her, so what if she had secrets of her own?" I narrowed my gaze. "If Alice knew my methods, she could have killed the man, making it look like I did it. And she could have drugged our drinks while you were telling us goodnight and trying to convince me to leave Kohler alone. We were so focused on each other, we mightn't have noticed."

"She must have found my notebook. All my entries about you." Jack dropped his head to his chest. "I didn't keep them in code. I hate the silly nursery rhyme code." He raked his fingers through his hair. "This is my fault."

I hurried to the door, picking up the bundle with my blouse and dragging Jack behind me. "We don't have time for fault-finding. We must get downstairs. Toussaint is interrogating Graves now. The shooting at the square may have made him bold or desperate, or both. If Toussaint confronts him—if he even hints or guesses—Kohler might turn on him."

We scrambled down the stairs and rushed to the closed door. Van Dyke sat on the bench nearby.

"Is Graves still in there with the inspector?" I asked.

The porter stood and nodded. "Yes, nobody's come out."

Jack rapped on the door. "Inspector, we have the blouse. May we bring it in?"

No answer.

Van Dyke furrowed his brow. "Nobody's come out. I haven't moved from here."

Jack tried the doorknob, but it didn't turn. "I'm going through." He nudged me away and took two steps back before ramming the door with his shoulder. It bowed a bit but didn't give way.

Van Dyke readied his position. "Together, then."

Both men moved into place, and with a nod, they charged the door at once. The frame cracked, and the door flew open, crashing against the wall inside.

At first glance, the room appeared empty. However, a French window on the opposite wall stood open with the curtains fluttering in the breeze. As we rounded the end of the couch, we found Toussaint. My heart dropped.

He lay sprawled on the floor in a pool of blood, with a knife in his chest.

33

MONDAY, MAY 7, 1945, EVENING

I knelt at Toussaint's side, feeling for a pulse. The blood from his wound turned his navy uniform jacket almost black, while his complexion had turned a waxen white. His lips moved but made no sound. I turned to the porter. "He's alive, Mr. Van Dyke, please call a doctor. There's not a minute to lose." I waited for him to leave the room. "Jack," I snapped. "Graves, or Kohler, rather, is out here somewhere. We must stop him before he's gone for good."

Jack rushed to the open window. "I'll find him. Are you all right with Toussaint?"

"Of course, now go." I shooed him away and turned my attention to the inspector. Blood spread onto the rug beneath us. "I'm here. Dash it all; we should have realized it was Graves sooner." Why didn't I see this earlier? This man protected me. Gave me more than enough time to figure this out.

Toussaint's mouth pursed a few times before words came out. "Graves... Louis... Kohler."

"Yes, I'm sorry it took us so long to see." I scanned for something to staunch the bleeding. "Hang on." I pulled a table scarf from the nearby console and bundled it over his chest.

He squeezed my hand. "He's here."

Tears blurred in my eyes. "Yes, we'll find him. Jack is searching right now."

The door bumped shut behind me, and Toussaint's eyes widened. "Kohler." His voice trailed off to a rattle.

I leaned closer to his face. "I know. Focus on me. I won't leave you."

"I think he's trying to tell you I'm here; I'm in the room with you." Kohler's voice sliced through the quiet. My blood went icy. I turned and slowly rose to face him. He'd taken off his jacket, along with the padding around his middle, and he'd rolled up his shirtsleeves, revealing bare muscular forearms.

My heart pounded, and I prepared for battle. "You won't get away with any of this."

"My darling, Miss Tompkins." His posh accent melted into a guttural hiss. "I suggest you worry about your situation and not mine." He stepped toward me with sinister intentions telegraphed in his expression.

I moved away from Toussaint, hoping to keep him from any further harm, praying he'd survive until help arrived. I studied Kohler's features. His hazel eyes, sharp jaw, the shape of his lips, and even the angle of his nose were a near-perfect match to the other man on the train. Why didn't I see any of this sooner? My gaze dropped to his watch.

He noticed my shift in attention and raised his arm. With a quick shake of his wrist, the timepiece slid back to reveal a lightning bolt scar. "Official confirmation? Is this what you needed?"

My heart slammed against my ribs. "Why go to this extreme?"

"My dear girl, don't you see? A person is never more deadly than when they're dead. When you're dead, nobody suspects you. Nobody looks for you. You can get away with murder. No one suspects a middle-aged pacifist." His lips twisted into a menacing smirk.

"And Alice Fairchild was your informant?" I shifted to put the couch between us.

His upper lip snagged into a sneer as he rocked his head. "Of course. I assumed that was why you killed her."

"What?" My mind whirred, I blinked at his accusation, and he reacted before I could clear my expression.

"*You didn't* kill her?" he asked. His hand went into his trouser pocket. "Perhaps Jack did. And the poor old lady, too? I suppose he wanted to be absolutely sure." He held out a garrote for me to see. A simple coil of piano wire with a wooden peg at each end. Simple and deadly.

Push the emotions aside. You must act now. "That method will take some time." I inched toward him and away from Toussaint. It would be easier to fight if I weren't worrying about the inspector. "I'd have thought you'd want a little more head-start."

He sucked on his teeth. "And I thought you'd appreciate this." He bounced the weapon in the palm of his hand as though he was weighing it, relishing it. "I know how you enjoy an intimate kill."

"You have no idea, but you soon will." I scanned the room for a weapon. I'd been trained to use anything, but I had a few favorites, none of which were particularly handy. I could have snatched the blade from Toussaint's chest, but doing so would surely kill him, and he was barely clinging to life as it was. I backed up to a console table and rested my hand on a book.

Kohler side-stepped the couch and let one end of his garrote drop. He was obviously enjoying the tease. "You know, Penny—I think I *will* call you Penny now. You and I are not so different from each other. You kill. I kill." He stepped toward me, staring like a lion about to pounce. "But I'm better. More efficient."

I gripped the book. "You kill innocents. I kill murderers."

He lunged, and I dodged, whacking the book against the side of his head. He grabbed my wrist and spun me under his arm. I kneed him in the groin with almost no effect. His muscles were pure steel. I was a rag doll in his grasp.

He threw me to the floor and planted his heel in the center of my back, knocking the breath from me. "You should at least put up a fight." He moved his foot to kneel down and straddle me, but as soon as his weight lifted, I rolled to my back and, in one motion, kicked.

This time, my foot landed on his inner thigh, sending an electric jolt from my foot to my hip. Kohler wobbled with the impact, though I was sure the blow hurt me more than him.

His lips curved beneath his narrow moustache, and he dropped to his knees, pinning my hands to the floor on either side of my head. He glared and lowered his lips to my ear. "Yes," he hissed. "I don't often get to watch the faces of my victims as their souls leave their bodies. I'll enjoy this."

With his face still next to my ear, I turned my head and snapped. My teeth caught his earlobe and latched on, drawing blood. He pulled away, but I held my jaw tight. He howled as a chunk of his skin tore off in my mouth.

He loosened his grip enough for me to free one hand and scrape the side of his face. I spat out the bloody chunk of flesh and scanned for another weapon.

My fingers found the book again, and I slammed the spine into his Adam's apple. Before he could draw a desperate breath, I jabbed the outside corner of the book into his eye.

This sent him reeling back, clutching at his face, the garrote dangling from between two of his fingers.

I scrambled to crawl from beneath him, but his other hand clasped my ankle and pulled me back before I was clear.

Kohler's weapon dropped over my head, but before he could tighten it around my neck, I positioned the book between my throat and the wire. He pulled me to him, my back pressed into his chest. The book offered slight relief—enough gap to allow my fingers to take hold of the wire. Enough for a labored breath to fill my lungs. *Keep breathing.*

His voice rasped in my ear. "Penny, relax. You're going to die now. Don't fight me."

The book blocked me from rocking my head forward, and I needed to do that if I was going to escape. My fingers pushed the wire out enough to let the book slip free. The wire sliced into the skin of my fingers and throat as he tightened the garrote. My own knuckles worked against me, crushing my airway. I couldn't breathe. Fear gripped my thoughts. *I couldn't breathe.* I squeezed my eyes shut to clear the intrusion. I only had one chance to make this work before I blacked out and died.

I lowered my chin to my chest, and with all the strength I had left, I threw my head back, butting the back of my skull into his nose. I felt the warm spray of his blood on my neck. He let go of the piano wire, but I did not.

Whirling around him as if in a dance, I wrapped the wire around his neck and pulled. He stumbled back from his knees, and his feet kicked in front of him.

I had strangled four other men in my life. It wasn't an easy task when I was at my peak. At this point, I was exhausted, spattered in slick blood, and soaked with sweat. He was strong; I was not. But I knew I had to win this battle. If I loosened my grip, even for a second, this Nazi filth would walk away.

I remembered my training, Jack's voice explaining the trick to know how long to hold the tension. I tightened the garrote as I whispered in Kohler's ear. *"Our Father, who art in heaven, hallowed be thy name; thy kingdom come; thy will be done on earth as it is in heaven."*

His fingers dug into the flesh on his neck, clawing at the wire. Blood from his nose seeped over his hands and into his shirt.

"Give us this day our daily bread, and forgive us our trespasses as we forgive those who trespass against us." I kept my arms up and out like wings; his shoulders shuddering against my breasts. My upper arms and shoulders ached for relief, but I couldn't relax for even a second.

His legs flailed now. His heels kicked and rattled against the wood floor.

"And lead us not into temptation, but deliver us from evil." The taste of blood and sweat filled my throat and threatened to purge itself. All I could do was swallow and pull harder.

Finally, his body flagged and stilled. But still, I held tight. These last few moments were crucial.

"For thine is the kingdom," deep breath, *"the power and the glory,"* breath, *"for ever and ever."* My muscles burned, but I held tight. *"Amen."*

Still no movement from him. I let the peg handles of the garrote drop. I gasped and gulped. My lungs ached. I rallied enough energy to push his limp body off mine.

Turning away, I crawled back to Toussaint's side. He still breathed, but he was unconscious.

Wiping the blood off my hands onto my skirt, I lowered my face closer to his. "I'm here." My voice was nothing more than a rasp. I slid my palm to his clammy cheek. "Please, stay with me, Henri. Please."

Where was the doctor? Where were any of the others? I heard movement behind me and released a relieved sigh at the thought of Jack or Van Dyke returning.

"Thank goodness, you're back," I said, but got no response.

The sound surged into a growl, and I turned to see Kohler, covered in blood, diving toward me.

Pop!

He dropped to the floor at my side. Behind him stood a familiar figure, with an arm outstretched, holding a gun. It wasn't Jack.

Dahlia?

34

MONDAY, MAY 7, 1945, EVENING

I squeezed my eyes shut, knowing they were playing tricks on me. And when I opened them again, Jack's silhouette filled the doorway. He crossed the room in two strides and knelt at my side. His arm wrapped tightly around my waist as he assessed the situation.

"We have a doctor on the way. He should be here any minute." He felt for Toussaint's pulse. "Hang on, man."

Before he finished his sentence, Van Dyke called from the inn's front door. "Right in here." He led an older gentleman into the room, and they both set to work on the inspector.

Jack scooped me into his arms and carried me to the open French window. "You need some fresh air." He propped me up to stand against the window frame. His finger traced the edge of my face and tucked a wilted lock of hair behind my ear. "Take a breath."

I inhaled as much air as my lungs could hold and let my shoulders drop as I released it. "It was…." The luxury of breathing again was almost too much.

Jack shook his head, and his deep brown eyes softened at the rattle in my voice. "I know. I should have been here for you. I should never have left your side." He placed a gentle kiss on my forehead.

"I don't know what I'd have done if you hadn't come when you did." He tried to interrupt, laying a finger over my lips, but I continued. "If you hadn't shot him."

"Darling, I didn't." His lips almost curved to a smile as he gestured to the hedge of roses in the garden.

From behind the roses stepped a tiny, round-shouldered, grey-haired woman wearing a grey tweed skirt set and a sympathetic expression. Dahlia approached with her hands stretched out to me. "My dear, I couldn't stand there and let him hurt you like that."

I hopped through the low window frame and ran into her snug embrace. "Dahlia, you're alive. I thought I was going crazy." My mind stretched to understand. "But how?"

She nodded her whole body as if she were in a rocking chair. "Dear Penny, you needn't worry so much about the how."

"But I saw you. You were dead." My thoughts panged with the memory of her grey face and purple lips.

"You saw what you were supposed to see." She patted my hand. "And so did everyone else. I have a few tricks up my sleeve, the same as you."

"But…."

"The same little pulse-slowing tablets as you have." With her demeanor so calm, she might have been sharing a mince pie recipe.

I swiveled my face toward Jack. "Did you know? Is Alice still alive?"

Jack shook his head and raised his hand in an oath. "I didn't know until after she'd shot Graves, erhm, Kohler."

Dahlia clucked her tongue and patted my hand. "And no, Miss Fairchild is dead."

My mind raced. I needed to calm down. "But how can we be sure? If you're—."

"I know she's dead because I killed her, dear." The old woman gently squeezed my hand.

I blinked in utter shock. "*You* killed her?" Perhaps I was swooning because Jack's strong hand propped me up again. "Why?"

Dahlia gestured back inside. "Let's sit for a moment. I'm catching a chill." She tottered inside to the sofa and lowered herself into the cushions, dragging us behind. "Sit here beside me, Penny."

I obeyed, and Jack and I filled the rest of the sofa. "I don't understand," I said.

Dahlia's gaze toggled between Jack and me. "You look so surprised, both of you." She glanced over her shoulder at the doctor and Van Dyke, carrying Toussaint out of the room on a stretcher. She grimaced and gnawed at her lip. "I think he'll be all right. I do wish I'd come in here sooner. I might have stopped the fiend from hurting the dear inspector."

I waved my hands to get her attention. "Dahlia, please. Help me understand. Why would you kill Alice?"

"Well, I shouldn't take all the credit. The sweet little French girl helped me. Slipped a little poison into her tea. Seemed the perfect opportunity for me to die, too, so we coordinated our efforts. Poor Madeline. She was a good spy, very dedicated to the

Resistance, but she was young." Dahlia shot a pitying glance at Jack. "I know you liked the girl, but I had to do it, you know."

He furrowed his brow. "You killed Madeline, too?" he asked.

"Oh, heavens, no. Kohler killed her." She looked as though she might spit the taste of his name out onto the floor. "No, I had to kill Alice. She was on my list." Dahlia drew a deep breath and blinked as though that was enough explanation. When we didn't respond, she added, "And she's the one who killed the double on the train and made it appear Penny had done it."

Jack pushed his lips in and out, working through a thought. "She found my notes?"

Dahlia nodded toward him. "Yes, I'm afraid so."

I shook my head furiously. This was too much to absorb in one day. "Wait. She was… You have a list? From whom?"

The old woman creased her brow. "My gracious. You must have suffered much more than I expected. You're such a clever girl, but your brain is struggling right now, isn't it?" She tightened her lips for a moment before adding, "I work for Mother, same as you two."

"Doing what?" Jack took the words right out of my mouth.

"The same as you two." She enunciated each word precisely. "You have a list. I have a list." She folded her hands together in her lap. "Well, I had a list. I've finished with it now, just as you have done, Penny."

I scrubbed my eyes with the heels of my palms, hoping to make some sense of it all. "You killed Alice, and you killed Graves… Kohler, rather. Anyone else we should know about?"

Dahlia chuckled. "Not on this trip. Not since my late husband, the general."

I almost laughed out loud. I was sure I was losing my mind. "You murdered your husband?"

"Of course, I did. Who else would they have do it? It's why I married him in the first place. It's why I married my last three husbands." Her calm, matter-of-fact demeanor triggered something in me.

"Of course." The words spilled out of my mouth before I could stop them. Another thought popped into my head. "But Kohler was on *my* list."

Dahlia's lips pressed into a tight, thin line. "Until last week, yes, he was." She laced her fingers together. "But someone back home decided he might be worth more alive than dead; they never met the bast—." She cleared her throat. "Excuse me. They never met him." She redirected. "They decided to remove him from your list and add him to mine, but I was not to move on him unless he got out of hand. I was a last resort."

"My… backup?" I rested my hand on her shoulder, in part to be sure she was really there.

"He was right about one thing. I was certainly more deadly to him after I died than before." Dahlia raised her hand to her hair and primped for a second.

There were too many layers to this for me not to ask questions. "What about the notes? This first one—the man in the iron mask—it was from Madeline?"

"Yes." Dahlia nodded. "And I wrote the last one. I thought you might have recognized my handwriting. Just a small way for me to let you know I'm still here. And I apologize for continuing the riddles. I know how much you dislike them. But I wanted to keep the secret from everyone else."

Jack leaned back on the sofa and blinked, like me, trying to comprehend everything he'd just heard.

Dahlia patted her knees. "I'm feeling a bit bedraggled. Keeping out of sight in such a small residence is quite exhausting. Hiding away in cleaning cupboards and under beds is for the young. I've had enough of it for a while. Would it be all right if I went back upstairs to rest? I suspect you two can manage from here."

Jack stood and held her elbow as she rose. "Allow us to escort you up."

As we went through the lobby, the doctor beckoned us over. "The inspector should recover. It appears that the blade missed the vital areas. The other man wasn't so lucky. The bullet went right through the heart. The man who shot him was quite the marksman. He was dead before he hit the floor."

Dahlia and I exchanged a smirk.

"Better than he deserved, then," Jack answered. "Nazi officer."

The doctor scowled at the word and muttered a French curse. He motioned to me. "May I examine your neck? Monsieur Van Dyke said the man tried to strangle you?"

"I'm fine, *merci.*" I allowed him to study my throat for a moment. "Please attend Toussaint. He is a great inspector, but more importantly, he is a good man."

"*Oui*, mademoiselle, I will see him to health. You have my word." The doctor bowed and hurried out to the ambulance.

My heartbeat steadied as we climbed the stairs with Dahlia holding one of Jack's arms and me on the other. We'd survived another mission. We were lucky, again. But, one day, if we continued this work for Mother, one or both of us, perhaps all three, wouldn't see the end of it.

"Listen, Penny, this has all been too much." Jack's voice hummed low. "The war is about over, and we've served King and country as much as anyone. More than a lot of others."

"Yes." The word came automatically, and I wondered if we were thinking the same thing.

"We've chased Nazis, collected information, carried messages, and killed. Me from a distance and you…too close. All this we've done for the crown. For a country that will never know our names." His dark, misty eyes stared into mine.

"What we've done." I swallowed hard, my mind and body finally starting to calm. "It was necessary. People like us will always be necessary."

"Necessary, maybe. But can we go on like this?" His hand slipped to my lower back. "You and I?"

I slowed on the step and gazed into his eyes. They pleaded. Or was that just what I wanted to see in them?

"When we get back to London, let's find a little cottage, if there are any left, and we'll quit this crazy life. We'll settle into an acre, grow tomatoes, raise chickens, or something. Wouldn't that be the life?" His words spilled out as we continued our climb. "I don't want to lose you to another madman. I can't lose you, Penny."

"It all sounds wonderful. Like a dream." I imagined a life without guns and knives and lists of people to kill. I conjured late-morning breakfasts with Jack and long walks to the market. No more nights spent stalking victims. No more bloody clothes to dispose of. No more secret codes or covert messages between us. No more heart-pounding chases in alleyways. Could I simply be plain Penelope Tompkins again? Or Penelope Vogel? Or whatever names we chose for ourselves? I wasn't sure. Part of me hoped.

We reached the top step, and Jack held me to his chest. His lips covered mine in a long, delicious kiss. When we parted, he gazed into my eyes. "Just say yes, Penny."

I leaned against him as we followed Dahlia to the bedroom door. "Yes."

Dahlia turned to face us; her eyes smiled knowingly at our lovemaking. "I suppose we're all quite exhausted." She shot a mischievous glance at us. "I, for one, will be going to bed directly and expect to sleep soundly. I dare say I won't hear the comings and goings of anyone else in the whole of the inn."

Jack opened the door for Dahlia and gave the old woman a wink as she went inside.

She put a trembling hand on my arm. "Penny, dear, I won't need help getting ready for bed, but I suppose you should freshen yourself before you take a moonlight walk with your young man."

I couldn't decide if she was upholding the charade for appearances' sake or if this was just her way. I no longer knew what to believe. I glanced at the blood on my hands and blouse and felt it drying in my hair and on the back of my neck. "Yes. I should clean up."

"Then I'll leave you two ladies to it." Jack bowed to Dahlia and then squeezed my hand. "I'll check in on you in ten minutes. Give her a little time to settle in, shall we?"

"Ten minutes," I answered as I shut the door between us.

AFTER A THERAPEUTIC SHOWER and a change into a clean dress, Jack and I spent an hour in the back garden, bathed in moonlight, making plans for our little cottage in the country. We talked through the last week's events while we finished a bottle of wine and a loaf of bread that Jack had found in the kitchen. We watched and noted as each light in the little hotel winked out for the night.

"Shall we retire to my room for more privacy?" Jack traced a line of kisses over my bruised throat. "We still need to *debrief*."

I followed him up the dark stairs, into his room, and into his bed. We spent another hour making love and making plans. Afterward, I lay on Jack's chest, listening to his heart thump as he drifted to sleep. With each heartbeat, I thought of all the hearts I had stilled over the last few years. A dozen? More?

Their deaths saved innocent lives. There was no way to know how many lived because of the deaths I caused.

I was good at death.

But now this war was almost over. Could I be good at life?

Jack's arms loosened around me, and his breathing deepened and slowed. I slid off his chest and to his side and stared out the window to the star-flecked black sky.

Every time I closed my eyes, I found myself back in Kohler's clutches, the wire closing tightly around my neck. I struggled to breathe normally. I struggled to breathe at all.

No matter how much I wanted to, I struggled to see a quiet, tidy future with Jack.

35

TUESDAY, MAY 8, 1945, LATE MORNING

The hotel bustled as our little band of travelers prepared to return to the train station and resume the journey back to London. There was enough activity to allow me to slip back to my room without attracting notice.

Even if anyone had seen me, their attention was soon redirected by the growing chatter about the events from the night before.

"Can you imagine that horrid Nazi pretended to be a pacifist?" One exclamation led to another. "Or that Mrs. Lundt wasn't actually dead?" Everyone had a theory, but we refused to give details.

The new inspector on the case handled all the questions with the same response. "You need only concern yourself with the rest of your trip home."

When Jack brought down the luggage from our rooms, Dahlia attached herself to his elbow and requested that we have our own car. The inspector obliged, sending everyone else ahead and away. He shook Jack's hand and said, "I thought you might like some good news. My office just called and told me there will be an announcement later today. Germany officially surrendered to the Allies this morning. The war is over."

The three of us released a collective sigh, and we shared warm hugs as our luggage was stowed in the boot of the car.

Allard met us in the driveway and took me aside for a moment. "I am so glad I caught you before you left, miss." He held out a note. "This just came from the hospital."

I thanked him and waited to open the missive until I was alone.

Dearest Mademoiselle Tompkins, thank you for saving my life. The doctors assure me that I shall recover without long-term damage. I hope that we will meet again someday under more amenable circumstances. Perhaps we can share a bottle of wine and reminisce. Please take care of yourself, mon chéri.

Sincerely, Henri Toussaint.

JACK GLANCED at the paper as I refolded it and tucked it into my pocket. "Dahlia's waiting in the car. Is everything all right?"

I took his elbow and squeezed. "Yes. Just word from Toussaint. He's going to recover."

"Good." He helped me into the car next to Dahlia and then slid in beside me. "He sent the note only to you?"

I retrieved the letter from my pocket and handed it to Jack as though it were nothing. But my heart swelled with gratitude that Inspector Toussaint—Henri would be all right. "I'm sure he sent it to me because I was the one with him as he lost consciousness."

Jack scanned the page and frowned as he silently mouthed the words, then spoke aloud. "Share a bottle of wine? *Mon chéri?*" His eyes flashed a jealous flicker of green.

"Of course, he's grateful to all of us. After all, it was Dahlia who saved us all." I patted her knee and tried to keep the focus off me.

"You're more than welcome, dear," Dahlia chirped.

"And you've nothing to worry about, Jack. We'll be in our little cottage chasing chickens, won't we?" I didn't want him to know I was having second thoughts. *Was I having second thoughts?* Of course not. If not a future with Jack, what would my life be? I had to start over one way or another.

I tucked the letter away again, and the action seemed to grab Dahlia's attention. "Oh, I almost forgot; I got a letter, too. Mother wanted me to ask you both." She dug in her pocketbook. As she pulled out a note, her hankie dropped to the floorboard. "Oh, bother."

Jack scooped up the linen square and returned it to her trembling hand.

"Thank you, dear." She tucked it back in place and held out the folded paper to me. "There's a new assignment for you." Dahlia hesitated, drawing her hand back. "But if you're giving it all up, maybe I should keep it."

My heart raced ahead of my mind. Another assignment? The mere thought of the fresh adrenaline triggered my cravings.

"No!" Jack and I said in one voice.

I snatched the paper from her hand, perhaps too eagerly. A flush of heat swept over my skin. "We should at least see what it is, right?" My fingertips sizzled with anticipation.

Jack pulled me close and read over my shoulder. The temptation was too great to resist. I tipped my forehead toward his with a singular message in my eyes. "One last job for Mother."

THE END

COMING SOON: THE WILLING
RESISTANCE

Justice has a new destination.

Penny may have cleared her name, but the war isn't finished yet. In the shadowed corridors of postwar Spain, Inspector Henri Toussaint follows a trail of secrets, sabotage, and survival.

The Willing Resistance continues the Traveling Companion Series with a twist of danger, a touch of romance, and a mission that may cost more than either of them is willing to give.

Read on for a preview of Chapter One.

THE WILLING RESISTANCE, THE TRAVELING COMPANION, BOOK 2

June -3, 1945

My dearest Henri,

I was so Pleased to hear of your release from hospital. I hope you Keep to your doctor's Advice for an eXtra walk eAch afternoon. The weather in LoNdon has been nice.

Dahlia, Jack, and I made a brief stoP in Paris for a gift for MoTher. We found a lovEly silK scarf Printed with aQua roses.

Please wrIte soon; I look forward to shAring that bottle of wine once you've fully recovered.

With love,

Penelope

3 6

FRIDAY, JUNE 15, 1945

The train car bumped along the rails at a constant thrum as it climbed the side of the Pyrenees mountains. The movement rocked me into a relaxed, meditative state and jarred the letter in my hands, making it difficult to read.

My dearest Henri. It was written as if from a lover. I knew better. Penny Tompkins was clever and dangerous; any man seduced by her should fear for his life. I had read her missive, perhaps a thousand times, before boarding the train. I memorized as I packed my valise. Recited it as I dressed my wound and donned my brown tweed suit for the journey.

This was my first train since the incident that ended my service in the trenches and began my career as a police inspector. Though I'd been apprehensive at first, I'd settled my nerves once I decided to take the trip. The doctor had instructed me to find a place away from the ravages of war, and neutral Spain seemed to fill his prescription.

I'd witnessed what the Nazis had done to the beautiful countryside of France as I journeyed from north to south. Villages and meadows were scorched into rubble in some places, while other vistas remained postcard-perfect.

Back to Penny's missive. Her coded letters stood out from the rest, so obviously, I wondered if it was a mistake. *She babied me.* I pulled the capitalized block letters out from her precise script with ease. P-K-A-X-A-N-P-T-E-K-P-Q-I-A. To begin, I shuffled them to no avail. Perhaps she wanted to give me a little challenge.

I read them backward and forward and used them as initials for other words. Penny Keeps An X-ray And Notes… Nonsense. *Mon Dieu!* What is she doing to me?

These letters must be a substitution code. But where was the key? It took me six days to find it. I made it more complicated than necessary, of course. Such is my way.

The date, *June 3, 1945.* But that is not what she wrote. She wrote *-3.* Ah, *mais oui!* The key glares at me from the top of the page. Take the block letters and go back three places in the alphabet. P becomes S, K becomes N, and so forth.

SNDADRSWHNSTLD. But how can this be correct with only one vowel? I sounded it out, desperate to make sense. I stared until my eyes blurred. I was ready to send the note to ashes when my eyes refocused, and I finally deciphered it. SND ADRS WHN STLD. *Send address when settled.* So simple. I *am l'enfant* to her.

With that enlightenment, I relaxed in my seat to enjoy the scenery. But my mind still pondered why she wanted my address. Our letters had been mere pleasantries after our initial experience together.

I pressed my hand over the scar on my chest where I had been stabbed by Yann Kohler, the Nazi officer intent on fleeing the punishment due to him for the atrocities he'd committed. My last memories after that were of Penny's beautiful face—her dark hair, sharp blue eyes, and full pink lips. I imagined she had kissed me as she pleaded for me to stay with her.

I expected that kiss would remain in the dim corner of my romantic French mind. But she now asked for my address. Would we share a bottle of wine someday? Soon?

After folding the note for the hundredth time, I replaced it in my breast pocket, and my attention returned to the train carriage. Most of the men around me read newspapers, both French and Spanish, with headlines ruminating over the Berlin Declaration, dividing Germany into four districts. I scoffed as I thought about last month. The day Germany surrendered was the same day Kohler drove a six-inch knife into my chest.

A woman passenger sitting two rows ahead, facing backward toward me, raised her head and closed a book. She tucked the small tome into her handbag and gazed out the window for several seconds before shifting her eyes to me. Her features were dark and comely, and she flashed a victory-red painted smile from beneath her wide-brimmed hat upon realizing my appraisal of her. I wondered if she would be staying at the hotel or traveling somewhere in Spain or even Portugal. Perhaps even away from the continent.

The pressure change in the air caused my ears to prick, and I yawned to ease the pain. I glanced at my watch and realized we were nearing the Somport tunnel. It was a mile-long spiral into the heart of the border mountain that dropped the train 190 feet to the valley where Canfranc Station would greet us in Spain. My final destination and home for the next two months.

The doctor prescribed relaxation for my convalescence, and the tiny village in the middle of nowhere was just what the doctor ordered.

Or so I thought.

To set the mood, diffuse this blend of essential oils while you read.

To hear the songs of the era,
several of which are mentioned in this book,
please scan the QR code for the official
playlist of *The Innocent Assassin*.

MORE PAGE-TURNERS AWAIT...

If you enjoyed this story, take a look at other novels by Kim Black. Each one is clean, compelling, and hard to put down.

Little Black Dress, The LBD Project, Book 1

Red Heels, The LBD Project, Book 2

Bare Essentials, The LBD Project, Book 3

Shooting Stars Traveling Circus

Drop Dead Dallas

And under Kimberly Black...

Historical Christian Fiction:

Lydia, Woman of Purple

Her Most Precious Gift

Children's:

Pockets

Sophie Louise Will Not say CHEESE

ABOUT THE AUTHOR

Kim Black is a genre-blending wordsmith who crafts clean, compelling stories where bullets fly, hearts race, and justice always has a shot.

Based in the Texas Panhandle with her husband, a fellow writer, and their opinionated pit bull Bonnie, Kim writes romantic suspense and historical thrillers that spotlight strong, smart women who don't need rescuing—but might choose love anyway. She's the award-winning author of *Little Black Dress* and the creator of the *Traveling Companion Series*, where spies, secrets, and second chances collide.

When she's not plotting twists, you'll find her encouraging fellow creatives as a board member of the Texas High Plains Writers. Her stories solve a problem for readers who crave action and intrigue without graphic content or vulgarity. Clean doesn't mean boring, just sharper, smarter, and more dangerous.